Night Moves . . .

A siren sounded from the control tower; lights snapped on all along the wire fence. If their radar was any good they'd have me pinpointed anyway—knee deep in mud and slime. It was only fifty yards to the nearest section of fence at the darkest point between two lights. The Land Rover was away in the distance. I staggered to my feet and ran. As I neared the fence I made a running jump that took me three feet up, then scrambled up the rest, thanking God for National Service that gave you these skills gratis.

At the top were four tight strands of barbed wire. Laying the flight bag across I swung my body up and over, feeling the knee of my left trouser leg rip as I went. Then, hanging, I freed the impaled flight bag from the top of the barbed wire, hung on for a second and jumped, hoping the earth beneath was soft.

It was, but my knees took the shock badly and for a moment I lay there gasping in pain. I looked back towards the terminal. Incredibly no one seemed to have seen my Douglas Fairbanks acrobatics, but I wasn't going back for Take Two. I rose groggily to my feet, picked up the bag and tottered over the rough ground away from the fence. Keeping a distance of twenty or so yards from the wire, I began to follow its circumference, aiming away from the terminal building towards the point where I said I'd meet Diane.

Dragonfire

Peter Graham Scott

PINNACLE BOOKS   NEW YORK

DRAGONFIRE

A Pinnacle Book, published by arrangement with the author and Macdonald Futura Publishers Limited.

First printing, May 1982

ISBN: 0-523-41697-0

Cover photo by Cosimo

Printed in the United States of America

PINNACLE BOOKS, INC.
1430 Broadway
New York, New York 10018

DRAGONFIRE

The white room was quite ordinary, barely furnished with just a table and a couple of chairs. There was nothing to suggest that it had been constructed and sealed deep in the earth's core at enormous cost.

The monkey, tranquillized and vacant, sat on the table gazing ahead. Behind, in a hanging birdcage, a yellow canary perched, waiting. Below, two rats scratched idly and unavailingly at the floor's hard leaden surface.

The explosion, when it came, was small and silent, emanating from a black box in the center of the room, causing wisps of almost colorless gas to float up gently in the still atmosphere.

The monkey reacted first, as the first wisp rose, leaping up from the table with a silent scream of anguish, desperately clutching its throat, gasping as a suddenly frightened heart pumped faster and faster in paroxysms of choking death. The canary, still as a tiny statue, fell abruptly to the floor of the cage. The rats chased madly towards the wall, tried to scramble up

1

the sheer surface, and fell back, paws outstretched, eyes wide, jaws distended, ugly, furry, and dead.

Then decomposition began. The hair on the monkey's body grew limp and gradually crumbled from the surface of the skin beneath, revealing a dead form that was suddenly horribly human. Then the pink naked flesh greyed over and wrinkled, falling softly away from the bones, which were rapidly transformed from youthful white to ancient yellow as they too turned to dust, even as the table itself collapsed.

The birdcage crashed to the floor, breaking into tiny pieces that soon dissolved as swiftly as the disappearing yellow bird-carcass it had housed. And where the rats had fallen were now two small grey heaps.

Only dust: no table, chairs, monkey, bird or rats. . . . The projection beam flickered and died. Dim light illuminated three faces.

The first man said, "The ultimate."

The second, "Makes neutron look like a Christmas cracker."

The grey man, "It goes on, multiplying?"

"Destroying all organic life, feeding and renewing like a cancer."

"The whole earth?"

"Not quite. Certain natural barriers prevent total global spread Oceans, deserts where plant life has ceased. . . ."

"And the inhibiting factor of the Earth's own cosmic radiation. . . ."

"Don't confuse me with technicalities," the grey man said. "It could take out the entire United States? Right?"

"Could have been designed for just that purpose. And it makes similar retaliation unthinkable."

"How's that?"

"Drop it on Moscow and you destroy the whole of Western Europe. There's no desert between there and Germany, or France."

Silence. The air-conditioning was developing a curious rattle.

The grey man said, "Duration?"

"Half-life, two to three days, minimum."

"Dispersal?"

"No chance."

"Protection?"

"You guess. There's fifty feet of lead on top of that test-chamber."

"Might hold it for a thousand years, might last ten."

"Monitored?"

"So far. No foreseeable danger."

Another long silence. . . . Outside, in the brittle Nevada sunshine a car-horn suddenly blared, brakes shrieked, in a still-busy violence.

The grey man said, "We can't risk another test."

"Hardly."

"Let's look at the "B" camera."

Traffic on London's Westway was heavy as usual. In the darkening afternoon the wipers smeared twin half-circles of flaring red neon and dazzle-bright oncoming headlights as I jostled taxis, forced the car past trucks and finally swung right for the outskirts of Wembley, to arrive at the barrier of the main gate of Video City.

"I.D. Card?" The commissionaire's voice was pure Dublin. I fished out the necessary bit of plastic complete with manic photo. Pure formality; my car park sticker should have been enough. "Carry on, sir."

Through the upraised barrier and straight into the center car park. Entry here was a true measure of your Corporation status, more than salary, more than the thickness of your office carpet.

The rain was turning to sleet now. I briefly looked up at the familiar grey building—a solemn colosseum of illuminated and identical windows; not one of the architectural marvels of our time—more like some vaguely Swedish institute for the mentally deprived.

Lunch with the man from the Home Office had been a success. I was to be given access to film recidivist prisoners without too many official preconditions. So one of Frimley's cosmetic objections to *Gateway* was settled.

I pushed through the heavy glass doors into the high-ceilinged entrance hall and turned right for the elevators. The doors of one opened, emitting a crowd of chattering typists.

"Dan. Just the man I'm looking for." I turned to see Dudley French, wearing that special look of eagerness they seem to need in Current Affairs. "I'm just about to run your Chile film. We're hoping to use a bit on tonight's *Mon-thru-Fri*."

"Are you?"

"Maybe you'd better come down to VT and see."

"Maybe I had."

I followed him down the escalator to the basement, to the humming center where forty or so video-tape machines were set up in small plastic cubicles.

"They tell me the picture quality's not so good," he accused.

"You know the story. The Pinochet mob wouldn't let us in to make a proper documentary, so I went in as a tourist and shot on eight mil."

"Mag stripe?"

"That's right. Then blew it up to sixteen."

His PA, earnest and plain, clipboard clamped de-

4

fensively to her bosom, was waiting in VT 11. "We've found the interview, Dud."

"Let's run it then."

The operator pressed a button. The two big spools of tape on the machine began to spin very fast. On the monitor jagged gashes of black and white suddenly settled down to a coherent color picture.

"Is this Maria—whatsit?"

"Maria Dolores Pereira."

Her face was barely visible—pallid cheeks, dark smudges beneath bright black eyes. "And then—?" I heard my own voice prompting her. Her reply, in English, was hard to hear over the hum of the video machine. "I was taken from the cell into another room. An officer was there, and two other soldiers. . . ." Her voice became lower, a mere mumble.

Dudley said, "What's she saying?"

"She was terrified."

"Was she raped?"

"No. They simply questioned her, very violently, for a couple of days."

"Is she communist?"

"No. She's a bank manager's daughter. She just happened to be on a campus watching a demo when they rounded her up."

Dudley was fighting his disappointment. "What's the point then?"

"My idea was to show how anybody in that sort of country can get picked up and done over. If I'd wanted something more sensational I'd have shot it."

On the screen the girl had broken down completely. The operator said, "Shall I cut it?"

Dudley nodded. The machine skimmed to a halt and sudden silence. He said, "I suppose I could use a bit of it."

5

"What are you after, anyway?"

"It's this new UN report on Human Rights. I need a punchy bit of good television from someone who's been tortured."

I looked at him, balding and fluent, able to talk of something being "good television", whether it was a soccer match or diabolical horror. It had been a struggle to get even that from Maria. What had happened to her in an obscure police station had been unimaginable in her life up to that time. I had persuaded her to talk of it. I wonder where she is now?

The PA suddenly said, "Didn't you get some sort of award?"

"Some sort of."

Dudley clearly felt I should give it back. "I suppose we can make something of it," he said gloomily. "We'd have to lay different commentary. Just keep the visual, the bit where she's crying."

I said, "You've no right to use it."

"You got a written clearance from her, didn't you?"

"I don't mean that. The interview was shot for a specific program, one the girl knew about. You've no right to snatch a bit of it and dress it up to fit some other argument." It all sounded terribly pompous.

Dudley went red. "We can use it how we like mate."

"No, Dudley. You can hustle other people's stuff. But not this. Get a bit of news film. Use a still. Not this."

"No need to be like that, Dan."

"I am like that."

The PA looked at him nervously. He looked at me for a moment, then said, "We'll get something better."

"Do."

I left them in VT and caught the elevator five floors to my office—a small room out of the way near the back staircase. Jill, my secretary, looked up from her paperback. "Good lunch?"

"Very. Home Office suitably docile."

"Frimley wants you."

"Anything else?"

"Dudley French—"

"I caught him. Briefly."

"And Patrick Timothy keeps calling."

"The agent? He knows I seldom use actors."

"I said you'd call him back."

"I will. Next year."

Through the rain-streaked window I surveyed the enclosed piazza below, hemmed-in by the ring of studios and offices. In the center was a sad bronze statue, *The Spirit of Broadcasting*, circa 1950, a slim youth long abused by sparrows and seagulls, streaked with ancient verdigris. In his upraised hand a limp wand designed as a fountain, which hadn't played for years, since some industrial psychiatrist identified it as the cause of alarming incontinence among the office ladies.

"Don't forget Frimley," Jill prompted.

"Don't bully me, love. Just going."

In his spacious office, furnished and carpeted to standard Grade Two, Anthony Frimley, Head of Vital Features, Television—HVFTV no less—surveyed the view from *his* window as I went in. The squat grey blocks, remnants of the Empire Exhibition of 1925, now patched and scabbed with odds and ends of industry, and beyond, in endless careful rows, the red roofs of surburban housing.

Normally the picture pleased him. "Those people out there," he would announce with something like awe, "They call the shots."

He turned and stared, one hand brushing his thinning sandy hair. "You weren't about when I came out of 'Offers.'"

"I was having lunch with that man from the Home Office. Prison access for *Gateway*. I told you about it."

"Ah—yes." Frimley began to jingle the small change in his trouser pocket—always a sign he was nervous.

"*Gateway*." He took a breath. "You know of course that the Corporation is having to make certain—economies?"

"I've never known a time when it wasn't. How much do they rake in every week—seven millions?"

Frimley was ready for that one. "Ah, but think of our commitments. Two television channels—four national radio networks. . . ."

"I've read the Annual Handbook, thanks."

"It's not just our responsibility to the British public, but our duty to broadcasting as a whole. . . ." Frimley was off, good for a five minute lecturette on the Life and Purpose of the Corporation.

I switched off, still watching Frimley's mouth opening and shutting rhythmically. A career bachelor in admin, he owed his rapid advancement to a soft-voiced friendship with his own personal Socrates, the mysteriously-tilted "D. Tech. A.," the Director of Technical Administration. Sailing blithely from committee to committee, never personally involved enough to be blamed for the odd program failure, Frimley always managed to be around for general compliments. He'd been head of the department where I made my programs for nearly a year, and we didn't, as they say, "get on".

"It's simply a matter of good housekeeping." He was well into his stride now. In Glasgow, as a boy, I used to see the tatty films made by Old Mother Riley—a

8

pathetic old panto dame called Arthur Lucan. And her daughter Kitty. Frimley suddenly began to look exactly like Old Mother R. Give him a stringy grey wig tied back in a bun and a little flat hat and he was there. "Oh daughter, daughter, they've done me again! Caught me right up the gusset!"

But Old Mother Riley had suddenly stopped. Seemed to expect an answer. I awoke. "How do you mean, exactly—?"

"I said we should prune our most ambitious programs first."

"Surely that depends on the program." What are you leading up to, Frimley?

The coins in his pocket jingled together.

"Controller One has made the decision."

"John has?"

"Yes. We're cancelling *Gateway*."

"It's scheduled for transmission in the spring."

"Not any more."

"But John himself suggested a series about prisoner after-care."

"Not the way you proposed to do it. All that foreign filming. . . ."

"The whole idea was to contrast our methods with those of the Americans and the West Germans."

"I know. But . . ." Frimley was a master of the knowing pause. And somehow that's what he seemed like. An actor, delivering some sort of rehearsed speech. Not a real man discussing a problem with a colleague.

"Listen," I said. "We're committed. I've contracted Cumber Brockley to front all six."

"An unavoidable write-off, I fear."

"Didn't you tell John we had a chance of a co-production? That'll solve the money problem, surely?"

"I doubt if that's serious. Simply an enquiry from some sort of independent trying to set something up with the American Educational Channel. Talk to him if you like. What was his name, Shine?"

"Krein. Herb Krein."

"Herb Krein." Frimley made it sound like a deodorant. "You haven't heard from him lately?"

"No."

"Well then."

And I knew Frimley didn't care. To him programs were those tiresome and difficult affairs that interfered with a smooth-running organizational life.

"Are any other series being cut? Or just mine?" I asked.

"I don't know, at the moment. But you're not being singled out, I assure you."

I wasn't so sure.

"So—what do I do instead?"

"Instead?"

"Is it Kiddies Hour, or News for the Deaf?"

"I must confess I hadn't considered an alternative yet."

"What do I do? Sit and meditate?"

"Er—no." Even Frimley was finding this bit difficult. Don't prompt him. Let him sort out his own clichés.

He managed it at last. "We have to make economies somewhere. We're not—renewing your contract." But he wasn't foolish enough to show his immense satisfaction.

For in the Corporation, while administrators are on the staff, complete with pension scheme, most producers and directors were freelance—and expendable.

10

And my present contract happened to be up at the end of the month.

"Has anyone considered the work I've done in the last five years—for *this* department? The Uganda report, the three Americas, the Bhutto interview?"

"They were before my time."

"They were still made for the Corporation. What more do you want?"

"No one questions your professional ability."

"Surely there's some other program I could take over?"

"Not until after next Offers."

"When's that?"

"March. Or possibly April."

"What would it be?"

"Nothing very spectacular I'm afraid. We're thinking of re-examining Britain's economy. Studio discussion mainly."

"Talking heads?"

"A carefully chosen panel of experts."

"No film? No OB?"

"Probably not."

"I see." Britain's economy. *Again*? There had to be somthing better than that. I looked at Frimley in disbelief. He didn't enjoy close inspection. He turned back to surburbia in sleet and said no more.

Then he did something that surprised me. He turned back to me and held out his hand. I looked down at it, soft and scrubbed, and took it. Now Frimley could look me in the eye.

"It may be for the best," he said, oddly.

TWO

Only the carefully shaded lights close to the large desk were lit. The orange telephone bleeped softly. The grey man put down his pen and lifted the handset. The electronic fuzz changed to clear speech as his fingergertip touched the scrambler key.

"Mr. President?" The caller sounded nervous.

"Speaking."

The voice at the other end began speaking faster, pouring out words in an eager torrent.

"Don't justify yourself," the grey man said quietly. "Just give me the facts."

The voice slowed, because calmer. The grey man listened, hearing confirmation of something he'd feared all day, ever since the early morning's screening in Nevada. Now it was certain. A technician closely involved in the test had disappeared, leaving no clue either to where or why he'd vanished.

Still listening, as his caller went into detail, the grey man got up and wandered towards the high windows, the telephone's extra long lead trailing behind him.

He pulled the thick curtains aside to look out. The winter night was clear and frosty. He could make out the light; these same lawns where not so long ago hordes of angry people had stampeded toward the White House, using their anti-war banners as weapons against the stone-faced National Guardsmen in steel helmets.

Much more recently, in his own term of office, another huge crowd had demonstrated again, more peacefully this time, demanding an end to the spread of nuclear power plants. A mood of scepticism and clear-eyed rationality was appearing, not just among the media exhibitionists, but in straightforward honest working people. . . .

But now the lawns were quiet, still, deserted, although still secretly patrolled and watched by a score of video eyes. And beyond there was America, where ordinary husbands were sitting down with their wives and families, or drinking with friends, or playing games.

And some—perhaps many, perhaps only a few— were planning to remove another president by any means available; whether legitimately or simply by getting dirt on his relatives or his private tastes. . . .

Out there, too, was one man who for some reason had broken all his oaths of security and run free, taking with him one of the most deadly and potentially dangerous secrets ever known within the four walls of this quiet room. In the end it was always other people you had to rely on, other people who didn't always get it quite right. . . .

Lonely in half darkness, the president patiently waited for his caller to end his apologetic stream. Then he spoke.

"Find him."

* * *

I walked out of Frimley's room at Video City and along the light blue corridor to my own office, still trying to put it all together. The loss of my contract wasn't so important, not at that moment; the loss of the program was. I'd been looking forward to making *Gateway*.

There was of course the man who'd come to London from California to talk co-production all those weeks ago—Herb Krein. Maybe I might get something definite out of him, and force Frimley into agreeing to a reprieve . . . I quickened my pace and reached the office. Jill had already gone. I needed Krein's home phone number and she kept her address book in the top drawer of her desk. It was locked. But I knew she usually hid the key under the telephone. (It's called Security.)

I dialled the number in Los Angeles, carefully sorting my way through the 0101 and the 213 for L.A. I could imagine the bell shrilling through the apartment with that peculiarly sharp sound from every Hollywood movie. It went on shrilling. It would be—what—half past nine in the morning over there. But Krein wasn't answering. I dialled for cables. The Corporation operator wanted a project number to charge it to. I gave her the *Gateway* number; let her find out tomorrow that it was cancelled. The message to Herb was quite short: "DANGER LOSING GATEWAY UNLESS YOU COME UP WITH FIRM CO-PRODUCTION OFFER STOP CONTACT ME URGENTLY."

It was a forlorn hope, but something. As I put the phone down it rang again.

"Dan Galloway?"

14

"Speaking."

"It's Patrick Timothy." He sounded confident and relaxed. Not like an agent trying to make a sale. "I've been trying to get you all day."

"I'm not your man, Patrick," I said. "I've no show coming up just yet."

"I'm not looking for business. I've something for *you*."

"What?"

Short pause. "Could you come round for a drink?"

"When? I'm busy tomorrow."

"Could you make it tonight?" There was some sort of suppressed excitement in the way he asked. My curiosity was aroused.

"Why not?"

Icy rain spikes drenched my head as I ran out to the car. I'd called Sally to tell her I'd be late home. Queen's Park Rangers had a match, so the traffic up towards Wood Lane had sludged to a standstill. I chopped a gap through the jam and headed towards Hammersmith. As I turned the corner I dimly glimpsed the news-posters—XMAS RAIL STRIKE. NEW TALKS. Nothing ever changed.

The address Patrick had given me was SE 1. Down through Knightsbridge and over Westminster Bridge. It turned out to be a smart new block on the South Bank, just past the National Theatre. The elevator sped me all the way up to the penthouse. A smooth young Italian manservant opened the heavy teak door.

"Mr. Galloway? Let me take your coat, sir."

He led me along a corridor, wine-dark with French wallpaper, relieved here and there with the glitter of ornate gilt mirrors, into the enormous main room.

15

Along the facing wall, so vivid that it might have been a sparkling projection of "London By Night", was a brilliant vista of the river and Westminster Bridge, with floodlit Houses of Parliament behind, seen through huge double-glazed windows. The room itself was darkish. Leather armchairs shone bronze against the blues and gold of the discreet curtains and wallpaper. Concealed speakers gently poured out Rodrigo. In the center, in a sunken square pit covered in sheepskin and dotted with cushions, Patrick Timothy reclined. He was dressed in a simple white Moroccan caftan and was sipping wine from a Venetian goblet.

"Come on in, boyo."

I didn't know Patrick Timothy that well; indeed I'd only met him once before, when I'd needed a top actor to read a commentary. A former actor himself, he'd made a speciality of character parts in American-backed films in the sixties, when they'd paid in real money, not hope-chits. Turning agent at exactly the right time with a few good friends as clients, he'd done well.

There was another man with him, youngish and good-looking, in a restrained worsted suit with a Via Condotti tie. Patrick said, "I don't think you know Piers Gaveston."

I shook hands. Gaveston didn't smile, but looked at me rather searchingly.

"Piers has just been appointed 'Mr. Television' for the Party," Patrick added.

"Party?" It didn't connect. "What's throwing one?"

Patrick forced a smile. "No one, boyo. Politics. Piers works for the Radicals."

Which explained the discreet suit. But how did an old fruit like Patrick come to know him?

"Drink, boyo?"

"Just a Bell's, with water."

The Italian looked puzzled. Patrick hissed, "Whiskey, *caro*." The Italian withdrew. Patrick waved his arm regally, "Do make yourself at home." I rearranged a couple of the cushions to make a space to sit down, aware of them both watching me closely. "You've been on our list for some time."

"What for?"

Patrick didn't answer immediately, watching the Italian return with a huge cut-glass tumbler.

"Filipo *caro*, how many times must I tell you not to put in all that *ghiaccio*?" Patrick looked at me. "I mean, you don't *want* all that ice do you?"

"Not particularly."

"Tip all that frozen muck down the sink and give Mr. Galloway a proper whiskey." Wordlessly Filipo retired. Patrick drew on his cigarette.

Gaveston suddenly said, "What do you make of the current political situation?"

"You mean 'When's the election?' You tell me." The Radicals had been in power for over four years, and the opposition were urging the prime minister, John-Henry Baskomb, to name the date.

"It could be any day," Gaveston said. "I've been asked to suggest a few names."

"Of whom?"

"Directors, like you. To handle our election broadcasts, Party Politicals and so on. Certain people—in the Cabinet and elsewhere—are anxious we make a good showing this time."

"I gather some of them fancy themselves as television personalities."

Gaveston permitted himself the slightest of smiles. "There's nothing so perfect that cannot be improved.

The other side uses advertising agents. We're keen to build a team and train up our own."

Filipo had appeared again with my drink, a full tumbler of whiskey. I took more than a sip. "Don't you want someone who's more of an actors' director?"

Patrick said sternly, "Politicians aren't actors, Dan."

"They still need rehearsal."

"They want *you*," Patrick said rather impatiently. "John-Henry saw the thing you did in West Africa—"

"Uganda. More like *East* Africa."

"*Africa*—what's the difference?"

Gaveston said, "I take it you're not—politically opposed?"

"Far from it."

"You're quite right in thinking that the election will be fought on personality—the conflicting images of the two leaders," Gaveston said thoughtfully. "Perhaps the bluff, no-nonsense John-Henry persona has been overdone. Now we'd like to project him as he really is—a shrewd, tough world statesman. And there are certain others we'd like to bring forward. That's why we need your sort of brain, your sort of hardness. How do you feel?"

"When will all this be?" I asked.

"Early in the New Year, I expect."

Patrick said, like a statement, not a question, "You'll be free."

"As it happens, yes. The Corporation cancelled my new series only today. I'm free as of now."

"Ah."

Gaveston looked at Patrick. He seemed to give the very slightest of nods.

"I'll need to talk to someone fairly soon about the exact kind of program you've got in mind," I said.

"That will be arranged," Gaveston said smoothly.

"There's time," Patrick said. "Plenty of time."

They both smiled. Again, as with Frimley, I had an impression of watching a couple of actors speaking lines, of somehow being involved in a play where everybody knew the script but me.

"Good," I said, for want of a better curtain line.

"Finding one guy," said the man called Budgen, "shouldn't be all that difficult." He waved the younger man to a seat, a comfortable imported Swedish chair with carefully matched folk-weave covering. Budgen enjoyed this room, priding himself on having made it look as unlike an FBI office as possible. The walls were decorated with pictures and small scale models of World War I aircraft—his consuming passion. "You got those mug-shots?"

"Sure. Already sent off by telex to all our main agencies." The younger man, Wrighten, wore gold rims and sounded like a college teacher. Budgen often wondered what old man Hoover would have made of an assistant like this. "Trouble is," Wrighten went on, "there's just nothing at all special about him." He referred to the paper in his hand. "Jeff Sadler, twenty-nine, white Caucasian, fair hair, blue eyes, five feet eleven, no distinguishing marks."

"I read all that," Budgen said almost irritably, easing his hefty bulk from one side of the soft chair to the other. "Did you get the extra stuff on his background?"

Wrighten produced a second paper from the sheaf in his hand. "Lived alone, on the project, on-site bungalow. Unmarried. No regular girlfriend."

19

"Some kind of faggot, was he?"

Wrighten looked up sharply. The term offended his liberal sensibility. "He was not—er—homosexual," he said primly. "Not as far as is known on the plant."

"So he spends every night watching Charlie's Angels. Politics?"

"Nothing unusual. Tacit supporter Civil Rights when he was at the University of Texas."

"Wasn't everybody?"

"Quite. He was cleared for top secret work in October '76."

"Foreign travel?"

"Europe—Britain, France, Italy—last fall. Mexico the year before."

"And he's not a gambler, a deviate, a druggy?"

"Not even a Moonie. Mr. Clean America."

Budgen yawned. The usual—no information. "Somebody wants him back on the job in Nevada pretty damn quick. This one's come straight from the President's office. Could it be a mob operation, do you think?"

"I very much doubt it." Wrighten began to look more confident. "None of the regular syndicates, Cosa Nostra or the rest, admit to knowing anything, bad or good, about him."

Budgen grunted. Only a bespectacled amateur like Wrighten would pronounce Cosa Nosta with a night school Italian accent like he did. He'd have to take the trouble to get a better replacement fairly soon. "Hasn't anyone any idea which way he was heading?"

"I'm afraid not. But at least we know he went." Wrighten permitted himself a slightly nervous smile. "He drove his own car, a '77 Buick, east to Winnemucca. The local police picked it up this morning. And a man of his description rented a Torino from the

20

Budget office right in town there, giving the name of Jones. He gave them cash for the deposit, no credit card—that's how they remember him."

"Was Jones the name on the driver's license?"

"Presumably. Maybe the girl didn't check too closely. He picked up a Freeway Guide from the desk as he went—that the girl did notice." Wrighten produced a map. "Like this one. So either he planned to shoot right down through Vegas and Tucson into Mexico—"

"Or—" Budgen let his eye rest on a perfect miniature replica of a Sopwith Camel on the wall. Beautiful aircraft, the Camel, took a hell of a pasting on the Western Front back in '17, '18. No wonder those old movies like Dawn Patrol were so great. . . .

Wrighten was looking hard at him, waiting for him to finish his sentence. "Or what?" he prompted.

Budgen said briskly, "All the border post have the number of the rented car?"

"They have. But we don't know if he's still using it."

"If not?"

"He might have made other plans."

Budgen shifted his weight in the chair once more and faced Wrighten with a bull-like stare. "And what plans have you made, Mrs. Wrighten?"

The elevator sped me silently down to earth from the exotic heights of Patrick Timothy's South Bank pad to the dark green heat of the foyer. I pushed through the heavy doors into the night. The wind and rain hit hard. Traffic was still grinding by in the gloom, people on their way home to warmth, reassurance and the T.V. Across the glittering river Big Ben and the Mother of Parliaments looked very solid and depend-

able. A Frimley-style commentary was all it needed—
"For centuries the British Democratic System has
been the envy of the World; Government for the People
and by the People."—and up above the elegant Patrick
and a friend called Gaveston were planning to
remodel the fireside projection of a product called for
Radical Party.

The car's lock was frozen solid. I blew hot air on to
it, forced the key to turn, opened up and set off for
home and Sally.

I'd met Sally Acres as a bright young researcher
fresh from the concrete campus of Sussex. For a couple
of years we'd lived in a basement in Earls Court
on take-out Chinese and Spanish food. Now we were
Cordon Bleu and married, with a cottage on the hill
between Stanmore and Elstree, in a brick forest that
had once been a village.

Somewhere in Camden Town I got stuck behind a
juggernaut. For the next few miles it mechanically
shovelled slush onto my windscreen. To the regular
clatter of the struggling wipers I began to worry
about my future. Despite my freelance status I'd
never really been out of work before. Sally and I and
the children lived pretty high off the hog. I'd need
those party politicals, if and when they occurred. Presumably
they paid market rates for directors—I'd forgotten
to ask.

The juggernaut suddenly swung off right, I cleared
the last crossing and finally drove fast up the hill past
yet another new development. The houses weren't
selling; agents' boards hung askew like loser's banners
above the miniscule gardens. And at sixty thousand or
more, no wonder.

I turned left into the unmade lane that led to our
house at the end. Originally a couple of farmworkers'

cottages knocked together and modernized in the fifties, it had been civilized by Sally's deft touch. By the end of the century we would actually own it. I drove into the open garage, tried to pull down the up-and-over door, but it was stuck again. As I went through the front door I could hear laughter from the room we had converted from a coal-store to a small playroom. A camp Scots voice from the television: "So I minced it up and stuck it in the Haggis!" Screams of synthesized mirth from the box. I looked in at Carey and Kim, curled on the sofa, laughing too. They were enjoyable kids—high-spirited but not impossible. We were lucky.

"Hallo Dad."

"Hi. Where's Mummy?"

"Upstairs with Sarah."

I went on up the narrow stairs, bending my head automatically to avoid the low beam midway. Sally was coming out of Sarah's room. I kissed her, enjoying the moment of her soft fragrance. Sarah called, "Daddy!"

I looked in. "How's the reading?"

Sally biffed me from behind. *"Don't."*

"Rotten." Sarah screwed up her face as I kissed her. A day or so earlier I'd heard an assured commentary from one of the recording theatres: "Slowly the problems of dyslexic children are being uncovered and analyzed. Gradually their difficulties are being overcome. For children, and for parents, there is more than a glimmer of hope. . . ."

But maybe not for *these* parents. At seven, Sarah, highly intelligent in every other way, hadn't begun to read. My eyes met Sally's as I turned out the light. I slipped my arm round her as we walked down the stairs. "Still no better?"

"No. The headmistress is dodging the whole thing. She's saying we should find Sarah a special school."

"Why don't we?"

"When are you ever free to look?"

"Any day. I saw Frimley this afternoon."

"He found you, did he? He phoned here."

"He found me. *Gateway*'s been chopped. And he's not renewing my contract."

She stopped and looked at me. "Why?"

"No reason. Just—no program. Economy time." We'd reached the living room. I went to the drinks cupboard and poured a Tio Pepe for her and a whiskey for myself.

Sally looked at my glass. "That's a big one."

"Need."

"You haven't—upset the old dear?"

"No more than usual."

"Has it happened to anyone else?"

"Not that I know of."

"What about Christmas?"

"We'll manage. As they say." I went on to tell her about the meeting with Patrick Timothy and his friend from the Radicals.

"Doesn't sound very definite." Sally got up and refilled her glass. Normally she had just the one before dinner. "There's a letter from the bank." She hunted among the unopened letters on the mantelpiece. "Here."

"Probably the usual from Misery." I slit open the envelope. The message from Misery Martin was short and only just polite, enclosing a copy of a longer letter from his local director. It was straightforward. The bank wished to cancel my present overdraft facility immediately, and would be grateful if I could arrange

24

to repay the current debit sum—viz. £7,593.47—
forthwith.

Sally said, "You'll have to go and explain to old Misery. Tell him you've just lost your job."

"I'm sure he'd be most sympathetic."

"Then what are you going to do?"

What indeed? "I'll think of something."

"And what about us?"

"Us? The family you mean?"

"You and me."

I knew well enough what she meant. Sally and I
hadn't been getting on too well of late. Within the
confines of a marriage as close as ours I suppose it
was inevitable that we'd have periods of friction. For
no particular reason we were into one now. I wanted
to avoid any sort of argument. I spoke much more
quietly than normal. "There's nothing wrong between
us." I put my arms around her and felt her slightly
resistant, not at all convinced. I said, "We didn't need
Frimley messing up our lives. Not just now."

"No. We didn't need that." She disengaged herself
and walked through into the kitchen.

Supper was the usual, boisterous family affair,
noisy and fun. Then, while Sally washed up, I began
to make a list of prospects. Tomorrow I'd spend the
morning at home and phone a few friends; maybe the
research I'd done on *Gateway* could be put to use on
some other program, for some other company. . . .

In bed Sally wanted to talk further. "Dan—" The
last thing I wanted to do was to analyze our problem
any further. I fell back on nature's good old remedy.

"I've got a better idea—"

"Darling—you don't have to—" But I sensed she too
was in the mood. I snuggled close.

"I love you—"

25

"I know. But you don't have to . . . sort of . . . prove yourself . . . just because of. . . . *Darling!*"

Sally's soft warm body, her specially silky skin texture, was a private naked delight. My hands found her firm orb-breasts and burgeoning nipples and gently caressed from narrow waist and full pliant thighs to moist downy antrum, my lips encouraging her mounting excitement. Soon our very substance joined, and together we searched for, and at last found, the strange dream that makes forgetting easy. That glimpse of the sublime that ends, gasping, all too soon. . . .

She whispered, "It's still very good."

"Better than just very good. . . ."

She slept almost instantly. I envied her that. I suppose in her world nothing could imaginably ever go seriously wrong. Disaster was something you watched on the News, happening to all those sad yellow people with their bicycles and bundles. For us, it would always be all right in the morning.

"That Starsky on TV," Officer Jabowska opined carefully, 'is a goddammed schmuck." With the windows of the patrol car wound right down, he and Officer Taflis sat parked in the space, in shirtsleeves, the sunny Florida afternoon warm and lazy outside. "Some cop he'd make if it were for real."

Officer Taflis nodded. He'd heard it before from Jabowska.

"Every time," Jabowska continued, "every time they go into the whole schmaloola of busting the case, finding the jerk that pulled it, real Ellery Queen stuff. Then they go get him and you're into the rooftop chase. Same chase, same rooftop, week after week. And what next? Bozo pulls a gun and fires. And guess

what, he misses. Course he misses. He ain't a regular in the show. So Starsky shoots him. One shot, no aim, dead. No arrest. No trial. No fuck-nothin'. Just—bang. No blood—out." He looked at Taflis. "Can you imagine what Lootenant Lafleurie would do to us? 'Sorry Lootenant I hadda shoot the guy.' 'You hadda what?' "

Taflis didn't answer. He was intent on some sheet of paper on his clipboard.

"Are you listening? Or do I haveta speak slower?"

Taflis said, "Did we ever get a cancellation on that Nevada registration Torino?"

"How would I know?"

"A Torino just drove by. Could have been Nevada plates."

"You lookin' for a commendation?"

"Black. Like the color they said on the special alert. Think we should tail him?"

"I ain't doin' nothin' else. Let's go." Jabowska switched on the engine and put his right foot down, swinging the patrol car out on to the road fast.

They drove towards the outskirts of the little town, as it sleepily came to life in the late afternoon sun..

"I don't see no black Torino," Jabowska said, unnecessarily, after a bit.

"Keep going."

"Maybe we should switch on the siren like TV cops do."

"Maybe you should shut your mouth and open your eyes."

They covered the length of the single main street, looking from left to right. There were plenty of people about, plenty of cars, parked and moving ahead of them, but no black Torino.

"Give up?" Jabowska said, as they came out into open country.

27

"Keep going."

Ahead the flat landscape slowly changed to more overgrown scrub—the beginnings of swampland. Jabowska, bored, put his throttle foot down; the speedo needle swung up through the seventies. In front of them, dim in the convection-shimmer, Taflis spotted a small shape, moving along fast.

"What's that? He's busting the fifty limit, whoever he is."

Jabowska pushed the speed up to eighty, eighty-five. Now they could begin to discern the outlines of the car ahead of them. Color dark, definitely a Torino. Now Jabowska really piled on the power, rapidly shortening the distance between.

The driver of the Torino must have, suddenly recognized his pursuers as police. With a tearing of back tires he accelerated rapidly, starting to pull away again. The road they were traversing was built like a causeway, at times standing well above the surrounding scrub and swamp, as it threaded into damp and heavy vegetation.

"Hope he knows his way," Taflis muttered.

Jabowska nodded. About a mile further on they both knew the treacherous Alphacola Bend, ready-sprung trap for speed merchants. The warning signs were already sprouting on the right of the narrow highway and were all ignored by the Torino up front. Grimly Jabowska ploughed in all his driving skills to stay on the guy's tail.

Then came the final huge warning sign, "Very Dangerous Bend". The Torino roared into the curve, overhung by limp trees, like an express train into a tunnel, and momentarily disappeared from their sight. Jabowska instinctively applied his brakes carefully, war-

*ily ready to steer out of a skid. At that moment they
heard the mad screech of tires ahead, an explosive collision, and the sound of metal ripping apart as if under a violent buzz-saw. As Jabowska braked hard,
both braced themselves for their inevitable scorching
stop.*

*As they slowed into the dark sharp bend they saw
the wreckage ahead. The Torino, right out of control,
had smashed into the front of a huge Mack tow-truck
grinding its way through the hairpin. The truck-driver
had taken the full force of the impact and lay,
smashed and bleeding, in the ruins of his cab. The
Torino had ridden up the front like a madman's bob-
sleigh, and hung now at ninety degrees, its driver's
door gaping. Jabowska threw his door open and made
for the wreckage at a run. Taflis grabbed his mike and
shouted the call-sign urgently.*

But of the driver of the Torino there was no sign.

I spent that Tuesday morning at home in Stanmore,
and the time ran by as I worked my way through my
list of possible new job contacts. Having become part
of the furniture at the Corporation this was a new experience, and I wasn't exactly in luck either. There
was a girl I knew at Granada who'd just been pro-
moted to producer, who might have been interested in
picking up my prison series. She was abroad. There
was a man at Thames who ought to have liked another idea I had about examining NATO in depth. He
was in a meeting, and didn't call me back. I'd heard
that London Weekend were setting up a new Documentary Department. But the man they'd named as
head was on leave.

The phone suddenly rang. It was Patrick Timothy, fulsome about last night. "Great success. Gaveston's completely sold on you, boyo."

"That's good."

Patrick said, "There's something else on the horizon. If you're interested. A man I know has just come in from the Far East to set up a big commercial, in a hurry. I mean, you did say you were free."

"A commercial for what?"

"Some sort of cigarettes, I think he said."

"They can't show cigarette commercials."

'They can in Hong Kong, apparently. He'd like to meet you."

Fag commercials? Had I come down to that already? "I'll let you know Patrick."

"Today?"

"Yes. Sure." I wouldn't of course. Party politicals were one thing, but I hadn't come down to cigarette butts. Not yet.

The phone rang again and this time it was Misery Martin, asking me to come and see him at the bank.

They'd opened a Tandoori restuarant right next to Misery's branch in Stanmore. An odor of curry now permeated the building. In happier times Martin would refer to "my Oriental bazaar". There were no jokes, however, this morning. Just a polite smile.

Misery was grey-haired and thin, probably right on retiring age. Thirty years and more after the Second World War he still sported a fraying Royal Artillery tie and a toothbrush moustache, memories of his best years as a Gunner Subaltern. Followed by more than thirty years behind a desk hectoring people like me. He actually opened with something like: "The bank isn't a charitable institution. I sometimes wish it were—"

30

I wasn't having that. "What *is* all this, Mr. Martin?"

"Have you ever computed the rate by which your current expenditure exceeds you after-tax income?"

"Not exactly, but—"

"Some months it's over eighty pounds. In a month." He sucked air in through a hollow tooth, savouring the idea of my reckless spendthrift life, like a wine-taster a rare Chambertin. "Twenty pounds a week more than you earn."

I said, "It's called inflation. We have three kids at school, two cars, an elderly mother-in-law and a cat."

"Have you any idea how you might—er—cut down on your living standards?"

"None. Short of sending the kids out begging." Joke, Mr. Martin.

"None?"

"The house is reasonably cheap to run. My car's three years old. Sure, I buy a few drinks for people here and there, but that's part of the television business."

Misery didn't answer. Again I could see his imagination wrestling with unbelievable Bacchanalian fantasies. "Yes. I've heard some stories of what goes on."

"Your letter says, I have to repay right away. What's the urgency? Why does the bank need my Widow's Mite?"

Misery looked furtive. "There's been a—a change of policy."

"Well—I suppose I could take out a second mortgage to clear off this sum."

"Not a course I should advise. You've still nineteen years to run on your present one."

"You looked it up?"

"Er—yes. Tell me frankly, what are your immediate prospects?"

31

I could wing this one. "Prospects? There's about to be a considerable pay-raise for directors, I understand. Our union's in negotiation—"

"But what about you personally? Your contract is, I believe, freelance?"

"That's right. It's better, tax-wise—"

"Negotiable on termination? Every year?"

"Roughly speaking, yes."

"*If* they decide to renew?"

"Naturally."

"When does the termination next occur?"

"As it happens, at the end of this month."

"The end of this month." Misery made a note on his pad. "And you have reason to believe the Corporation will renew?"

"No. I have every reason to believe that they won't."

"Ah." Misery had simply seen too many of those terrible British war films on the late, late show. He was playing this like the man from the Pinewood branch of the Gestapo. He took a deep breath for the climatic bit.

But I got in first. "I've been offered something else. Something very lucrative. An important commercial."

There was no other way.

THREE

It had been getting darker all afternoon, the rain slashing across the bay, the wind driving black-foamed waves up the oil-stained sand. Then early nightfall brought total darkness, suddenly broken by vivid flares of lightning—vanguard spears of the coming storm

Inside the small police station it was sauna-hot. . . . Minute beads of perspiration trickled from the forehead of the girl doctor as, sickened despite her training, she attended the young man's wounds to head, chest and stomach. A couple of fishermen had picked him out of the inshore surf more dead than alive. It had been easier for them to bring him here to the police station than to call a rented ambulance to take him all the way to hospital in Fort Lauderdale.

Ronson, the young sergeant, black face sweat-polished, walked quietly over to watch as the girl's deft fingers firmly wound the heavy bandage around the man's beaten skull and neatly taped it fast. He'd seen them like this before; junkies who missed their footing off a yacht and were washed up nearly drowned.

Behind him, Officer Montes, face like carved mahogany in an Aztec museum, put down the phone he had been using, made a further note on his pad and wandered across to join Ronson.

'Find anything?'

"He's a hot tamale." Montes flipped through the pages of the pad in his hand. " 'Jeff Sadler'—that was the name on the dog-tags he was wearing round his neck. Turns out he's a technician in some nuclear project over in Nevada; been listed as missing several days. But they want him kept here."

"Here? This ain't no hospital, man."

"It's a definite order from headquarters. Hold on to him, make him comfortable, and at all costs keep him alive."

Ronson turned to the girl. "What are his chances, miss?"

She shook her head quickly. "No way. Not here. We've got to get him to a hospital."

"Sorry," said Montes. "We have to await the arrival of the FBI."

"Those jerks? Screw them for a start." Ronson looked at the young doctor again. "How bad is he? For real?"

The girl shrugged impatiently. "You can see. Multiple head injuries—I won't know just how extensive till I get an x-ray—certainly a skull fracture somewhere. And further massive injuries to chest, spine, pelvis, and both legs. Either he had a terrible fall or—"

"Someone put him through the grinder." Ronson grimaced. "What should we do?"

"We've got to get him to intensive care. There's no other hope."

34

"You heard the orders."

"He won't last." The girl seemed almost close to tears. Ronson frowned. It wasn't his responsibility, but the guy was dying. The girl watched him anxiously as he tried to think clearly. He held out his hand to Montes. "Let me see that stuff you've got."

Montes handed over the papers. "Those are my notes from headquarters just now. This is the original 'Wanted' circulation. 'Top Priority' and 'Top Secret.'"

The air in the little room was thick and stuffy as Ronson looked the papers over, wandering back to his desk. The wind was still angrily rattling the slats of the shutters outside the windows; distantly they could hear the grumble of approaching thunder and then, quite suddenly, the light drum beat of tropical rain on the roof.

Montes said, "Hell of a blow coming up."

Ronson looked up. "What do you think?"

"Me?" Ronson didn't usually ask his opinion.

"Yeah. What the hell do we do?"

"Well," Montes said, slowly. "He's a hot tamale like I said. Run out of some nuclear plant. Don't take much imagination to guess why the Feds want him back so bad. He's made a heist of the 'great big secret'."

"Just like in the movies. OK, big brain—if he's gonna die any minute like the lady says—what do we do?"

"The question is—has he got the—whatever-it-is—on him now?"

"There's nothing in his pockets," the girl doctor said quickly.

"So he must have delivered it," Ronson said.

"To some guys on a boat, maybe?" Montes added.

35

"And they took him to sea, killed him—or thought they had—and dumped him overboard?"

"You said it. Just like the movies."

"It could just be. Then we need to ask him only the one question." Ronson walked thoughtfully back towards the scarcely breathing figure on the bench, and leant over him, looking down at the bandaged head, the sorely battered face. "Jeff," he murmured.

"Please!" The girl grasped his arms and tried to pull the heavily built sergeant away. "You can't start asking him questions. He's dying!"

"Just the one." Ronson bent close to Sadler's blood-dried cheek, easing one eyelid open with a gentle thumb. "Jeff," he whispered. "What was the name of their boat?"

It took time, and patience, but in the end Sadler managed to mouth one word. "Pasquello."

Far out to sea, the big blow had started for real. The United States Coast Guard cutter Farragut was punching her way back to port through seas already approaching force six or seven, steering on radar. The skipper, Tad Colby, standing beside the helmsman, his face etched with crystallizing salt, peered at the unremitting blackness ahead, vision clear through the huge spinning spray deflectors, despite the relentless hammering of rain on the windscreen. Bracing his knees automatically as he felt the bows strike and dig through each succeeding big wave, Colby was tired, but content.

It had been a good season so far with not too many sinkings. Maybe the drug-runners were finally getting the message: the Coast Guard, well-armed and better informed, with a new surveillance-system over the whole of the eastern seaboard, had finally made the Miami Run unprofitable. Or that was the way it was being reported to Congress.

"Radio message, sir."

Colby turned to the young operator and took the yellow slip. "Thanks." He scanned it quickly. "Pasquello." The name wasn't familiar but few of them ever were. "Seventy foot fisherman. In your area. Under no circumstances to leave U.S. waters. Sink if vital." Christ, they sure picked some weather for a seasearch.

He read off the position given in the message, moved over to the radar scanner and rested his face easily against the thick rubber cowling over the screen. He set the figures given from master radar; the regular green sweep showed no more than a few freaks and shadows. He flicked a switch for greater magnification. Now he could see more clearly, a couple of dots to the north east, just about the position given, either of which might easily be a seventy-footer.

Colby straightened up, face red from the brief enclosure in the cowling. "Helmsman, bring her back to sixty, east, nor' east."

The helmsman repeated the order before swinging the wheel over. As their bows swung, the little ship caught the full force of the wind and the sea head-on, the huge waves pounding the groaning metal hull. Then the strength of the cutter's powerful diesels surged through the propellers, and the rolling, bucketing vessel surged forward again into the blackness.

The ship had been designed to do thirty-five knots in weather as bad as this. Inevitably it would overtake the boats ahead. All that remained was to stay up-

37

right, as she hammered her way through the sea's violence.

The horizon was momentarily lit by sudden flashes of lightning when they made contact over an hour later. Consequently, Colby could occasionally see the outlines of a sleek white fisherman against the greasy grey of the sea. Probably a seventy-footer, more than likely the Pasquello.

Still holding his handgrip and wary of the ship's sudden lurching, Colby picked up his radio handset. "Channel 16." A click in the earpiece and a voice.

"Channel 16, sir."

"Pasquello, Pasquello." Colby spoke carefully and slowly. "This is U.S. Coast Guard vessel Farragut approaching you aft. I call on you to stop and be identified." He paused, then repeated the same message.

A bright lightning burst showed the vessel ahead, hopelessly continuing at full speed. In the end the coastguard must overtake her. Colby knew roughly what to expect and didn't relish the prospect. Another fine boat, product of the latest technology and craftsmanship, superbly equipped with electronic devices, envy of thousands of make-do sailors, would shortly be raked by gunfire and sent to the ocean's depths. And all because she was a vehicle for drugs: a pawn in a game that created cripples and criminals with factory-like certainty. It was the waste, the senseless abuse of fine boats, that stirred Colby's very soul.

They were definitely closing in now, within the last two hundred yards. He lifted the handset and called up again on another channel. Same message—same lack of response. If anything, the Pasquello seemed to be trying to put on a last burst of speed, seeking a sort of shelter in the rough heart of the approaching storm.

Colby gave his orders quickly. The cutter had two

fast-firing cannons mounted fore and aft, and a further two machine guns midships. Seamen staggered along the heaving deck to uncover and arm these weapons. The bosun, heavy in outsize oilskins and over-trousers, clambered his way forward to a powerful spotlight up in the bows.

The other boat was now less than a hundred yards ahead. The bosun switched on the spotlight and focussed. In the brilliant beam the words "PASQUELLO, San Juan" showed clearly on the stern, black on white. On deck a couple of dark figures seemed to be working on the lashings of a large inflatable amidships.

"Sir." The helmsman nodded over to starboard.

Colby peered through the greying light. About a mile away, he could just make out a black mass, like a billowing rainstorm, or a heavy squall, approaching fast. Colby said, "Hold full speed."

"Aye, sir."

Eighty yards now. In the spotlight's remorseless glare, the two men abruptly left the inflatable and disappeared below. Colby lifted the microphone for one last appeal. 'Pasquello, Pasquello. Coastguard approaching. Please stop and be recognized. Continue at your peril."

The sleek white boat sped on.

Colby switched on the intercom to the gunners. "Prepare attack. Prepare attack. Warning only. Single rounds." The shivering gunners released the safety mechanism. Ready lights showed up on the panel on the bridge.

"Take aim," Colby said quietly. "Warning shots only."

In the bows the bosun raised a loud-hailer. "Pasquello, Pasquello. Stop now or we attack." His voice echoed in the darkness unheeded; the Pasquello thundered on.

Expressionless, Colby gave the order.

"Fire." The two cannons spat single shot, red tracer sailing like mad mosquitoes well above the white cabin into the eclipsing distance.

"Second warning."

The bosun repeated his loudhailed ultimatum. The cutter was breasting the leading boat's wash. Colby ordered a deflection to starboard, bringing her bows level with the Pasquello's stern. There was movement on deck now. "Second warning," he ordered, "Aim."

This close, the gunners had even more difficulty aiming well clear above the glittering sea-thrashed deck of the runaway.

"Fire." Again the cannons reacted, bright vermilion dots speeding into the dark infinity above the deck.

And at that moment the squall hit both boats simultaneously. For seconds the Pasquello vanished from sight in a black ferment of sea, wind and driving rain. Then it reappeared, speeding away from the cutter hard to port.

"Port forty," Colby rapped.

The cutter heeled over in the very gut of the violent squall, then came round square, catching up on the Pasquello rapidly. Colby grabbed a hand-hold. "Aim to sink," he ordered clearly. "All guns. At will. Fire."

The gunners, hands frozen and streaming, bracing their bodies and legs against the enveloping seats, fought to keep the white hull just below the waterline, in the cross-hairs of their sights.

Then they fired. Again and again the streams of brilliant tracer flew and tore into the side of the retreating Pasquello. Bits of fibreglass flew up from the water like shrapnel. As the sea began to pour into her

40

bilges under the continuous attack, the Pasquello *started to yaw dangerously, suddenly swinging round in the path of the pursuing cutter.*

And then it seemed to Colby as if a great fist heaved their ship right out of the foaming sea and spun it around on its axis. He stared in horror at the towering grey wall of water that suddenly surrounded them, engulfing them.

"Christ! It's no squall—it's a water-spout!"

Colby rushed to the helmsman's side and added his weight to try to regain control of the wildly spinning wheel. The bows were swinging from side to side. The ship reared up, only to smash down again into the tumultuous waves. Desperately the two men fought the wheel, and at last felt some response.

A white shape loomed above them on the crest of a massive wave that broke over their bows. With a searing, explosive sound, the nose of the coastguard vessel cut right through the hull of the Pasquello *like so much powder-snow. A spar slammed into the bridge windscreen, crazing the safety glass into a million icicles. With one hand Colby brought the engines back to "Slow," as he felt the ship answering the helm again, and the whirling power of the water-spout passed on and over them.*

Now, and only now, could he look aft. There was no sign of the Pasquello *in their foaming wake. Grimly he ordered the helmsman to turn about. The cutter heeled once more is it came downwind. . . .*

Pulling up the hood of his oilskin anorak, Colby slid open the door of the bridge-house, feeling the cold lash of sea and savage rain on his face as he stepped on to the violently pitching deck. He staggered foward to where the bosun, fortunately unharmed by the collision, still crouched beside the spotlight, swinging it

41

across the waves ahead, lighting nothing but the end-less blue-black waters.

Then they saw the wreckage. The Pasquello had split neatly into two halves, the stern section barely afloat, the bows a sad pyramid slowly subsiding into the rough foaming depths before their eyes. There was no sign of any other wreckage, not even the inflatable.

Colby took it all in. He'd seen similar sights many times before, though not in weather as bad as this. He knew the required drill.

"Search procedure."

If I was going to solve Misery Martin's self-imposed banking conundrum I needed to move quickly. It took just one call to Patrick Timothy to fix a meeting that very afternoon with his advertising friend from the Far East. His name, it appeared, was Mike O'Neill.

We met in his hotel, a suite, not a room, overlooking Hyde Park; a centrally-heated view of bare trees, rain-sodden earth, and the occasional muffled-up walker.

O'Neill was a confident heavy: face like a boxer, sallow and suntanned, exuding exotic confidence in a lightweight Dacron suit that looked as if it had been knocked up overnight by a tired tailor in downtown Kowloon. His handshake was soft and fleshy, hard-centered with thick, gold rings on most of his fingers. Indeed, gold featured plentifully in O'Neill's ward-robe—a hefty watch, a name-bracelet on the other wrist, even a gleaming 22-carat toggle holding the silk scarf around his thick neck.

While the inevitable waiter poured lukewarm cof-fee, O'Neill spelled it out. As he spoke I tried to place his accent. It was nearly, not quite, Australian. He'd started his advertising agency in Hong Kong eight years ago and done well. "Ever been there?"

"Only briefly." My first impression had been of the evercrowded streets of Kowloon and Victoria, the busy moving mass. Then a snatched trip to the border had shown me the other picture—the still lagoons, the great empty vastness of China beyond.

"I bet you've never heard of Expert cigarettes?"

"You're right. I haven't."

O'Neill produced a flashy-looking pack, all gilt and purple. "They're the top sellers in H.K. We've had the account for two years." He flipped it open. "Try one."

"Sorry, I don't smoke. Not even Experts."

"Well that's the product."

"Why come all this way to make a commercial?"

"We thought we'd do it properly for a change. We've been offered some air time over Christmas at a discount, so we need a sharp-looking promo in a hurry."

"Just the one?"

"That's right. Just a well-shot thirty seconds. You see, all the ads we run about Experts suggest they're made in the States and smoked by top men everywhere. In fact we import the tobacco from Red China and roll them in a factory up in the New Territories. But our Hong Kong people are peculiar. Tell 'em it's local-made and they'll piss on it. So we kid them that Experts are high-class imported, and you get tri-shaw runners buying one or two at a time in the hand for the same money they'd pay for a whole pack of genuine Chinese gaspers."

The script, it seemed, was still being written but he'd have a copy tomorrow. "It's a guy on a yacht in the Caribbean, the guy that's got everything. But we want it looking tough and real—none of this poofta soft-focus. That's why we want you. Patrick tells me you have a reputation for ballsy shooting."

I nodded. No point in playing humble. "When is all this?"

"You leave tomorrow."

"So soon?"

"I told you we were in a hurry, fella."

"Are you coming over for the shoot?"

"No. You'll be on your own."

"Where?"

"We've set it up in St. Thomas."

"Where's that? Near Barbados, somewhere?"

"The U.S. Virgin Islands. You fly on from New York. The camera crew's been booked in the States. They'll join you Thursday, shoot Friday, travel back Saturday. We're processing the film here, so you take a can of raw stock with you, and bring it back, sealed, for developing and printing. I want the whole thing cut and dubbed and into show copy by the end of next week."

"How about casting? Have you an actor in mind for this yachtsman?"

"No we just get some sort of good-looking American. I've contacted a casting director in New York I've been recommended, name of Mort Sleeman. You know him?"

"No—but then I don't use that many actors. And I've never worked out of New York."

"Well he's doing it. He's set up the auditions for eleven-thirty tomorrow—that's about an hour after your plane ought to get in. You grab a cab into town, pick which ever guy you like the look of best, then fly on to St. Thomas. The actor you take flies down with the crew next day."

44

I thought, I can do it standing on my head. I nodded. It all seemed settled. Apart from the fee. And I made sure that *that* was big enough to bring the roses back to Misery Martin's cheeks, and take care of Christmas.

"Don't answer it." The pretty freckled woman with the chestnut hair frowned slightly as she spoke. A lunch table had been set for two in the small conservatory. Weak sunlight added to the centrally-heated illusion of spring-like weather, though deep snow lay the other side of the bullet-proof double-glazing.

"I just wish I didn't have to." The grey man smiled affectionately as he took the telephone from the butler and dismissed him with a quick nod.

"President speaking."

A confident voice began to report. The grey man listened carefully.

"Has the cause of this man—Sadler's—death been clearly established?"

The voice in the earpiece gave him details—violence to the person reduced to flat medical terminology.

"And the boat?" Again the grey man listened, for some time, as his caller read out Colby's verbatim account of the pursuit and sinking of the Pasquello. *Despite the stilted prose of the coastguard's report, the grey man could imagine the whole scene. After four years in the wartime U.S. Navy he didn't need flowery adjectives to conjure up vivid images of boiling black seas, huge waves abruptly rearing like fearsome mountains over a frail craft which is somehow supported on a treacherous surface that might open at any minute and swiftly suck it down to oblivion.*

"Any survivors?"

45

Only two bodies had been found. But the normal complement of a boat like the Pasquello must have been at least four. And the inflatable had disappeared. . . .

"Thank you." The grey man replaced the telephone and thought for a moment. Probably everything was under control again as he'd been assured. The runaway technician was dead, his accomplices all sunk with the secret.

"Come and eat, darling," the pretty woman said. "This was to have been our quiet lunch together, remember?"

The grey man smiled at her warmly. Somehow, some instinct made him unsure. The problem was not properly resolved, was still ticking on. He'd pass it on to Waldorf. . . .

After wrapping up the final details of the commercial with Mike O'Neill, I dropped off at Video City on the way home. Frimley wasn't in his office, but I found him in the fifth-floor toilet, anxiously combing his thin strands of hair across the top of his forehead. His eye caught mine in the mirror as I explained I'd need the rest of the week off. He didn't seem surprised. "Don't bother about filling in a leave form," he said affably. "Just go—wherever it is you're going."

"Thanks." I wasn't going to enlighten him further.

I watched as Frimley's comb streaked across his head once more, sending a small shower of dandruff, like midget confetti, all over his collar. He still looked furtive. "About April," he suddenly said.

"What—about April?"

"The series I mentioned—"

"Britain's economy?"

"That's right. It—ah—looks more than possible. No firm date yet. But—possible." He smiled rather oddly, and left the small room abruptly.

I drove home to find Sally bathing Sarah.

"A commercial?"

I'd half-expected opposition from her. We'd always had reservations about my touching commercials. Several or our friends were deeply into advertising, but Sally had strong views about getting involved in the superficial end of an ephemeral medium like television.

I said, "I leave tomorrow for the Caribbean."

"What for? Sticky coconut chocolate?"

"No." Spit it out. "Cigarettes."

Silence as expected. Sally was heavy on antismoking.

I said, "We need the money. It solves the immediate problem." I gave her a quick run-down on the Misery interview.

"Silly old fool. He must know the cost of groceries these days."

"I wonder if he does?"

"He must have some sort of wife, a family."

"I doubt it." I could imagine Misery Martin living in a frosty one-room flat on a diet of macrobiotic brown rice and sterilized apple-juice. "Anyway," I added, "The whole job will take a week."

"And then?"

"Back to the Corporation in April. Frimley said so."

Sally brushed her hair away from a face steamy with bathroom heat, and lifted Sarah clear, wrapping her gently in warm soft towels, cuddling her as she rubbed her dry.

47

Our eyes met. Sally said, "It's not going to become a habit, is it?"

"One off," I said. "Do it, take the money and run."

"Good." She didn't need to say more. Part of our mutual, unspoken deal was shared attitude of something like integrity towards an, alas, very tatty medium—television.

I watched in silence as she settled our daughter in bed, gave Sarah a lusty goodnight kiss, and followed Sally down the stairs.

Sally said, "It's a bloody nuisance, you going off like this. I'd arranged for us both to look at a new school for Sarah on Thursday. You did say you were going to be free."

"Well—now I'll be working."

"In the Caribbean. Tough."

"Would you rather I turned it down?"

She stopped and looked at me. "Don't make *me* decide. You said we needed the money."

"We do."

"Well then."

I drew a deep breath. "We'll look at the new school next week. When I get back."

"If you can tear yourself away."

"I will. Promise."

But the old tension had come back between us. I never quite understood exactly what Sally was afraid of when I took off on a foreign location. As it happened, I didn't sleep around that much and she knew it, but perhaps she had some other instinct that our bond might one day be subjected to an irresistable pressure, and break.

So, both of us, alone and separate in the same bed, were restless and occasionally sleepless that night.

I made my farewells to the kids over breakfast cereals, but my goodbye to Sally at Heathrow was fairly strained. We kissed passionlessly at the passenger entrance, as people do in public places. I had a moment of regret for all the things I hadn't been able to say, as I watched her walk away through the hustling crowd and disappear into a moving kaleidoscope of faces, bodies and shiny luggage.

Then I was claimed by a friendly shipping agent, carrying a bumper parcel from O'Neill; the flimsy script which would take me all of a couple of minutes to read on the plane, a bulky package of Experts in cartons specially polished up for pack-shots, and the thousand-foot roll of 35mm. Eastmancolor negative film, sealed, docketed, and stamped for re-entry into Britain by HM Customs.

"The only other thing," the agent asked, "is, do you want to stay in First Class?"

"Is there a choice?"

"The clients have booked you into First."

"The Corp always send me Tourist."

"I know." He was helpful, not supercilious. "Knowing you came from there I just wondered. Quite a few people swap for Tourist and get the cash refund."

Why not? I could survive without flat champagne and erastz caviar at thirty thousand feet. He had it all fixed by the time the flight to New York was called, thrusting a useful handful of bank notes in my direction. Clutching my briefcase, my can of film, and my cardboard box of Experts, I queued and trudged with all the other aerial refugees towards the opening in the jumbo, and finally slumped into a window-seat at the back, and relaxed at last.

49

It was still, I realized, only Wednesday morning. Less than two days ago I'd been lunching with a man from the Home Office trying to argue my camera into a top-security prison. Now that was all over, yesterday's problem, and I was off in the opposite direction. Doing what? That feeling of unreality was here again.

The plane wasn't that crowded. My whole row remained empty until the doors were closed. Strapped in, I flicked through the flight magazine, heard the engines roar for take-off, looked out briefly to see the roads and reservoirs disappearing below through low cloud, watched the hostesses' gangway pantomine with life-jackets and little yellow oxygen masks. I'd seen the in-flight movie, and I didn't need eight hours of Golden Moments with Rentovani in both ears, so I avoided a plastic headset. As the machine at last emerged into high altitude winter sunshine, I took the short script out of its envelope to find out just what I was into.

It only filled a page, and had been written, in a hurry, by the office-boy. It was no less than your old-fashioned Man-of-Distinction in a fit: the "gleaming" yacht in the blue Caribbean, the "expensive" stainless steel fishing tackle, even his "Swiss chronometer" wrist-watch, and "hand-made Gucci deck-shoes," all reverently and enviously copied out of some yellowing back-number of *Vogue*—1960s style. "A man of superlative taste, of judgement, of skill, and style, naturally chooses only the best for his smoking pleasure. . . ." Cut to—guess what?—a pack of Experts as his well-manicured hand selects one. And cancer comes free.

Bogus and unoriginal. If I'd had any doubts about what I was doing for the money I had none now. I put the paper down and made for the rear toilet.

When I came back, there was a girl sitting in the

seat next to mine, calmly reading the single page of script. She looked up and smiled. "Hallo."

"Hi."

"I didn't think they could show smoking commercials any more."

"They can in the Far East. So I'm told."

She smiled again, and stood up, so that I could pass across to my seat by the window, letting her breasts gently brush my shoulder through her shirt as I moved by. As she sat down again her long blonde hair fell forward, almost over her startingly clear blue eyes, that smiled again as she said, "My name's Gisela Braun."

"Dan Galloway." I wasn't going to ask to what I owed this honor, but she answered as if I had.

"I was bored. Looking for company. Do too much flying I guess."

"Don't tell me—you're an air hostess?"

She was. Coming back from vacation in London. "You look surprised."

"I am. Most of the flying nuns I seem to travel with don't use your kind of perfume."

"You like it?"

"They don't wear it on Aeroflot."

The sheet of script had fallen to the floor. She bent to pick it up, and handed it to me. "You're really making this—cigarette junk?"

"I really am. Not, I hasten to add, what I usually do."

"And what *do* you usually do?"

I started to tell her. She'd seen quite a bit of British television and, with a certain amount of help, began to make herself believe she'd even watched some of my documentaries. We entered that curious pressurized-air-induced euphoria that happens on long flights

—a sort of rapture of the depths in reverse, enjoying each other's company for that exact moment and no more.

Closely observed, she wasn't as young as I'd thought, maybe all of thirty, or even thirty-five, but her glamour was undeniable. Her accent was somehow not American, as though it had begun somewhere in Europe.

She said suddenly, "Why aren't you in First Class?"

"Why should I be?"

"Surely an advertising agency would send you First on a job like this?"

I confessed about the London shipper and the refund he'd fixed. She laughed in a way that sounded almost relieved. "I should worry. It's all Chinese dollars to me. We get our flights at ten percent of the going rate."

Drinks arrived, then more, then lunch. It was no hardship talking to her. At 40,000 feet we chatted our way back and forth across the globe, telling stories of places we'd enjoyed—Jaipur and Patnos, Jakarta and Fez, Omdurman, Bangkok and Leningrad. At last I asked her the question I'd been saving. "Where were you born?"

She frowned. "It's called Prieczin nowadays. It used to be Halmstadt, and something else when it was part of Czechoslovakia, but the Germans had taken over by the time I was born." She stopped, seeing the furious addition going on in my mind. "That dates me exactly, doesn't it?"

"Must have been a vintage year."

It wasn't Neil Simon but it would serve. She smiled again with those amazing eyes. "Thank you. Anyway, after the war it became Polish, so I could have stayed Polish if I'd tried."

"But you didn't?"

"No. I'm American now. I married a soldier—but that didn't last. So here I am—a simple working girl."

"Working very nicely, too."

A hostess was passing. Gisela asked, "Jane—how long till landing?"

"Less than an hour now. Everything OK back here?"

"Fine." Gisela turned back to me. As she raised her hand to brush her hair back I noticed a small gold ornament on her bracelet, some sort of symbol, a circle with a double cross motif inside. She said, "Can you see anything down there?"

I looked out of the window past the silver and oil-slicked wing through the murky cloud. We were already flying over land again. Heaps of brown and dark green showed up amid flat white patches of snow, the occasional lake and a few roads or houses. Nova Scotia could it be? It looked very cold and distant.

It was warm in the cabin though. Gisela asked, "Are you stopping off in New York?"

"Only a couple of hours, for an audition. Then I fly straight on."

"Pity. Still, I've a couple of days vacation left. The Caribbean isn't that far."

But I didn't follow through with the obvious invitation. I was supposed to be working, after all.

The jumbo hit the ground hard at Kennedy. Outside the steamed-up windows there were biting winds and patches of frozen snow on the runways; men in earmuffs drove up in small tractors to collect the baggage. And snugly within, we gathered up our odds and ends to musak memories of the appalling thirties—

Glenn Miller style—and trudged through the long concertina-way to baggage claim.

We waited, suddenly strangers again, until at last the long conveyor rumbled into action and cases bounced like starlets through the ragged rubber curtains, to be grabbed off by porters.

"Gisela! How you been?" The voice behind was loud enough to make me turn. A man had come up to Gisela and taken her hand. I'd noticed him when we first came through, one of those grey characters that seem to stand around in every airport customs area, vaguely watchful, sent there by who-knew-what curious agency of surveilance.

"Hallo." Gisela spoke quietly, not smiling back.

"How about a drink?" the man said. "I can take ten minutes out."

"Sorry. I have to go."

"Aw, come on honey. It's been a long time—"

"No," she said. I couldn't understand why she was suddenly so angry.

The man didn't either. "Gisela, what's wrong, baby?"

"I'm busy."

"*Too* busy? Too busy for *me*?"

Gisela didn't answer, simply walked away. I saw my case appear and went forward to take it. As I swung it clear Gisela was beside me again. "Who was that?" I asked.

"Oh just a guy I know—or one I don't even want to know. He used to work for the airline."

"In Security?"

"Something like that. How d'you guess?"

"The way he looked. What's he do now?"

She shrugged. "No idea. I didn't want to get involved anyway. Not when I'm working."

"Working?" She'd said she was on vacation.

She looked confused for an instant. "All travel's like work if you do it as much as I do." She pointed. "Those are mine."

Her cases were real hide with fancy locks. "Are we sharing a cab?" she said.

"Where do you have to go? I've got to see some actors on East 38th and then come straight back."

"Couldn't be better. You can drop me off at First and 44th, right by the UN building."

We trudged through customs. I had to go through the formality of declaring my roll of undeveloped film, but the agent at Heathrow had done all the work. The top copy of the carnet was stamped, torn off and kept, and I was handed the film back with the rest of the papers. Provided the paperwork's right you can swan all over the world with a sealed package of film—and no questions asked.

We found a porter and followed him through the automatic doors from dry warmth into the bite of instant Siberia. Taxis were crawling in through the slanting sleet, nibbling slowly at the huddled queue. Our turn came at last and we settled into the steamy comfort of a Checker back seat. The driver, fur-hatted, unshaven, hunched in some sort of hairy bomber jacket like a prehistoric ape, took charge of the luggage, swearing to himself in a continuous and profane litany about the weather as he resumed his seat and took us off into the blizzard.

Gisela gave me a quick smile, then relaxed, looking out at the misty white curtain streaming past the windows. The road was a rutted mixture of salted slush and treacherous ice as we reached the highway, with its lonely airport hotels standing like huge tombstones in the white flat wilderness. We passed the frozen

55

remnants of the World's Fair of '64, where I'd seen President Lyndon B. Johnson descend by helicopter into an unexpected riot of Civil Rights protest; it was now naked of humanity, bland and frozen. At last we crossed the iced-up metal lattices of the Queensborough Bridge, with the black East River brooding below, and finally reached Manhattan.

We fell into line with slow lanes of traffic moving downtown and eastwards. "Just here," Gisela said abruptly, tapping the perspex shield behind the driver's head.

He braked in a slither of brown slush and opened her door.

"Don't get out," she said to me, and suddenly came close and kissed my cheek. "I hope I see you again. Sometime."

I mumbled some form of vague assent. We hadn't even exchanged addresses.

"Might even see you in the sunshine," she said as she got out, her cream leather coat suddenly flurried white with flakes. She headed towards the entrance of what seemed to be a new and very smart apartment building, the driver ambling after.

And then again, I thought, you might not. How many times does one strike up a quick plane-time relationship that ends as abruptly as it began? I went on watching as a porter took care of her luggage in the opulent doorway. Air hostessing must certainly pay to provide her with a pad like this. As she waved a final time and the glass doors slid to behind her, I realized what I'd noticed back at the airport. All her bags had First Class flight tabs on them.

"Nice-looking chick," the driver grunted as he slammed back in and we rumbled forward again.

"Nice big ass. I like a broad with sump'n I can move right into."

Thus, having lyrically declared his personal erotic stance, he relapsed into moody silence again all the way to the address I'd given him on 38th.

It seemed to be a fairly run-down building in a churned-up area. I found Sleeman Casting down a flight of steps to a basement office. Holding on to my bags and my carton of Experts I pushed at the door of a place that looked more like a sleazy barber's shop in Lower Paisley—except that it turned out to be full of girls. There were a half a dozen or more, who all perked up as I entered—crossing their legs, licking their shiny lips, sticking their boobs out and flashing on the old neon smiles—all for little me, Big Director of a thirty-second gasper plug.

"Hi. I'm Mort Sleeman." An ancient hand grabbed mine, and I found myself facing a little old man in a ginger rinse and a bright purple golfing jacket, with "Morty" writ large on the patch pocket. "You must be Dan Galway."

"Galloway."

"Not 'Galway' like 'Galway Bay'?"

"No. Like some other place."

He smiled. At least the teeth were fresh and new. "All this has been kind of short notice, even for a pro like me. This is the best selection I could raise." He waved at the girls sitting and standing uncomfortably in the hot, cramped room.

And among the faces watching me with false hope I could see those of three men, one bald and nearly as old as the crapulous Mort, the others fairly nondescript.

I said, "There's been a mistake. I don't need any

girls. Just the one guy, driving his yacht in the Caribbean." It sounded even worse when I spelt it out.

Mort winked, and nudged me like a red-nose in burlesque.

"Sure thing. Driving his yacht. Great. And these young ladies are the scenery. Lying around on deck. You know—bikinis—topless—bare-ass—you name it."

I couldn't see even a slob like O'Neill paying for that.

"We'd never see them," I said. "It's just the thirty seconds."

"No broads?"

"None. Sorry." I sneaked another look round the crummy little room, the walls festooned with yellowing images of hopefuls of the forties and fifties, avid smiles now cracking up as the glossy paper crumbled. If O'Neill had needed to convince me how tacky this job of his was, he needed no better advocate than good old Morty. "Just the millionaire, that's all."

Mort nodded. He was clearly no stranger to the turn-down.

"OK kids." He clapped his hands the way dance directors did in *42nd Street*. "Nuth'n for you today."

The girls all groaned a bit as they picked up their action props, their huge square folios of photographs. One or two managed to produce the ghost of a winning smile or a whispered goodbye as they left; the others just switched off and went. Leaving me with Mort's three genuine contenders, the men. As I inspected them more carefully Mort must have seen my face. "I told you I didn't have much time," he said warily.

The first man, the bald one, had a sad tired look about him that had no place in a commercial's dream.

I told him as politely as I could that he needn't bother to stay. He knew that routine all too well, and left.

The second, name of Lou, younger but with hair dyed unnaturally black, began on the long history of his stage experience, a lifetime in bit parts, tour, stock, off-off-Broadway, a tiring journey to nowhere. He mentioned a play I'd seen and named the part he'd played. Alas, I wished I could have remembered him. So I shook his hand, thanked him for coming, and watched him leave with that optimistic smile actors always manage to paint on when they know the audition hasn't been theirs.

Which left Sheldon, the third one. Tall, reasonably good-looking, around forty-five, he said he'd been both a model and a straight actor. But he was more cautious about revealing exactly what and where. And he knew I didn't have much time—or much choice.

"I'd need to know what the part was," he said. "See a script. Discuss it with my agent."

I told him it was a morning's work, blowing a couple of smoke-rings.

"He's a millionaire, you say? That could be interesting, at least. Who's doing the clothes?"

I turned to Mort. "Did O'Neill say he'd pay for any special clothes?"

"Not to me," Mort said quickly. At that minute he didn't look as if he could finance a quick trip round Gimbels on the last day of the sales. "No clothes. No way."

"You're a millionaire with eccentric tastes," I said quickly. "Just bring whatever casual stuff you've got."

"You mean you want me to take on the role?"

"That's what I do mean. I'll see you tomorrow, in St. Thomas." I turned to Mort. "Fix a deal at whatever

59

money O'Neill said you were to pay. Can you get me a cab?"

A few minutes later I made my way up the cramped steps to the beaten-up green Ford that Mort had conjured. It had stopped snowing, and more people were moving round the streets again, muffled against the weather like extras in *Anna Karenina*. The whole second-rate scene with Mort Sleeman had shaken me somewhat. What was it about this set-up that didn't ring true, that insisted it had to be done in a hurry, and with the cheapest and nastiest people? Was it simply that O'Neill didn't *know*? And what on earth was the result—god help me—going to be like?

I hadn't found any sort of credible answer by the time the taxi deposited me at the right terminal building, Sub-Station Zero, at JFK. I made my way to counter three for the on-flight to St. Thomas, Virgin Islands. I checked in and eventually found myself strapped into another back seat, this time on a 707. I looked at my watch. I hadn't yet changed it to New York time and in London it must be already evening.

But the daytime show must go on. In frosty half-light the plane thundered down the runway and lifted clear. Another performance of the oxygen and life-jacket act, a plastic meal and coffee, and suddenly a miracle was happening outside. Like some theatrical effect the heavy winter clouds dissolved, the sky all round brightened magically to bright blue. Ahead and below I could now see the radiance of the brilliant ocean, and later the small green humps of the islands, lace edged with white beaches, breaking the gentle surface of the clear azure water.

Midnight my watch said, but still bright day here. I tried to count the number of in-flight whiskies I'd

had, clearing my brain for the business of the afternoon to come.

As the plane landed, the heat was already a gentle
embrace within the cabin, but the doors opened to
oven-temperature. I put on my sun-glasses, picked up
my briefcase, my box of Expert goodies and my
jacket, and joined the queue of blue-rinsed, green-
veined ancients of America waiting to disembark.

All I could see of the airport looked very flat; a few
small sandy hills one end and the sea's horizon the
other. But I could already hear a steel band tinkling
away in the distance assuring me I was in the tropics,
man. And that inevitable feeling of insouciance was
mine once again. For a moment or two, no more.

At the bottom of the aircraft steps, a man was looking up seriously at each arrival. He was about forty,
short and leathery, dressed in a pair of grubby shorts
and a khaki singlet which still bore traces of an army
number. His face hadn't enjoyed the razor's touch
lately either. As I reached the burning tarmac he said,
"Mr. Galloway?"

"That's right."

"You're doing the Expert promo? I'm Doug Haskins." He extended a fairly dirty hand.

"Are you our Production Manager?"

"Hell, no. I'm a shipping agent. Haskins International. I got a call from my guy in New York to look
after you."

"I expected a production man. There's a lot to set
up in a hurry."

"We'll manage, buster. Ain't much in these islands I
can't fix."

Haskins was already leading me swiftly into the low
building that served for both customs and immigra-

tion. It wasn't any cooler inside and was crowded with people waiting for the return flight, shouting and laughing, hot and sweaty. Haskins said, over his shoulder, "We'll grab up your bags later."

I flashed my passport open briefly and we walked out into real heat, bouncing unremittingly off the concrete. By now I was tired and dehydrated. And wary, for some instinct was flickering again, telling me all was not quite right. Haskins was holding open the passenger door of a beaten-up yellow estate car. I got in. He started the engine and drove out into the little feeder road bordering the airport fence.

I asked, "How much did they tell you about this shoot?"

"You need some kind of a boat, that right?"

"We need a spanking great yacht, millionaire style."

"New York never said nothing about no millionaires. Just a big sailing boat, they said."

"And you've got one?"

"Kind of."

"How—kind of?"

"You'd better take a look."

We rattled on out of the concrete driveway on to a main road, over a low hill down towards the bay of Charlotte Amalie, through a hooting shouting muddle of antique traffic; horse-carts and people on bicycles fighting it out with weaving snorting little Japanese runabouts. Through the window drifted the unmistakable magical aroma of the tropics—petrol fumes, sour cooking fat and strong urine. Now the palm-fringed road led us through an outcrop of tin shanties, then we swung left and right again to aim through an avenue of old stone warehouses, tricked out as duty free gift shops.

Little grey men in oversized Bermuda shorts,

white-kneed, straight off the cruise ships, trotted duti-
fully along the sidewalks laden and stooped with
heavy plastic bags full of Korean transistors and Tai-
wanese perfume, after their heavyweight floral wives
striding on in search of Today's Best Buy.

We emerged into sight of the glittering bay again,
with its mixed flotilla of fishing boats, cruise-ships at
anchor, and sharp white pleasure craft. Here and
there were venerable ketches and topsail schooners
quietly sinking into seedy retirement. Ahead of us the
square shape of the Red Fort, besieged on all sides by
traffic jams. The volume of metallic argument grew
as we grated round in low gear.

Haskins nodded. "Yacht marina's just the end of the
bay."

He skimmed the backside of an old woman on a
moped, handlebars crammed with mangoes and ba-
nanas, and accelerated. The engine rattled in protest.
"Don't go too well in this heat."

Suddenly he pulled off the road on to a dirt track
on the seaward side, and drove dustily through what
looked like an abandoned building site. A few dented
and rusty cars lurched at all angles at the water's
edge. We parked alongside. A narrow concrete causeway led past a small hut-like office and flyblown bar,
where half a dozen scruffy men sprawled, right hands
welded to beercans. They watched us glumly, as Haskins led me onto a narrow pontoon between lines of
moored sailing boats of all sizes. He stopped and
pointed. "There she is. The *Flying Danskman*."

She was a big old-fashioned Baltic trader, with a
beaten-up black hull and patched sails in all shades of
dun. I said, "*That* one?"

"Been a fine ship in her time."

Her time must have been the turn of the century,

63

before the rot set in. I was back in Amateur Night. I said, "Didn't they brief you at all from New York?"

"Uh?" Haskins started to look defensive.

"It's for an expensive commercial. The guy in the story can afford the very best."

"A fifty-footer they said. The *Danksman*'s fifty-three. She sails like a clipper—and she don't cost much either."

I couldn't be too hard on him. The poor jerk obviously hadn't done this sort of work before. I took a quick walk round the rest of the boats in the marina. There were all sorts, some shiny and polished, some truly grotty. But there was nothing that would look impressive enough on the screen.

I turned to Haskins, "Is there somewhere else on the island? A proper yacht club?"

Haskins paused before answering. "There's *the* Yacht Club."

"Where's that?"

"Across the hills. Red Hook way."

"Let's try there."

"You definitely don't want the *Danskman*?"

I didn't even bother to look again at the broken-down old schooner. "Definitely not."

Haskins spat into the water, then turned and led the way back to the car. One of the men at the bar called, "How's it going, Doug?"

"Lousy," Haskins muttered, doubtless for my benefit.

He barely waited for me to get into the car before slamming it into reverse and spinning it round in a cloud of angry dust, to clatter back on to the main road. We hurtled up a sharp hill, the ground falling away on our right to reveal a magnificent vista of the whole huge bay, the tongue of a long green island

64

lying across it, with the misty suggestion of another in the distance.

In the bright sunlight, an old-fashioned passenger seaplane ploughed gently through the water traffic, lazily taking off southwards towards the dim line on the horizon that must be St. Croix. The low sun kicked brilliance off the water, as the residual bow-wave spread among the moored boats, rocking them almost in time with the rhythmical sway of the palm trees framing the view.

Haskins said, "Don't expect much help from those stuck-up bastards at the Yacht Club. Never go near them myself." There was a curious, perverse dignity about the way he said it—Humphrey Bogart in a dud take.

"We'll see."

The road became rutted. Mangroves and weeds, odd unkempt trees sped by on either side, in empty uncultivated land. "Doesn't anyone try to grow anything on this island?" I asked.

"Who needs to? They can grow all the fruit and stuff we need in Florida. 'Sides, none of the locals want to work. Not in fields, anyway."

A sign directed us up a sandy lane. The Yacht Club was a low modern building at the end of the drive. Haskins let me lead the way in. Inside it was air-cool after the clammy heat. There was no one in the main room, not even a lounging figure in the bar by the water's edge. I saw a door marked "Club Steward", knocked and looked in. But that too was empty. I walked through open sliding doors on to a verandah overlooking a white sand beach. The sea beyond was an unbelievable blue, and right there before me I could see at least three boats that would be suitable. But no one was about.

"Still siesta time," Haskins grunted.

I walked along the length of the veranda. "Did you want something?" A woman's voice rang clearly. I turned. She stood in the doorway we had just come through, darkly framed in the shadows. She was middle-aged and coarse-skinned in a sixties sundress, a couple of irritable little dogs yapping around her bare brown legs.

I went over to her and explained quickly. She didn't seem all that interested. "You'd better talk to Tom."

"Tom?"

"My husband. He's Commodore right now. I'm Kate Blakey."

As if on cue, a grey-haired man appeared, coming in from the car park behind her, a friendly father-figure from a Chase Manhattan ad. "Hi. Tom Blakey."

"Dan Galloway. From London."

Kate said, "He's shooting a commercial. Wants a boat."

"You don't say?" Tom brightened. "Well, you've come to the right man, Dan. Ain't no one knows more about shooting commercials than old Tom Blakey."

"How's that?"

"I was in Madison Avenue for twenty-two years with my own agency. In the sixties that was, with all the great names, David Ogilvy, that crowd. Then I sold up and came down here."

"You have a boat?"

"Do I? Let me show you."

He led us down to the jetty, handing us into an inflatable. As we motored out towards the mooring I filled him in on what I needed. He nodded. "Like that one?"

We were coming alongside a great gleaming Sparkman Stephens designed sixty-footer, built in glass

66

reinforced plastic. Rigged as a sloop in nylon and stainless steel, she combined the lines of a racer with the comforts of the QE II. Tom said, "This the sort of thing you had in mind?"

The name, *Fantasy,* shone proudly on its bows. I climbed up the short spotless ladder onto an immaculate deck. The cockpit was amidships, the tiller a shining ring of balanced steel. I jumped down and took the wheel in my hands for a moment, living the daydream of every faint-hope punter at the Earls Court Boat Show, the sky above azure, the sun strong, the sea ahead pure crystal. There was no sound at all except the syncopation of the wind in the rigging above, the light drumbeat of nylon rope on aluminium mast.

I looked at Tom. He knew exactly how I felt. "Could we have it for Friday?"

"Five hundred bucks for the day and it's yours. All in."

"You've got it, Tom." I turned to Haskins for some nod of support but he merely scowled.

We set up the details of time and readiness on the short trip back in the Zodiac. Haskins added nothing. Even back in the club bar, downing his fifth gin-fizz, he still seemed put out.

"You've got to admit it's a better looking craft than the one you had lined up," I said.

"Don't know why you have to be so goddammed persnickerty," he mumbled.

I turned to Tom Blakey. "He'd booked me some old tub called the *Flying Danskman.*"

"The *Danskman?* You've got to be joking."

I wasn't prepared for what happened next. Haskins suddenly grabbed my shoulder from behind and swung me round on the barstool to face him, his eyes red-rimmed, and for a moment, mad. "Listen, smart-ass. Don't start making any cracks about what I did or what I didn't do. You're getting *paid*, OK?"

The little scene was as stupid as it was unnecessary. I straightened my jacket as he released it. "I'm being paid to do a job properly," I snapped.

He turned to his glass and drained it. Tom said awkwardly, "Come on, fellas—"

Haskins got up. "We've done the business."

Tom said, "One more?"

Haskins ignored the offer. "Let's go." He didn't wait for me but walked out towards the entrance.

Tom smiled easily, as if used to this sort of rudeness. "Shall we see you tomorrow?"

"Probably. I want to see something of the islands."

"There are a lot of nice little bays round by St. John's. I could run you over in the Chris-Craft."

"Thanks. Sounds great."

"Call me when you're ready. Where are you staying?"

"I don't know yet. Mr. Haskins has fixed it." I glanced towards the unfriendly figure silhouetted in the brilliant doorway. He didn't answer.

Tom said, "If you need any more help—anything at all—tell me. I'm pretty well known around here."

"He don't," Haskins said loudly from the doorway. "I got it all set up. Now, are you coming?"

I shrugged. "See you tomorrow, Tom."

"Look forward to that."

I followed Haskins out to the old station wagon. A few more cars had now joined it in the car park; a shining Mercedes convertible, an old Lincoln and a new Toronado. Haskins pressed the starter and slammed into reverse, carving ruts in the gravel as he sped out.

"Was it really necessary for you to be so rude? The man's helping us, and in a big way."

Haskins spat out of his window. "You got your boat. Leave it at that."

There was no point in arguing with the man. My complaint could wait until I saw O'Neill back in London. We bounced along the narrow broken tarmac road which wound its way back to town through the small hills.

"Where am I staying, by the way?"

Haskins grunted. "Booked you in at Cokey's. OK?"

"Cokey's?"

"Ain't one of your smart tourist rat-traps. Probably ain't the place Mr. Commodore Tom Blakey would ha' put you. But folk that know reckon it's the best place to stay on the island." He sounded pretty defensive, but I wasn't rising.

We drove on in silence to the airport to pick up my bag. Then we returned to the town, suddenly swinging left down a street close-packed with seedy wooden shacks and sharply uphill again, leaving the shabby buildings below as we sped through deep shaded foliage, emerging into the harsh sunlight once again to find a carefully tended drive leading to what must once have been a colonial mansion. "Cokey's," Haskins said.

I dragged my bag from the car and started following him up the wide newly-painted wooden steps, glancing back for a moment at the new superb view of the bay and the islands, framed in yellow magnolia and purple bougainvillea—a travel poster come to life.

Haskins was already embracing a big, brown, motherly soul who ran the place. "This is Maggie, Dan. A very good friend of mine."

69

"Pleased to meet you." I shook her soft friendly hand, and knew at once from her smile I'd be happy here.

Haskins seemed to be over his bad temper. Indeed, up here he was quite a different man from the suspicious character he'd played out at the Yacht Club, laughing and slapping Maggie's well-upholstered buttocks with all the brio of a Neapolitan tenor.

A taciturn and aging porter, Victor, emerged from the back somewhere to carry my bag to the room on the first floor. It was high and full of old-fashioned cane furniture, with a brass double bed. The balcony, with French doors open, offered a repeat of the fabulous view of the harbor.

"OK?" Haskins asked from the doorway.

I smiled. "Very pleasant. Oh, I need to send a cable to my wife. Can they handle it downstairs?"

"I doubt it. Better give it to me. I'll get it off tonight. Full rate or night letter?"

"Full, I think." I quickly wrote out an "arrived safely" message for Sally and gave it to him. "When do the film crew get here?"

"About midday tomorrow."

"Good. I'll have time to look round some locations before they arrive."

"Boy, you're a beaver."

"I never stop." But I was feeling tired now. I looked at my watch: 2 A.M. British time—not even sunset here. "I think I'll turn in."

"You don't want dinner?" As he said it I was aware of the pleasantly spicy smell of cooking coming from below.

"No. Just sleep."

"See you tomorrow then. I'll be here just before twelve."

"Fine." Haskins left. I took a quick shower and dropped into the big bed.

But, irritatingly, sleep wouldn't come. Not at once. Somewhere in the back of my head were these jigsaw pieces that wouldn't fit. I tried to break them down into known facts. One, at the very moment when I was unexpectedly being dropped by the Corporation and pressed by my bank, an agent I scarcely knew had come up with a job—the sort of job I didn't normally do. Two, a girl travelling First Class on a transatlantic flight had taken the trouble to come back into Tourist just for the pleasure, it seemed, of picking me up. Three, this commercial, costing someone a hell of a lot of money, was being left in the hands of people like Mort Sleeman and this—frankly—hopeless shipping agent Haskins, who really hadn't the first idea. . . .

Then, mercifully, the sleep I had been denying myself overtook all further conjecture, and I went out for some hours. . . .

If you're fifty-five, short, bald and divorced, and you've only just made Grade Two, General Duties (Diplomatic); you might be excused for thinking some of life's real riches have eluded you.

Irving Passman was such a man. Duty Officer on the all night shift, he gloomily watched the hands of the electric clock move from 3:46 a.m. to 3:47. After San Diego, Langley had not proved the sort of posting it had been cracked up to be. It was cold, it was wet and it was unfriendly. Before San Diego there had been Europe: parties, foreign chicks and a few laughs. He drew hard on the night's seventeenth Marlboro, and waited for fortune to smile. . . .

71

The phone shrilled. Irving reached out mechanically.

"Duty Officer."

"Irv? It's Oscar."

"Oscar who?"

"Oscar Quartley, dumbo. How you been?"

"Oh, fine, fine." And so on through the usual conversational hoops before Oscar got to the point. "Guess who I saw at JFK today?"

"Who?"

"Gisela."

"Gisela Braun?"

"Who else? Still looks great."

Gisela. Bonn. A couple of winters and a summer. Happy memories.

Irving said, "How'd she look?"

"Great. As ever."

"What's she doing these days?"

"I didn't ask. I got no chance to. She was with some other guy. Didn't want to stop and talk."

Irving felt a pang. Could it be stirring jealousy—for something so dead, so long ago? "Who was the guy?"

"Search me. I was only with her for a coupla minutes."

"Yeah." They chatted on about other times, other friends, until Oscar signed off. "Thought you'd like to hear about Gisela, Irv."

"Thanks."

"See you around then."

"Sure." Irving replaced the phone on its rest. Why should Oscar have called him like that, out of the blue? Had he felt put down by Gisela not wanting to stop and talk to him? Or was he simply playing a professional hunch and dropping a word in the right quarter?

Who was she working for these days? There'd be no harm in checking her out. He'd nothing else to do. He'd just run her name through the system and see what came up. . . .

FOUR

Moonlight still filtered through the shutters, but my London-orientated body-tempo knew better and aroused me like an alarm clock. Wide awake in seconds, I walked to the balcony and looked out. The view of the bay below was even more breathtaking in clear, sharp blue, ringed by thousands of tiny points of light reflected by the still, black water.

A splash from below. The aquamarine rectangle of brightly lit hotel pool below was disturbed by a couple of shadowy swimming figures. One, paunchy in Hawaii-jazz boxer shorts, looked up as he clambered out. "Why don't you join us, fella? The water's great."

"Why not?" There'd be no more sleep for me that night. I slipped into my trunks and ran down the outside staircase. I waved to the couple, middle-aged comfortable Americans, now settled back in reclining chairs to watch as I dived in and swam the requisite number of lengths. The water was like a warm bath, bitter with chlorine, but refreshing. I climbed out and approached the man and woman.

"Just arrived?"

"Yesterday," I said.

"From New York?"

"From London originally."

"British? We don't get many of you people here in the Virgin Islands."

I explained about the commercial. They introduced themselves—Lou and Nancy Greenly, from Queens. Retired from their antique and curio business, they wintered every year in St. Thomas.

Lou said suddenly, "Wasn't that Doug Haskins came in with you?"

I nodded. "You know him?"

"Do we know him?" said Nancy.

"Friend of yours?" Lou asked.

"Not really. Someone booked him from New York."

"Crooked as a crab," said Nancy.

Lou added, "We used to use him to ship out curios when we had the shop on 27th."

"Then he got himself mixed up in a smuggling case," Nancy said. "Lucky he didn't go to jail."

I didn't answer. The picture fitted my own suspicions too easily.

"Just keep an eye on him," Lou said.

The day's beginning, which had been stealing up on us, suddenly turned the pool and gardens from indeterminate purple and green to brilliant crimson.

Lou yawned. "Time for breakfast, hon."

Nancy said, "Nice meeting you, Dan. And pardon me for talking to a perfect stranger like I did but—"

"I got the message."

"See you around." They ambled back to the hotel. I lay back on the recliner, feeling the sun already at work on my body. I didn't want to think any more,

75

certainly not about Doug Haskins, past or present. Just lay back and enjoy it. . . .

Breakfast on the patio—paw-paws with lemon juice, overfried bacon strips with midget eggs—revealed Cokey's to be full of eager American couples and triples, plus the odd Germans and Swedes. Maggie seemed to be running the place on her own, with the sad-eyed Victor as her one and only assistant.

She came and sat at my table as I was finishing the toast and marmalade. "How was breakfast, then?"

I explained about the bacon. "Just fry it very lightly. You don't have to turn it into a cinder."

"You do for these folks."

"Not for me."

"Whatever you say, man," she chuckled, going away.

I called Tom Blakey at the number he'd given me, making a date for nine. The cab Victor called for me was one of those square old Studebakers that haven't been seen in the States for years. The driver—"Call me Robert, man"—offered me the back seat, but I preferred the front and got in beside him.

"Staying long?" The obvious question as we rattled downhill towards the town.

"Just two or three days." We were already in among the shanty-lined streets, brakes squealing at every suicidal chicken making the crossing. Then, as we came to a main road, a truck full of goats shot across our front. Robert slammed on his brakes and swore. "Some of these guys—"

We cleared the frantic town traffic, passed the Red Fort and the curiously Bournemouth-type bandstand on the green behind it, speeding up the hill road back to the Yacht Club. Tom was already there, greeting me with a broad smile. "All set?"

The Chris-Craft was a beauty in shining polished

mahogany. I stepped down into the cockpit, sinking deep in the comfort of the white leather passenger seat.

Tom said, "We'll make for St. John's first. That's the next island heading east. Got all the best bays—it's where they used to shoot all those pirate movies with Burt Lancaster and Yvonne de Carlo. After that you've got the British islands—Tortola and Virgin Gorda—but I guess you won't have too much time—"

"Right. I'll take St. John's."

"Congress set it up as a nature reserve a few years back, and I must say they keep it pretty nice. You can scuba at Cinnamon if you want to. I've a couple of snorkels in the trunk—"

"Another time, maybe. I have to be back by midday to meet the crew."

"Let's go then." Tom roared the engines, and the boat took off, planing out of the mangrove-lined lagoon towards a wider bay, past a couple of conical green islands, a glittering blue-gold horizon ahead.

"Better put some cream on your face," Tom shouted above the engines. "Sun gets to be a real furnace."

I took the tube he gave me and started daubing my face. I thought, I'm actually getting paid for this, feeling the cool rush of the wind, the scatter of spray, enjoying the sparkling luminescence of the incredibly clear air. I looked over at Tom, pudgy middle-aged schoolboy, face brightly-lit by the scintillating water, letting all his old ad-man's aggression out in the wildly revving power of the engines, as the streamlined craft tore across the waves. For him there was no novelty. He could, and probably did, go for a careless spin through the water every day. But I suspected that today my presence, my enjoyment, added something to his own pleasure. For life in this small island community must be boringly predictable. Yet Tom looked contented enough.

We soared through a narrow gap between the mainland on our left and a long narrow tongue of amber sand. Tom pointed ahead at a flat green smudge. "There's St. John's."

A red light suddenly started winking on the dashboard. Tom saw it, swore suddenly, and brought the boat to a shuddering halt. Our wake caught us up from behind and almost swamped us. "What's wrong?"

"Goddam fanbelt." Tom clambered over to the back of the cockpit, lifted a hatch, and revealed a pristine engine. Plunging his hand into the intestines he fished out a few remnants of mangled rubbery string. "It'll be OK. I've got a spare."

Within seconds he'd ripped the new belt out of its wrapper, looped it round the alternator below, and was forcing the top of the belt round the rim of the fan-pulley. Too tight, it wouldn't go over the rim and slot into place.

"Don't you have to slacken it off?" I ventured.

"Oh screw that. Listen, I'll hold it on the pulley, and you just give the starter a quick jab—"

It sounded horribly dangerous. We were drifting on the open sea, no other craft in sight. I had visions of a nasty accident. "You'll lose your fingers—"

"Course not. I've done it before. Just go ahead and jab the starter like I said."

I went forward and nervously touched the starter button. As the engine fired, Tom deftly flipped his hand sharply upwards. The fan-belt jumped right over the flange of the pulley and ran on smoothly. Tom grinned. "Trick I learned in army transport."

He lunged back into the driver's seat, revved the engines and we sped away towards St. John's. "You

78

get in the habit of doing jobs like that down here," he shouted. "None of the locals would ever lift a finger to help out."

"Still—you don't seem to have a bad life here."

"Maybe not. When you look at it from outside, when you see it on a short visit. But I guess it's like everything else. After you've got it, like Marilyn Monroe said in the song, you don't want it." He slowed the engine revs so that he could talk more naturally. The boat slid into a gentle glide, water slapping pleasantly along the gunwales. Peace was all around us, strong warm sunshine, the occasional note from a passing bird. "All those years I spent, thumping up and down Madison and Fifth, hustling air-time," Tom said, "I was dreaming of all this. Come frost or blizzard I'd think, 'Wait till I've made a million, then it's goodbye gentlemen, nice to have known you.' But of course I made a million and found a reason not to go. I made two millions—still found excuses. But at five millions I quit. And I guess not a day goes by that I don't kind of regret it. I keep remembering the good times."

"Everybody does. You must have been under terrible pressure."

"Oh sure. I was the original Willy Loman. Death of a goddammed salesman. Most of the time. There were company vice-presidents I'd have murdered, PR men I'd have gone to the chair for, fools of copywriters, men in my own setup. Schmucks, all of them." He drew a deep breath. "But, boy, they were *living*. And so was I."

"And now?"

"I wait. For the inevitable. The one thing written into life like an unbreakable guarantee."

I started to feel uncomfortable. This was as morbid as a *Time* think-piece. "You must have had a great time back in the sixties. There was a kind of reckless optimism—"

"Oh sure there was that all right. But we also had bad government and a lunatic war that cost us millions."

"And incidentally killed hundreds of thousands of quite innocent Asians."

"Oh sure. 'War is hell.' That's what General Sherman said way back, and it hasn't changed any since his time. A realist fights a war hard, for real. So, having gotten ourselves into a fight we didn't want, we took the opportunity of trying out all our latest weapons under combat conditions."

"And that's good?"

"I don't defend it. Trouble was, that guy Lyndon Johnson just couldn't be told any different."

"You preferred Nixon?"

"I had to, I'm a Republican—always will be—and he was the man we wanted. At the time." He looked ahead, and pointed. "See over there?" We were approaching a lush bay with tall palm trees overhanging a white coral beach. Running back from the sea were a number of neat wooden bungalows, like a superior army camp, linked to a large main building by flower-lined paths. "Caneel Bay. Where Richard Nixon used to come for some quiet thinking." He slowed the engine to a whisper.

We drifted inshore, the wind gentling the palm-fronds, humming-birds now just audible. In the sun's morning warmth, it was as near as anyone might ever get to paradise. But with that conscience. . . ? Tom watched me for a moment then smiled his easy smile. "Didn't do him much good." He pushed the throttles forward and the boat responded, leaving the water like a let-loose greyhound, confidently surging ahead on its cushion of glittering spray.

We raced around a curiously hump-shaped island into the next bay, a small curve indenting the green land, a midget lagoon that changed color delicately from hyalescent blue to the cream shallows of coral sand. Single pelicans hung suspended in the cobalt sky, watchful for the merest glint of silver in the translucent depths below. Then, sighting, they would dive with stuka-suddenness hard into the sea, and strike, fish tails writhing and disappearing in their great pouchy beaks as they soared again cerulean high.

Tom didn't say anything. He knew, and I knew he knew, that he'd brought me to the perfect location for the particular piece of junk I was perpetrating: a quiet bay, safe, free from trippers, easy to work in. "This is it," I said unnecessarily.

"Thought you'd like it. I could sail the *Fantasy* over here in less than an hour."

It all made sense. I nodded agreement.

Tom said abruptly, "Where's your friend Haskins today?"

"Waiting to collect the crew when they arrive. We seem to do better without him anyway."

"Could be." Tom released the gear, letting the boat drift. He reached for a couple of cans of beer from a neat refrigerator under the dash and tossed me one. The amber liquid tasted cool and good. There were worse places I could have been in mid-December. . . .

"Do you know Haskins well?" I asked.

Tom took another drink, and wiped the back of his hand across his mouth before replying. "Scarcely at all. I see him about here and there—at the wharf near the old submarine base—and at the airfield if I'm meeting someone—but I can't really say I know him."

81

"Did you hear about the smuggling case he was into?"

"Where did you get that?"

"Some people at the hotel. This morning."

Tom looked at me very straight. I could see the sweat shining on his temple. "You don't have to believe every goddammed thing you're told. Particularly down here."

"He just seems an odd choice to set up this commercial."

"You're a long way from home, Dan."

"What's that supposed to mean?"

"You're a perfect example of what the army used to call over-involvement. Haskins isn't the world's best, but he's *here*. Don't get yourself so screwed up, man. See the thing for what it is—a crappy little one-day shoot for some jerk from the Far East who can't be bothered to come over and do it himself."

"So he gets me to put my name on it." I remembered what I could—and should—be doing at this moment. *Gateway*—a serious program about prison reform, something I really cared about.

"Forget it, Dan. No one'll ever know. Do it as well as you can, take the money, and if they don't like it, they can do the other thing."

He was good to be with. Reassuring. He pressed the starter again and let the engines idle. "Time to get back if you want to meet your crew on the midday flight. Oh, and—Kate asked me—can you make dinner with us tonight?"

"Why yes. Thanks. I've no particular plans."

"Bring some of your crew if you want to—your cameraman—or whoever."

"I'll see."

"I'll pick you up about seven. OK?" He let in the

82

throttle and we sped forward in a surge of power, leaving the beautiful bay behind, cleaving a furrow through the calm blue ocean. In less than half an hour we were tying up among the mangroves at the Yacht Club.

Tom drove me on to Cokey's in his well-preserved Lincoln. Maggie came bustling out. "Doug's been up here looking for you, Mr. Galloway. Said he'd see you at the airfield."

"Come on," Tom said, opening the car door again. I didn't argue. And although Tom was a much more cautious driver than Doug Haskins we still made it through the traffic to Lindbergh Bay in ten minutes flat. As we approached along the feeder road I saw the plane had already landed; people were coming down the steps.

Doug was in the customs hall. "Where were you?"

"I told you I was going out to look for locations."

"Find anything?"

"All set."

Tom said, "See you tonight, Dan," and left. Haskins showed some sort of pass at the gate and we both walked through on to the hot tarmac. The film crew were easy to identify—a huddle of bewildered-looking people at the foot of the aircraft steps. Sheldon was in the centre, our one and only star, all flashing smile and Harper's bazaar. Quickly they were introduced, and became individuals—Paul the lighting camera-man, ebullient and overweight, enthusing about the clear light—Gary, his assistant, long-haired and white faced as the star of an Andy Warhol quickie—Renee, continuity, harassed and unattractive, as they always are—Suzy, makeup, casually assessing the value and availability of each member of this cargo of spare male-crumpet, and finally Crosby, the grip, relaxed and Harlem-cool.

While Haskins took Gary and Crosby off to see the camera gear through customs, I shepherded the rest of them to a shady bar I'd spotted just near the entrance. I could see they were the kind of film crew you'd pick up for a day's shoot anywhere—professional and outwardly friendly, unlikely to develop any temperament. They came into the tiny bar and suddenly filled it with color, laughter and vitality. Only Sheldon might become tricky. I watched him as, self-obsessed, he chose a stool just where he could observe himself in a handily-placed wall-mirror. He was already developing his self-imposed role as a pain-in-the-ass.

"I'm still worried about clothes, Dan."

"Did you bring any?"

"Just a few old casual numbers I had in a drawer."

"I'll take a look at them when we get to the hotel." The O'Neill organization didn't seem to run to a costume supervisor. But I could always take Sheldon shopping in town later. I didn't want to get bogged down; I wanted to find out more about Paul, the cameraman.

It appeared he knew one or two acquaintances of mine in London, and a couple more in Paris and Munich, but he mainly worked on news in New York, either locally or as a stringer for foreign TV stations. His main interest was food. He'd already eaten his way through three Gourmet Guides in the States and halfway through Michelin in Paris. "How about this place? Found anywhere good yet?"

"I've been here less than a day."

"Virgin territory, huh?"

Suzy, on the next stool, snorted. "Boy, it's the way you tell them, Paul."

I could see they were going to be all right, though it turned out in conversation that they'd not worked together before. Paul was used to this sort of operation; whenever he needed an assistant he picked a freelance like Gary. The others in the team had simply been found by an agency. I quickly told them what was involved on the shoot and gave Paul the single sheet of script.

"Oh my, I shot this one twenty years ago," he said as he looked at it.

"Didn't everybody? It's crap, but let's make the cooking beautiful."

"No dialogue?" Sheldon pouted.

"Strictly mumming. Just flash the old smile now and again."

"I spent three years at the Actors' Studio for *this*?"

Suzy spluttered Planter's Punch. "'Actors' Studio'? When *was* that? Where'd'you get this guy, Dan?"

"Audition. We set it up in a hurry—long distance."

"I bet you told them it was a fag commercial."

"Get *laid*, darling," Sheldon said, pleasantly.

"I'm ready when you are, sweetheart."

I looked quickly round at the laughing faces, relaxed and ready to go. Perhaps yesterday's feelings of unease were unfounded after all. . . .

Then Haskins and the boys came in. I set up another round. Crosby and Gary both took beer.

"That can of negative film-stock you brought out from England," Haskins said. "Where is it?"

"In my room, at the hotel."

"Customs papers all made out for the return?"

"The man at Heathrow did all that."

Gary said, "I'll pick it up soon as we check in and get it loaded into a magazine for tomorrow."

The party looked ready to move on. Suzy, Renee,

Paul and I piled into Haskins' station wagon, the others found a taxi. I'd told them all I could; they could spend the rest of the afternoon by the pool.

On the way to Cokey's I mentioned Tom's dinner invitation. The girls weren't too keen, but Paul agreed to come, though he'd heard of a genuine Creole restaurant near Magens Bay that we ought to try another night. When we arrived I went up to Sheldon's room to look over the stuff he'd brought. There was plenty of choice, and I settled for a pair of white slacks and a fancy top. He hadn't any Gucci shoes, but we'd never see them anyway.

Back in my room tiredness overtook me and I slept till late afternoon. I was showered and changed by the time Tom showed up. I found Paul in the Bamboo Bar with Suzy and Renee, and made all the introductions. Tom invited the girls once more, but they'd already set up Gary and Crosby for dinner somewhere else. Sheldon appeared, still whining about his wardrobe. I told him not to worry. Dissatisfied he set off towards the harbor to look for a sailor.

I joined Tom and Paul. Darkness had descended with tropical suddenness as Tom drove us away from the lights of the town, up the Mafolie Road and across the central mountain that divided the island from east to west. The headlights picked out banks of bright red earth at each curve, startling small creatures that ran back into the black haven of night. The moon hadn't risen yet; the heavy foliage above us scarcely registered against the inky sky as we followed the road's curves to darker heights.

At what seemed to be the summit, we approached a pair of heavy iron gates that suddenly opened effortlessly as the car came near, and were clanged shut by two ghostly, linen-clad figures as soon as we had passed through. Now the lights revealed a constantly changing floral spectrum—magnolias, bougainvillea, azaleas, even rhododendrons of all colors—that momentarily came to life in passing, then submerged into nocturnal gloom again. The house was solid but splendid; an architect's adventure in stone and polished wood and glittering glass.

Kate came out to meet us in the wide doorway, a different woman from the sunscorched matron at the Yacht Club. Generous and welcoming, she was dressed in flowing white silk and appeared to be far more attractive under the kinder light of evening.

"Come in, both of you. Glad you could make it," said as if she meant it too.

Tom introduced us to the men drinking from frosted glasses on the wide verandah: Ed Liveright, a banker, Harry Lloyd, in real estate on the islands, Carl Buderus, whose father had perfected and patented the Buderus Bed, (the "American Way to Natural Sleep"), and Maurice Flint, who was said to "have a few stores in Maine".

Inquisitive, red-faced and glassy-eyed, the top people of St. Thomas in their bright shirts and pajama-stripe trousers, inspected Paul and I like a couple of zoological specimens. Conversation was difficult. Once they'd established what the commercial was costing and who it was being made for they collectively lost interest. There were no dollars to be made from what I had to tell them, so talk faltered.

Their wives descended in a sudden drapers' riot of bright printed silk—Peg, Meg, Alison, and I-didn't-quite-catch-it. The chat became even more superficial, interspersed with a few good locker-room jokes.

Dinner was soon announced, and we drifted into a long cool dining room, where insects played like tropical fish round each subtle light-source and vast windows revealed an epic view of thick, lush greenery all the way to the brilliant, distant bay. A huge table, of what seemed to be one single piece of polished mahogany, was set with gleaming silver, each place named in silver letters on tiny white ivory billboards. Somehow Kate had even got Paul's name right.

The superb Vichysoisse was followed by red snapper in a hot fragrant sauce, tempered by a sort of Californian Riesling. Conversation petered out altogether with the roast beef, fried yams and batter pudding, aided by Chateau Lafitte, but revived with the almond-flavored sorbet. By then we'd been treated to a review of most of their prejudices about foreign parts. The Middle East was in danger from communism and so was Africa. Europe itself was now heavily exposed to the virus and even easy-going Australia might succumb. Worse still, the disease once again threatened the United States.

Brandy appeared, and the ladies retired to the drawing-room like characters in some Somerset Maugham opus of half-a-century ago.

Ed lit a cigar. "I can't think what that screwball President of ours thinks he's up to." He blew out a thick cloud, his words emerging from a dreamlike mist. "*Wage restraint.* Who needs that? In our economy for God's sake?"

"You're right." Beside him Harry sounded equally bellicose. "We've always lived on expansion. And look at the fuck-up he's made of energy. Shortages, rationing, people waiting in line for hours for a few gallons of gas—"

"You can't believe it," Carl said. "In a country like the United Staes—with all the oil resources we've built up over the years—Texas, California, Mexico, Alaska, that tar-sand place in Canada, what's it, Athabascar, off-shore wells all over—"

"Not enough." Paul suddenly spoke up from across the table. "None of it's enough, not all the production of all those places. We still have to import more than half the gasoline we burn, and we've simply got into the habit of buying cheap, and expecting it to stay cheap. Now the price is rocketing we're in a jam."

Ed looked at him seriously, as if seeing him for the first time. "So what do you suggest?"

"We start lookng for it in the States again, in areas that were previously thought too costly. And seek out more ways of making synthetic."

"Easier said than done," Carl said. "Believe me, I've lost millions in that game."

"There's no other way," Paul said. "The world supply isn't inexhaustible. No matter how much we economize, in the end shortage will force the price up so high that as a nation we'll be spending more than we earn."

"So we're back on the old crud about balance of payments," Ed said. "You sound just like some hick politician."

"If the cost of oil goes up that much," Carl said through a haze of cigar-smoke, "then we have to do something about it."

"Like what?"

"The stuff comes from the Middle East, right? Saudi Arabia, Kuwait, those sort of places? What did they ever have before we found the oil? Camel-shit. What will most of them ever have? I ask you."

"So where does that lead?"

"I tell you where it leads, my friend. If those guys, those Arabs and those Libyans get too greedy, we move their asses right out of there and take over.

89

That's what. If we hadn't drilled in those deserts while they sat there covered with flies, they'd still be picking their sores."

Paul said, "How do you figure we could just 'take over'? Do you think the Russians, for instance, would stand by and watch us walking in?"

"*Russians?* Why do we have to be so goddammed scared of the Russians? Listen, I've been to Russia—you can't even make a Stateside telephone call without a screaming match. Technically they're crap, light-years behind us. All they've got is peasants, millions of them, Mongols, Ukrainians, Siberians—all stupid."

"I don't agree. They were first with super-sonic flight, first with satellites—Sputniks—remember?"

"Sputnik schmutnik! You some sort of red? Sure we've been sold short by our politicians, and those Russians have been let believe they could take us on and win, but I tell you we're years ahead, in sheer destructive power. Believe me, I've got friends who know just how far our research boys have gone. Laser-beams, death-rays, real Flash Gordon stuff—"

"And radiation," Ed said suddenly. "That's the real big one."

"How do you mean?"

"Kills everybody, everything. But leaves the buildings standing."

Carl said, "You ask me how we take over the Middle East? I'll tell you. What's an oil field? A desert full of pumping equipment. The only thing that spoils it are the locals. So you get yourself a way of getting rid of them without disturbing the oil wells."

"And we've got it," said Ed. "Believe me."

"I do believe you," Paul said. "I'm terrified that everything you've said is true."

Harry stubbed out the end of his cigar and looked

across at Paul. "You want to destroy the whole of the American economy—our standard of living—frozen food—long-distance transportation—make us all cave-dwellers like Pakistan or some place?"

"I didn't say that. But how can anyone countenance mass-murder—after the century we've all lived through?"

"What do you do?" Ed said suddenly, "For a living?"

"I'm a cameraman, shooting news, mainly."

"Then you should take more notice of what you shoot. You work for someone else, right?"

"Sure, on assignment."

"Well none of us here do that. Wait for another guy to assign us. We run businesses, take risks, set up the game, so that guys like you can make a living with no hassle and go home safe to the wife and children, OK? What Carl's been saying will happen, because guys like us will make the decision to make it happen, not some two-bit president."

Paul didn't answer. He simply looked very hurt. After a time he muttered, "You know it all."

"Aw, don't be like that, Paul—" Tom said.

Paul rose from the table. To Tom he said, "Could I call a cab?"

"Now come on Paul. Ed was just giving you his opinion—"

"I heard it. I've heard those opinions before."

"Are you boys ever going to join us?" We all turned at the sound of Kate's voice from the doorway. "We're all set up with the backgammon, and wondering what's become of you."

"It started to get heavy," Tom said. "We're coming right now."

"Maybe we'd better go," I said. "We've an early start in the morning."

"Are you sure? I mean—"

"I think it's best." I wanted to rescue Paul before someone threw a punch.

"You're the boss." The farewells took us some minutes, while Tom roused his chauffeur from somewhere at the back of the house. Ed and the other men didn't seem at all put out at Paul's discomfiture; we might as well have been concluding a discussion about the weather. They were just as affable at the end of the evening as they'd been at the very beginning, saying they hoped they'd see us again, wishing us luck with the shoot next day.

As soon as we were back in Cokey's I led Paul to the deserted Bamboo Bar, found Victor in the kitchen, and had him set up a couple of large Whiskey Collinses.

"I'm shaking, you know that?" Paul said.

"I saw."

"Those bastards up there. That crap, that absolute shit they were talking. Christ, I almost punched that Ed on the nose."

"Violence," I said, suddenly aware from the thickness of my voice how much we'd drunk, "only begets more violence—"

"And bastards only beget more bastards." Paul's face looked very red. "Did I dream it? Or did that schmuck really say all that stuff about taking over the Middle East?"

"You didn't think he was serious, did you?"

"Sure I do. You hear the same thing all over America. If the dollar goes down two points everybody shouts, 'What's wrong?' 'It's those goddammed Arabs again,' they say, 'charging us too much for their oil.' So what's the answer, the big, clever, well-thought-out answer? Bomb them, napalm them, kill their children, *anything*, just so we don't have to go back to walking. You really *do* hear people saying it. Even after Vietnam. They forget that whatever it was we went in there for, we just didn't manage to do. It's *lunacy*."

His anger seemed to exhaust itself. I ventured to speak. "Come on. It's not *all* you hear in America. You're not insane. Those people up there are completely out of touch. They get down here to a remote island and start arguing global solutions. They forget how much they have to be thankful for."

"The American Dream," Paul said bitterly. "Material prosperity beyond anyone's needs, advanced technology solving your problems before you even know what they are—and that's the result—that sort of dinner-party for dangerous nut-cases."

"The food was good—"

"Oh sure. But the conversation—" Paul suddenly drained his glass and got out of his chair. "Moralizing won't get the cotton picked. I'll see you in the morning."

"Bright and early." I watched him as he walked out of the bar, rather unsteadily, but with a certain curious dignity. He was worth meeting, and I was glad I'd come.

"I want results."

General Waldorf surveyed the roomful of assorted faces, mainly men, mainly white, the occasional female, black, or Asian, added here and there with condiment care to the general mix. And for all the effect his words were having on their blank expressions, he might well have been talking of life on Mars. It was a veritable textbook on non-communication.

"The President's worried. I'm worried. And by god you'd all better start worrying too. I've given you the picture. On the face of it, it all adds up—but something's still missing."

He paused. Nobody even blinked.

Any fact, any fact at all, you think might be relevant to this matter—report it. Is that clear?"

Empty assent. Almost imperceptible nods, murmurs.

"OK. Same time next week."

Waldorf picked up his single sheet of notes and left the briefing-room with his aide. One row from the back, as others around him rose and left, Irving Passman remained seated for a moment. Facts were the demand. But all he had to offer from the whole of last week was a single paragraph:

"BRAUN, Gisela, born April 1945. Nothing known since memorandum PHT/RWS 657 (West Germany) May 1972. Believed now working as air hostess, Pan American."

Non-information could never be offered as positive information. . . .

94

At seven next morning, Victor knocked at my door with breakfast and crossed to the window to pull the shades.

"Another goddammed sunny day," he muttered as he left.

I drank the juice and the coffee, ate the scrambled eggs and toast, but left the burnt and frizzled bacon and went down to find the crew.

Sheldon, baggy-eyed and whey-faced, was cutting up rough in Suzy's room while she was attempting to make him up. Obviously his adventures in the harbor last night hadn't had the delicate charm of Marcel Proust. I told him roughly to cut out all the big star rubbish and get his body down to the hotel entance, ready, in five minutes flat.

Robert was already outside with his old Studebaker and Doug Haskins with his estate. Gary and Crosby loaded the camera gear into the back and Sheldon appeared looking sheepish with the girls and we set off.

I watched the possessive way that Suzy looked

across at Gary; last night's encounter must have been satisfactory. He smiled back at her in a lazy temporary-owner's fashion. They at least, weren't complaining.

Tom was waiting at the Yacht Club ready to motor us out to the *Fantasy* in the inflatable. Doug was not coming with us and took his leave, saying he'd see us at the hotel later. Tom had lined up the Chris-Craft as a camera boat and Paul, Renee and I set ourselves up among the rear seats.

To get the best advantage from the clear morning light, I wanted to take the establishing shots of the *Fantasy* sailing first. Quickly I explained to Tom. I'd shot boats before and it's no use taking them in full sail running along at the boat's own pace—the results look flat, like a still. The only way to get an impression of speed is to have the sailing boat come towards you and aim the camera boat head-on towards its bows, veering off at the last moment. Tom understood. "No problem. I'll be driving the Chris-Craft."

We motored out towards the big white sloop. Kate, silent and hung-over from the night before, was already aboard with a couple of local crewmen. I laid the plan out for them. Sheldon was to go aboard straight away and stand behind the tiller, with a hidden crewman actually managing the steering. We'd sail over to St. John's and film the long shots on the way. I told Suzy to go aboard with Sheldon and hold his hand.

It all worked well. We stood off in the Chris-Craft while they upped anchor and motored *Fantasy* out through the swampy bay to the open sea. As they began to haul up the canvas, we closed in so that Paul could pick up a couple of back-lit angles of foresails rising against burnt-out sun and sky. Then, as both boats emerged from between the small islands at the edges of the bay, Tom drove the Chris-Craft ahead and turned to wait for the *Fantasy* to appear. With sails now set, all white, lean and beautiful, heeling slightly as the onshore breeze caught her canvas, *Fantasy* was a cameraman's gift.

Instinctively Tom and Paul, strangers two hours ago, became a perfect team, communicating in short sentences, single words sometimes, Tom maneuvering instantly to Paul's needs, hurling the Chris-Craft straight towards the huge sailing boat almost right under the bows and swinging clear at the moment when a splintering violent crash seemed inevitable. After this trick had been repeated two or three times Paul was satisfied. "Anything else?"

I'd made a shot-list and given it to Renee. "Just the shots of Sheldon at the wheel and the pack-shots and that's it."

We came alongside *Fantasy* and climbed aboard. Tom sent one of the crewmen back to the club with the Chris-Craft, while we lined up a mid-shot on Sheldon at the wheel. It was getting very hot now. Kate, looking healthier and more cheerful, appeared from the galley with a tray of ice-cold Bloody Marys, which disappeared fast.

Sheldon was still fussing Suzy about his hair getting blown about and I suddenly realized that he had a transplant job. I consulted Paul and he suggested making it a low angle. Sheldon demurred: the problem now was his double chin. Finally we settled on a compromise a couple of inches below his chest. As the camera rolled Sheldon seemed to take on a new image. Gone was the camp, middle-aged spoilt child; somehow he became the millionaire owner of this beautiful boat, assured, confident and relaxed.

"OK. Cut. How was the hair, Suzy?"

"Fine as far as I could see."

We did another take, then Paul had an idea for a shot reflected in the hub of the tiller wheel and we took that, then another through the rigging and finally we went into the pack-shot routine. I fished a glistening pack of Experts out of the cardboard box and we photographed Sheldon selecting one and lighting up, this way, that way, every way. Paul was good—really professional and fast.

Sheldon's hands got sweaty and had to be washed and made up again. Suzy had to do another manicure job on his fingernails; in the very close shots his hands started to shake. We did it again and again and finally got a steady shot of him holding it close to the lens.

I was getting paid for this, I reminded myself, and paid very well, but it wasn't like directing; it was simply and relentlessly achieving a series of corny images for the wrong reason. They didn't need me or my special talent—whatever that might be. The ridiculous hack who'd written the script could have shot it all just as well, if not better. But here I was living like a millionaire in the middle of a strange winter dream of warm sunshine. So—save the questions.

We'd finished shooting, covered my shot-list many ways, given the editor enough material to make a thirty-second commercial several times over, and we'd used up the thousand-foot roll of Eastmancolor film I'd brought from London.

"What now?" Paul asked.

"Wrap," I said.

"Wanna go back," Tom asked, "or stay and make a day of it?"

"Where could we go?" I asked.

"Virgin Gorda. If you've never seen the Baths over there it's quite an experience."

"Why not?"

Tom took over the wheel and the boat seemed suddenly to take on a new life. He called out a few orders, shortened sail and the boat began speeding eastwards, close-hauled, through the narrows and into the broad reach of Sir Francis Drake Channel. For more speed he started the engine and we ran up to ten or eleven knots. Suzy and Renee were now down to bikinis, sprawled in the brilliant sunshine with the rest of the crew stripped off on the frying-pan deck. Tom called out the names of the islands as we approached and passed each one; Jost van Dyke, Great Thatch, the long mound of Tortola on our port side, Peter Island, Salt, Ginger, Fallen Jerusalem, Beef, Scrub, Great Dog, and at last the curious domed sandstone rocks of Virgin Gorda. Flanked by palm-trees and sea grapes, this was *Treasure Island* come to life, with its rich foliage and white sand beach running down to a glassy, clear aquamarine sea.

Tom throttled back the engines and neatly brought the ship to a lazy drift in the bay. The sails rattled down and were carefully stowed and tied by the crewmen. The motorized anchor slid swiftly into the albescent water. Lunch—delicious cold seafood and salad—appeared effortlessly from the galley, and I suddenly thought of Frimley sadly playing out his mean little ploys in the cold, back there in the Corporation.

Tom tapped me on the shoulder; he'd opened up a locker at the back. "Want to dive?" Sated with sun I nodded. He threw me a mask, snorkel and a pair of outsize flippers. I put them on and jumped over the side into a marine production number of bright, crazy-colored fish of all sizes, jostling in the blue element and suddenly shining incandescent as the light from the sun caught them. Parrot fish, trumpet fish, squirrel fish and rays, in identical groups or alone in solitary beauty, with shapes and sizes as various and evocative as the brilliance of their many hues, as they swarmed and swam in an endless kaleidoscope of flashing and hectic chromatic change. Gary and Crosby were already in the water ahead of me. Around the strange khaki caves they called the Baths, the fish were even more exotic and numerous. Flashing amber and copper, aquamarine and red, they traced their many patterns and offered a glimpse of the endless variations of marine forms—strange shapes, glittering dragons, sparkling-sighted monsters dazzling the unaccustomed eye with their endless variety.

At last I surfaced, throwing the mask off into the boat and climbing in. "Fantastic," I said.

"The only word," Tom said. "Fantasy—all so near, and so few people get to see it."

After a while the boys returned and climbed aboard. Tom started the engines and lifted the anchor, heading the boat north round the east of Tortola. He handed the wheel over to a crewman and produced a couple of fishing rods. "Interested in a blue marlin?"

Paul grabbed one rod. "Sure." I took the other and cast.

Away to starboard, a disturbance above the water turned out to be a shoal of dark blue flying fish, momentarily breaking surface. I watched them lazily, paying no attention to the rod in my hands.

"Hold it!" Tom shouted suddenly. My line was suddenly spinning out violently. Tom grabbed the rod from me and slowed the wild revolutions, then began to reel in, fighting whatever it was that had taken the bait.

"What is it, a marlin?" I asked.

"Could be," he grunted. "Could be a wakoo or a cobla. Doesn't feel like a barracuda."

At the helm, Kate had slowed the boat down to a walk. Tom went on reeling in. "There it is!" He pointed. A huge silver form broke surface and dived again, violently tautening the thin line.

"That's a tuna, Tom!" one of the crewmen called.

"You reckon?" Tom was holding on with all his strength. A thick vein began to stand out on his forehead as the perspiration flowed and all I could feel was the sense of missed opportunity. If I'd been making a documentary this was the drama I'd have captured on film, not the tailor's dummy charade on which we used up all our film stock.

Gradually, foot by foot, Tom brought the great fish nearer to the boat. Then beside him, Kate pointed. Behind, quite near, a black triangle suddenly broke surface and disappeared again. Like a silver projectile, the shark homed in on the dying tuna at the line's end. In moments the clear water boiled with violent movement and then became bloody red. The silver shadow was gone into the depths and the line became limp.

Tom, no longer having to fight, reeled in fast. The crewmen stuck boat-hooks over the side to lift the huge, savaged fish aboard. As its body rose we could see the extent of the shark's attack—a great gash from below its mouth practically to its tail, white bones and bloody entrails all horribly exposed.

Tom put the rod down heavily. "Let's get back," he muttered.

The crewmen chopped the remains of the tuna into portions and carried them below, quickly swabbing

101

over the decks to remove all traces of fish blood. But somehow in that moment the calm happiness of the day had disappeared.

We came back past the many islands through the narrows by St. John's, the sun still hot but lower, its light growing greyer as the afternoon ended. I started to thank Tom for the wonderful day but he just said, "Forget it." As he brought the boat through the gap where St. Thomas began, the sky grew slowly more yellow, then orange, and finally red as the low building of the Yacht Club came in sight. A single figure in white showed up against the dark wood—a woman, somehow familiar. Eyes straining in the failing light, I at last made out enough of her features to recognize her just as she saw me and waved.

Gisela. . . .

I couldn't remember mentioning St. Thomas to her but she said I had. She'd taken the rest of her leave and come on down as she'd threatened. "I could be scheduled for flying tomorrow, but the airline knows where to find me."

She'd taken a cab to the obvious place, the marina, and by elimination on to the Yacht Club and so found us.

"Why do all this?" I asked, deadpan.

She smiled that amazing smile. "You're not going to embarrass a girl by asking *that*."

"The least I can do is to invite you to dinner."

We were standing on the veranda at Cokey's. It was quite dark, but there was enough moonlight to see the bay and the lights of a cruise ship making its slow way out of the harbor. Paul and the rest of the crew had left us and were planning to dine in Magens

Bay; we simply stood there enjoying the view. Stronger than the scent of the poinsettias and magnolias, I was aware of Gisela's perfume, her nearness and her unquestionable availability. Behind us someone came out of the hotel. I turned to see Maggie. "Do you happen to know a good restaurant, Maggie?" I asked.

She came down the steps. "What's wrong with my cooking then?"

"Nothing Mag, but—"

"Jess cos I fry your bacon a bit crisp don't mean I'm a dunce in that kitchen, man."

"No, of course not—"

She broke out into one of her great belly laughs. "Jess you try the Golden Gourmet down the Submarine Base Road. Tell that lazy slob Louie that Maggie sent you. He'll fix you up."

She disappeared back into the hotel. I looked at Gisela. "The Golden Gourmet it is. Just give me time for a shower. OK?"

We walked up towards the lighted doorway. Doug Haskins was just coming down to the hall, a taped-up can of film in his hand.

"Dan," he said, "Gary's just unloaded your rushes—here." He thrust the film can into my hands. "You got all the paperwork for British Customs?"

"I told you that I had." I couldn't quite see why he was so worried.

"You're booked on the direct New York flight at two tomorrow. I'll be there to see you off." He looked curiously at Gisela.

I said, "This is a friend of mine, Gisela."

He extended a grimy hand. "Pleased to meet you." He nodded to me and drove off in his wagon.

The Golden Gourmet was obviously in fashion.

Built on the harbor edge with huge warehouses for neighbors its small gravel frontage was packed with parked cars. As we approached we could hear a small steel band beating out a carnival from within. Inside the lighting was sparse and flickering. An ebony face appeared. "No tables."

"Maggie sent us." It was like a replay of a scratched old ganster movie.

"From Cokey's?"

"That's her."

"Wait."

We waited, crowded into a small bamboo-lined bar with a few other hopefuls, glimpsing the four perspiring panplayers in the darkness of the restaurant beyond.

"Twenty minutes, OK?" I turned to see an ivory smile in the ebony face behind us. "Have a drink."

The drink became three, but at last we were shown to a table overlooking the ink-black ocean. From here you could see all the way down the long channel between the two dark masses of islands that broke up the main bay. The wind was rising; the multi-toned xylophonic sound of so many nylon ropes rhythmically striking so many aluminium masts set up an alternative percussion to the insistent busy bell-notes of the steel band behind us.

Our food arrived; some sort of highly-spiced fish for Gisela, a steak-au-poivre for me. All through the meal Gisela was more than flirtatious, positively and unmistakably amorous, as though we were picking up some long-ago affair. When we got up to dance she slipped into my arms easily and naturally, a highly acceptable feminine package, all soft, switched-on and ready-when-you-are.

104

She held on to my hand as we returned to our table. The dark waiter closed in. "You Mr. Galloway?"

"Yes."

"Call for you."

"What? From the hotel?"

"No sir. Long distance."

"Excuse me." I left Gisela and followed the man through a door into a midget office, thoughts racing. It had to be Sally. It had to be bad news.

"Dan?" A confident man's voice crackled as I picked up the receiver.

"Yes, who's that?"

"Boy did I have trouble locating you."

"Who is this?"

"Didn't you get my cable?"

"What cable?"

"It's Herb Krein—in Los Angeles."

Herb Krein—the possible co-producer for *Gateway*.

"Hallo Mr. Krein."

"I got your cable and called your office at the Corporation—your late office that is. They said you'd left."

"Only temporarily."

"Then I called your home. Your wife—was that?"

"Yes, Sally."

"She gave me your address. Hey, what sort of flophouse are you into over there?"

"It's very old, very comfortable, called Cokey's."

" 'Chokey's' Sounds like it. Some jerk with no roof to his mouth answered—"

"That would be Victor—"

"Then I got some old broad—but she at least knew where you were dining—" He paused for breath. "Listen, there is interest over here for *Gateway*. Meaningful interest."

105

"How—meaningful?"

"Like—one of the major oil company Foundations."

"That's good."

"Sure it's good. How soon could you fly to L.A.?"

"I'm on my way back to London tomorrow."

"Then you can fly straight here instead. I've had Hester check the flight. If you can get to St. Croix by ten-thirty tomorrow morning, you can take the connection through Puerto Rico to Miami and pick up the direct flight through to L.A."

"But I have to get my rushes in for processing in London by Monday night."

"You can still make it. You arrive here tomorrow—Saturday night—we meet for breakfast on Sunday, then meet the guy from the Foundation for lunch and you can be on your way by Sunday night, back in London Monday."

I thought fast. It *was* important. "Right, I'll see if I can catch that flight. How about a ticket?"

"Do you have a credit card?"

"Yes."

"What sort?"

I told him.

"Use that. We'll reimburse you this end. I'll book you into the Beverly Hills tomorrow night and have a chauffeur service meet you, OK?"

"OK."

"What time is it there?"

"About a quarter to nine."

"It's a quarter of six here, I'm glad I caught you."

"So am I."

"Nice talking to you. See you Sunday morning. So long."

I cleared the line, dialled for the operator and asked for the airport. Luckily the girl on duty was taking trouble. Yes, I could have a seat on the seaplane out of St. Thomas at nine tomorrow with through connection to L.A.

The band had stopped playing when I walked back to the table.

"Who was it?" Gisela asked. "Some other girl trying to date you?"

I told her my news—my good news—the chance that I might be able to get a program I cared about back on the air, and watched her expression change from teasing sensuality to bewilderment.

"What is all this? I thought you had to rush your film back to London as soon as possible."

"I do. And I can. And go to California on the way."

She looked at me strangely. "I don't understand."

Behind us the band clanged into melody again. I held out my hand. "Dance?"

"Sure." I held her close again, but something had happened. Earlier on her warmth, her evident desirability had seemed perfectly natural. Now I had an uncanny feeling she was simply acting.

Halfway through the number I said, "Do you mind if we call it a day? I'm tired."

"Call it what you like," she said easily. "Though I was just getting my rhythm back."

"We'll find it again." I led her back to the table picked up the check, and took her arm as we went out into the velvet night.

A little old Japanese banger with a taxi-sign drew up. In silence we got in. "Where to?"

"Cokey's."

"No," Gisela said, "I'm not in your hotel. Could you drop me off at the Leeward first please?"

"Sure thing, ma'am."

We drove along the coast road without speaking,

that same road that had been so full of lively traffic when I first arrived about thirty hours before. The cab swung off left in front of a solid-looking block. "The Leeward, ma'am."

I got out after Gisela, half-expecting the offer to be still open, but she stopped short of the entrance and put her arms around me.

"Goodnight, Dan. Thanks for a lovely evening, as they say."

"Goodnight? But—?"

She smiled fleetingly. "Another night, Dan. When we're both—more in the mood—" Her eyes were shining and the invitation was still undoubtedly there. I tried to draw her to me but she resisted gently. "No, please, Dan. We'll see each other again. I promise."

"When?"

"I'll find you. Look, I'll see you off tomorrow morning."

"Do that."

"Goodnight, Dan. Get some sleep." She leant forward and tenderly kissed my lips.

And then she was gone.

The crew were waiting for me in the Bamboo Bar at Cokey's, but after a couple of quickies I remembered I hadn't phoned home about my change of plan. I knew there was no telephone in my room, but Victor directed me to a callbox under the stairs. I dialled the operator and sat down to the major battle of getting through to Sally in London. The connection was made at last, a sleepy voice said, "Hello."

"Darling, how's everybody?"

"Asleep. It's—God, it's *four* in the morning. What's up?"

"Sorry about that, love. It's just that—I've heard from Krein—"

"Who?"

"Herb Krein—the man who wants to co-produce *Gateway.*"

"Ah yes, he rang here—"

"He wants me to go to Los Angeles to meet some oil man about the program."

"But you said Frimley had chopped it."

"Only because of the cost. Don't you see, if I can bring in Krein as co-producer with some money I can revive it. Possibly."

"Or possibly not. How long will you be away?"

"Just a day longer. I'll get back some time on Monday."

"Oh blast."

"Why?"

"Because I had a look at that school for Sarah today—I mean yesterday—and it's not bad; not *good* but not too awful. You ought to see it."

"I will."

"But I made an appointment for Monday."

"No way. I'll be cross-eyed with jet-lag after all that flying."

"Don't I know."

Another voice echoed from God knows where. "Three minutes, do you wish to continue the call?"

"Call me in Beverly Hills. I'm at the Beverly Hills Hotel from tomorrow," I said quickly.

"What's the number?"

"I don't know. Ask directory."

"What time shall I call you?"

"I don't know. It's about seven or eight hours back from you, say about four o'clock on Sunday afternoon your time, that'll be around eight o'clock in the morning—"

The line suddenly went dead. I banged the receiver rest up and down and finally got the operator. "I've been cut off—"

"International cleared you. Did you ask to continue?"

"No, but—"

"Long distance calls are terminated at three minutes unless an extension is specifically requested," the girl said in a sing-song voice. "Do you wish me to reconnect?"

"Don't bother."

Victor was hanging about in the corridor. "Finished with the phone?"

"I think so."

"I'll just switch it off. Maggie don't like taking no calls at night."

There was laughter from the bar. Somebody called me in to join them. I wavered for a second but it had been a long and funny old day; bed was the best answer. On the way up the stairs I wondered why Gisela had acted as she had. I never liked guessing games. I didn't want to puzzle it out. Not now.

The hotel ballroom was alive with steaming faces, straw-hat enthusiasm, cheer-leaders banners, placards. "WE WANT MORE"—carefully researched and selected ad-man's slogan to ensure the president's re-election hung in red letters on white above and alongside.

Souza boomed bellicose and brassy from the speakers. It was still loud in the little room behind the stage, where the grey man, his wife and entourage

110

waited. But the president seemed distracted, remote from all the confected euphoria.

"What is it, dear?" his wife asked. "What's wrong?"

"Nothing."

"Don't pretend, dear. I know you too well. Is there anything?"

"Waldorf," the grey man said. "Have Joe Humphries call General Waldorf."

"And say what?"

"Just ask him if there's any news?"

"Right." The chestnut-haired woman slipped from his side to find the secretary.

The president relaxed a little. Out there was the first tangible evidence of what observers were now calling his "nationwide support"—the first platoon of a massive army he must inspire and drive to secure electoral victory once again. Dismally he thought of the year-long round of such loud meetings, coca-culture hysteria that lay inescapably ahead. In that context, the disappearance of a single technician mattered little or nothing. . . .

And Humphries was back. "General Waldrof says not to worry. Everything possible's being done to solve the problem."

Out in the ballroom the regular cheering had now started, waves of sound, a sea-storm's beginning. The president braced himself, switched on his media-smile. He took his wife's arm.

"Shall we go in dear?"

SIX

There was a message pushed under my door next morning in, I suppose, Maggie's writing, "Please call Mr. O'Neill in London." He probably just wanted to know how the shoot had gone. I didn't want to tell him about my change of route home and anyway I hadn't time to go through all that call-booking routine with the local telephone operator this morning. I tried to get through to Haskins but his line didn't answer. In any case I didn't need him to see me off; he would have enough trouble dispatching the crew on the later plane to New York.

I showered, shaved and picked up my bag and the sealed can of film and left the unused packs of Experts for Victor to try out on his cough. I saw Paul in the entrance, said my goodbyes to him and to Maggie and was at the airport ticket desk before eight.

The flight was all one class to Miami, but I decided to take First for the long flight to Los Angeles. I joined the bus-load of tourists who were taking the seaplane trip to St. Croix, alighting on a concrete strip by Hassel Island where the plane was drawn up on wheels, looking frail and World War II out of the water. Up a ladder into an old-fashioned bucket seat; I chose a place near the front. As the last passengers entered I saw Gisela among them.

"Thought you'd overslept."

"I'm flying with you."

"How come?"

"There was a message waiting for me at my hotel last night. I'm scheduled on a day flight from Miami to L.A."

I paused before answering; the coincidence seemed too much. "The flight I'm on."

"It must be."

I stared at her. "Pan Am must be short of hostesses."

"Short of good ones." She smiled.

A steward came up behind her and asked her to take a seat. The one next to me was already taken. She said, "See you later," and moved on up the gangway.

And the idea that had already half formed in my mind put itself together neatly—all too neatly.

The little plane's engines started coughing and then revved to a roar that vibrated the whole fabric of the fuselage. Propellers whirring, the pilot edged her down to the water and she entered like a duck. A bit more revving and we were suddenly speeding across the bay. As the hull took off from the sea the noise decreased and we climbed clear of the glittering spray. Peering through the porthole I saw the green islands rapidly disappearing behind us, the lazy ships and tiny craft all left in our wake.

The seaplane bumped through a couple of air pockets as if to remind us that this was flying nineteen-thirties style; no food, no musak, no pressurization, but a great feeling of traveling through the sky in a small, claustrophobic, vibrating tube of aluminium.

The tourists chatted away and soon we were descending. Pain shot through my ears as, with a sudden onrush of metallic sound, the hull cleaved the water, the engines slackened and the little aircraft slowed to a stop. In moments we had taxied up another ramp and were stepping out on to frying concrete. I waited for Gisela to alight.

"Seems you can't get rid of me."

"Must be my lucky day."

She was almost inviting me to interrogate her, to challenge this coincidence, but I wasn't ready for question-time. Let her go on thinking I'd accepted it all. We fell back into that friendly and relaxed relationship we'd had on the plane from London. Gisela had recovered her normal gaiety, but the coquettishness and promise of our dinner last night was missing. Perhaps she was waiting for me to make the first suggestion—I wasn't going to. Not yet. I needed time to puzzle it out.

There was Coke, there was coffee, then we trailed on to the 727 for Miami. No delays, just sunshine bouncing off the superlative sea below and a gentle landing at San Juan and one more take-off.

Still no change of mood from Gisela. As the orange juice arrived she asked me, "You're staying just the one night in California?"

"That's right. Then I fly back to London tomorrow night."

"Pity." Yet she seemed to say it with relief.

"That's what you said about New York, remember?"

"Yes. I remember." She looked at me rather strangely for a moment, then left it at that.

We stayed silent for some time. Perhaps this would

be the right moment for me to ask her about herself, in the hope that she might let some clue slip to why she was tailing me.

"Tell me about your husband," I said.

"Martin?"

"Was that his name?"

"Yes. It's not very—interesting."

"It is to me."

"Why?" She was already on the defensive.

"So that we might know each other better."

She flashed me a look with those expressive eyes. "Well—" She took a deep breath, then said, "Martin was your typical country boy. From Rapid City, South Dakota. When I met him he'd made Sergeant in artillery. He was stationed near Garmisch. I was waiting tables at a little snack bar just outside the town, where skiers used to come at the end of the day, weekends mostly. It was the usual 'Hi, good looking, what time d'you finish work?' sort of pickup, but he did it with a sort of style. He was gentle and attentive. I fell."

"How about your family? Did they like him?"

"Family? Didn't I tell you? I didn't have much of a family left after the war."

"What happened to them? I mean—you don't mind telling me do you?"

"No, I don't mind. They weren't heroes—not like in all that resistance junk you see on your British television. Just ordinary people. My father was called up into the German Army and got himself killed somewhere in Russia quite early on. My mother died in the first winter after the liberation, and my brother—much older than me—took off for Italy or some place and just never wrote home."

"So what became of you? You must have been just a baby."

"I was. I was taken in and brought up by some people my parents had known in Halmstadt. Then when I was about fifteen their pimply-faced son caught me in the log-store." She stopped and looked out at the bright blue sky stretching into infinity beyond the window.

"And then—?"

"Do you really want to hear all this?"

"It's fascinating."

"Yeah, well it wasn't all that fascinating getting inexpertly and incompetently raped by a fat Czech schoolboy with advanced acne and dragon's breath. So—as in all the best soap opera—I was thrown out of the house because I was a 'bad influence' on little Karel—*little* Karel—my God what a pig!" She drank a little of her orange juice.

"So you found a job?"

"I found a job. There I was, waiting table, all of sixteen, and terrified of men, when Martin said, 'Hi.' "

A passing hostess scooped up our empty glasses and folded the trays into the backs of the seats in front. "Go on," I prompted. "About Martin."

"Martin." She paused as if wondering how much to say. "He was—beautiful—those first few years, really beautiful. He showed me how two people could truly love each other, helped me lose all my inhibitions about my body, about sex, and about life, about not being sure whether I was German or Czech or Polish or what. Then the time came for him to be sent back to the States, so he decided to quit the army, marry me, and settle in Germany for good—not just for my sake but because he really liked it there. He used all

116

his money, and a lot more he didn't have, buying a restaurant in Mittelwald. He'd never done that sort of work before, but I guess he liked the notion of playing 'mine host' to all his old army buddies. He never discussed it properly with me, but he figured I'd be happy to be out back cooking the dumplings and apfelstrudel while he was out front in the bar." She paused again.

"How did you make out?"

"We started. We didn't make much money—in fact we seemed to be losing out, getting further and further in hock. Then I found I was pregnant. I told Martin. 'No problem,' he said. He organized the doctor, the hospital, everything. But there *were* problems. It seemed I was going to have trouble delivering. I was sent for tests. *Tests!* Don't ever let anyone you love fall into the hands of the German medical profession. Tests, they call them. They went on and on. Hands, rubber gloves, forced up and round everywhere." She shivered. "I'd be sitting there stark naked with four or five of these white-coated butcher-boys inspecting me like a rotting carcass—"

I said, "How was the baby, when it arrived?"

"Late," she almost snapped. "Martin had had to take on another girl for the kitchen. The loan company was giving him a bad time. I went into hospital for a couple of nights and stayed there four weeks. While I was in there you can guess what happened."

"Martin made it with the new girl." I was beginning to wonder how much was fact, how much carefully laundered legend.

"Right in one. At last I had the baby, a little boy, beautiful like Martin. But the whole of German medi-

117

cine, tests or no tests, couldn't keep him alive. He died within the day. So there I was—no baby, and as it turned out, no restaurant and no husband either."

"The loan company?"

"Called in the loan. And Martin was off back to Rapid City, South Dakota, real rapid. Leaving me, as a German resident, to clear up the mess."

"What did you do?"

"What any girl that has to make money in a hurry does."

"Hooking?"

"Not quite. I thought about it. I was that desperate. I tried a couple of clubs in München, but they weren't short of that sort of talent. So I went out to look for the kind of job that paid well that most people don't want. Night telephonist, hotel clerk, you name it. And there was a guy, a former client at our restaurant, who helped out, too." She sighed. "We became lovers of course. What else is new? Then when I'd got some money together I went round to see the loan company and made a deal to pay off a percentage and call it quits."

I was ahead of her now. "And then Martin turned up again?"

"You read the synopsis," she smiled. "I was settled in München by then with this guy, Gerhardt. I was willing to blow it all, take Martin back and start again. But he cut up rough about my shacking up with Gerhardt—God knows how he thought I was supposed to have made out all those months—and then of course I started on about the little waitress he'd been knocking off all the time I was nearly dying in the hospital trying to have his baby—and he blew. And I've never seen him since."

She sat back, suddenly quiet. Beside her, frustrated,

I was still in the dark about what she was involved in *now*, and where I fitted in. I had to keep her talking; somewhere there might still be a clue. "What happened then?"

"I got a divorce by post—years later. Gerhardt left me for someone else. I did a lot of other jobs—ended up flying. End of story so far."

"Mmm." So she could have been into anything. Spying, smuggling, who knew? I certainly didn't.

She looked at me clear-eyed. "You're quiet suddenly. Are you sorry you asked?"

"Far from it."

"Everybody has skeletons. I hope it hasn't—"

"Put me off? Not at all. Intrigued me."

"Because when we first met, I kind of hoped—" She smiled her delightfully charming smile then looked away.

"Keep hoping", I said.

She didn't answer, keeping her head turned away, looking out of the aircraft window.

And the answer, the only possible answer to all this, clicked together like Lego in my head.

I looked out of the window once more. We were approaching Miami, miles of tower blocks on the sea's edge misted over with a sort of money vapor. The plane banked and descended and soon we felt the heavy thump at the moment of landing. As the engines slowed to a whisper and silence Gisela said, "I have to leave you now to get showered and changed. See you on the plane."

She moved off out of sight down the aisle. In no hurry, I let the crowd off before me and wandered down the aircraft steps towards the terminal building.

119

The air here on the mainland was clammier than in the islands, there was no faint scent of tropical plants, no distant steel band. I simple had a faintly sick feeling that somehow I had been and was being duped.

I went into the terminal bar and drank a beer. It tasted sour and fizzy and my mouth was still dry a few moments later. I found the bookstall but there was nothing I particularly wanted to read. At last the flight to Los Angeles was called. At the security check I opened my briefcase, showed them the taped-up can of film and the customs papers; the security man lifted the can to check the weight, nodded and handed it back. I replaced it in the briefcase.

As I mounted the front steps of the aircraft I saw Gisela waiting in the rear entrance in trim blue uniform. She saw me and started moving forward. I showed my boarding card and was shown to my seat. Gisela appeared beside me. "What's this, travelling First Class? I'm serving back in Coach."

I said, "Lucky them."

She said, "If you'd said you were travelling First—"

"I'll see you in L.A.," I smiled.

She forced a smile back, "It's a date." She walked away back into the rear of the plane.

But her face had given her away for just the instant I needed. And I knew beyond further doubt that her presence on this flight was more than just coincidental. I reached into my briefcase to find a paperback; the film can got in my way. I lifted it on to the seat beside me.

"Is this taken?" I looked up to see a woman of about sixty with carefully set silver hair smiling down at me rather nervously pointing at the seat.

"No." I whisked the can off the seat and put it back in my case. "Be my guest."

"Thank you." She took off her neat linen jacket and handed it to the stewardess waiting to offer us yet more iced orange juice. "I don't travel all that much," she said, "I like to find a friendly-looking person to talk to."

"Oh."

"My name's Ellen Hawkins. Been staying in Miami have you?"

"No, I'm just passing through. I've been working—in the Virgin Islands."

"Making a movie?"

"Just a quick commercial."

"You live in Hollywood?"

"No, near London."

"You don't have an English accent—not what I'd call an English accent."

"It's Glasgow. What you'd call Scotch."

"We used to meet a lot of movie people back home living in Berkeley—my husband was a professor you know."

"Was? Is he retired now?"

"He passed away last summer. This is the first real trip I've had since then. My son—he'd got a good job in the State Department—he gave me this holiday. Paid for everything he did."

"In Miami?"

"No—in Puerto Rico. Didn't I see you on the plane there with a girl? A blonde? Your wife maybe?"

"No. She wasn't my wife—just a friend."

The engines started and mercifully made too much noise for further conversation. I knew I was trapped with this garrulous old party with no way out for the rest of the long flight. But First has its compensations. There were enough interruptions—drinks, peanuts, more drinks, lunch, coffee—to occupy her for the next hour or so.

We crossed the long Gulf of Mexico and came back over land somewhere west of Baton Rouge, running into low cloud before we reached Texas. Ellen Hawkins rattled on about the loneliness of being a widow, the cost of living, why don't they cut welfare payments for all these shirkers ad nauseam. At last I made excuses and got up to go to the john halfway down the compartment. The busy lights were on up front. I went back into Tourist; the toilets were even busier there with queues. I caught sight of Gisela in fancy apron hurrying past to the galley. She gave me a quick but far-away smile.

I parted the curtains to go back into First. I'd nearly reached my row when I realized that Ellen seemed to be riffling through my briefcase. She actually had the can of unexposed film in her hands as I said behind her loudly, "Looking for something?"

She looked up in alarm and gasped, "I—"

I saw with relief that the band of adhesive tape sealing the two halves of the tin together to keep out the light hadn't been tampered with.

"Give me that."

She handed over the can. The envelope carefully taped on to the side (containing the camera-sheets that Gary would have filled out, giving the name of the production and simple developing and printing instructions) seemed to have some adrift. I carefully stuck it back on again, taking my time.

"I—was looking for a cigarette," Ellen said.

"This is a can of film."

"I know. It was on top. I thought you might have a pack underneath."

"I'd rather you hadn't touched it. If it had been opened to the light or got fogged in any way all my work of the last week would be down the drain."

The woman looked afraid again. "Silly of me. I needed a smoke so badly—"

I wasn't enjoying it either. "This is the no smoking area," I said.

"Oh—I'm sorry." She quickly gathered up her things and clumsily moved forward to find another seat.

I watched her go then eased myself into the seat by the window, the can still in my hand. I shook it. It sounded like a tightly-wound roll of negative should. Maybe it was all right. I started to put it back in my case.

"What was all that about?"

Gisela was standing beside me. I snapped the case shut. "Some woman—wanted a cigarette—poking around in my bag."

Gisela laughed. "I told you you should have travelled Coach class."

The stewardess from First appeared. "Everything OK sir?"

"Of course. Why?"

"The lady who was sitting here, she seems upset."

"A misunderstanding, nothing more. Give her my apologies will you?"

"Yes sir." The stewardess looked hard at Gisela; Gisela got the message and left. "Anything else you'd like sir?"

I looked at my watch; it was ten o'clock St. Thomas time but now we were going back another three hours for California. "Just a sleep."

I shut my eyes for a moment or two to let her clear, then looked out at the darkening red sky. Could it have been coincidence? I didn't know. That was the trouble. I desperately wanted someone who knew to let me in on the secret.

It was dark when we touched down at Los Angeles. There was a welcoming feeling about the warm velvet air and the spaciousness of the airport. A chauffeur found me, gave me a note from Herb Krein: "The chauffeur will drive you to your hotel. A central car will be waiting for you there ready for tomorrow. See you for breakfast. Warmest regards, Herb." It was thoughtful and promised well for our meeting. I gathered my bag from the inclined rampway and nearly bumped into Gisela.

"Going my way?" The seductive mood was back in her voice.

"Which way's that?"

"You're booked in at the Beverly Hills aren't you?"

"Yes."

"I've never been to the Beverly Hills." The message in her eyes could have been read by a five-year-old.

She handed her overnight bag to the chauffeur and took my arm as we followed him out in to the warm night and the waiting Cadillac. She snuggled up to me in the back of the car as we were driven the length of La Cienga Boulevard towards Beverly Hills, calf and thigh all transmitting powerful and irresistible messages of promise. It was so obvious I smiled all the way, as we drove up the beautiful tree-lined avenue to the moonshaded entrance.

And who was I to turn down this sort of offer? I had begun to laugh after we had checked in and were following the bell-hop up the stairs to the room Herb had booked. I found him some folding money and shut the door.

"Is it a private joke?" Gisela asked.

"No, it's meant to be shared," I said, putting my arms round her and drawing her into a kiss.

Whoever designed the air hostess uniform made sure it would come off in a hurry; her jacket slipped from her shoulders to the floor, three buttons let go their hold on her shirt, a single bra-hook parted to reveal her white rounded breats and rosy tumescent nipples; the skirt zip descended and a two-handed thrust down her hips peeled her like a peach. Naked, with strong supple fingers, she did the same for me. Still kissing we fell in slow motion on to the bed; she broke free and stretched out upon the soft sheets. My mouth found her earlobes, her nose, her lips again, her hardening nipples. She began to gasp already, quickening her rhythm as her vulva opened to receive me; I felt her come to a shuddering first orgasm almost as soon as I entered, and then her rapture really began as she started to redeem in full the promises her eyes had been making ever since our first meeting. By turns sensual, tender, animal and shy, she continuously sought different ways of love, consistently searching for more and more subtle pleasure. Slowly, I travelled up and down her yielding, active body, tasting perfume and salt, tongue-testing each and every acrid-sweet mound and crevice in the controlled panic of desire. And momentarily as she reached up to grasp my ear, I saw again the distinctive bracelet with its pendant pattern of two entwined crosses, before my lobe was violently pulled down for a split second of biting pain between her foaming teeth, and at last pleasure mounted to climax—long drawn, delayed till unbearable, and again, until by joint consent we parted and came to rest.

"Again?"

I must have fallen asleep. She was kneeling above

me, her breasts swinging from side to side across my chest and arousing me with fiendish precision. I murmured, "I have to make breakfast with this man Krein—"

"There's plenty of time till breakfast." I reached up to her shoulders and rolled her over and down. . . .

Down further, down into sleep that was dark and strange. I was aware of running figures and movements and pains inside the ears from pressure and depressure and suddenly consciousness. . . .

I tried to remember where I was—in bed—but *where*? Then I made out the figure of a woman, dim and naked in a small morning light, expertly searching through my briefcase where I'd thrown it down on the floor by the wardrobe.

"Gisela."

She spun round.

"It's here, what you're looking for." I flicked on the light and pointed down beside me. Wedged under the leg of the bed nearest my head, half hidden by the bedside table was the taped-up can of film.

Gisela gasped.

I said, "I put it there when you went to the bathroom sometime during the sex olympics."

She made a dive to grab it. I was out of the bed like a greyhound, bringing her down and twisting her round to grip her wrists together in one hand, the way I'd learnt in Cowcaddens Junior years ago.

"Would you mind—just—telling me why you need that can so badly?"

"Darling—you're hurting me."

I relaxed my grip a little but still held her firmly. Gisela grimaced. "Do you usually go in for this kind of wrestling?"

126

"Not with girls. But I'm enjoying the practice. Now—what's so special about the can?"

Gisela shook her head. I tightened my grip again, "Tell me." Gisela set her mouth closed firmly, tears formed in her eyes, "I had to do it; my parents—"

"You told me they were dead."

"I lied. They're still there. In Czechoslovakia. Please believe me—"

It was too pat. "I don't believe you Gisela; I think you're in this for the money. What is it you're smuggling? Drugs?"

She didn't answer, looking at me now with pure hatred.

"Let me help you Gisela. You were sent to tail me on the plane from London, even if it meant your changing from First where I should have been to Tourist where I was. Then you followed me to St. Thomas. Why? To see me off safely? With my can of film? Or whatever it is?"

She gave a small nod.

"What's in the can? Tell me."

"Film, that's all I was told—a film that had to be got back to London for processing."

"Are you sure?"

"That's all I know. Please—I'd tell you if I knew any more." She was looking at me as fearfully as if half expecting me to hit her. God knew what sort of sordid situations she'd been into before, but she must have known I wouldn't use violence. I wasn't some sort of super spy who would sleep with a girl one minute and slap her around for information the next.

I let her go and got up, not sure what to do next. Somehow it didn't seem as if I was being used for ordinary smuggling. But what else could it possibly be?

Gisela had picked up her clothes and was starting to dress, the bathroom door behind her open. I noticed a straightforward lock on the outside. I grabbed her and pushed her in there, throwing her clothes in after, taking a key from inside and locking the door.

I picked up the film can. Whatever was in it was almost certainly not the film Paul had shot for me in the Caribbean yesterday. Doug Haskins must have made the substitution. Of *course*—he'd have had time after Gary had unloaded the camera and before he'd handed it on to me. But if it was film, undeveloped film, I couldn't risk fogging it by peeking at it in daylight now.

I looked around the room; early morning sunlight was making bright streaks on the walls. The wardrobe was big enough to walk into. I went in, pulling the door after me. Light still shone up from under the door. I found a small rug near the bed, took it in and set it against the inside of the foot of the door as I closed it, sealing off the light to give me a makeshift darkroom.

I carefully peeled the tape off the can, sticking it on the wall beside me to use again. Then, nervously, I opened up. What felt like a thousand-foot roll was in a black paper bag inside. I pulled it out gingerly and tore a couple of inches of film off the end, and put it in my top pocket. To the touch the roll felt as it should have felt, the plastic bobbin in the center intact. I put the whole roll back into the black bag, and the black bag into the can, closed it and resealed the sides with the tape that I retrieved from the wall. On the face of it the film was as it should be.

It was getting stuffy in the wardrobe. I pushed the door open, blinking at the sudden light again. I examined the piece of film I'd torn off the end of the roll;

it looked exactly like an exposed piece of 35mm East-mancolor negative should. The envelope was still taped to the side of the can. I prised it off and opened it.

Instead of the normal camera-sheet was a typed note: "*IMPORTANT*—THIS FILM IS HIGH SPEED HSPD7 (MODIFIED) *DEVELOP ONLY TO CORRECT FORMULA.*"

A sudden crash from the bathroom, in three steps I reached the door and unlocked it. Inside the window was smashed and gaping. I looked through and just glimpsed Gisela on the garden path eight feet below as she ran round a corner and out of sight. She obviously had friends nearby, probably someone in on the deal. I threw my clothes on rapidly. I had the film but who could I take it to? The police? To tell them what? The CIA? How do you contact The CIA? I had no idea. No, I had to get the film developed to see what was on it before anything else.

Where? A laboratory. Think of a name. Constellation—the biggest lab outside the major studios. On a Sunday morning? I couldn't wait and I couldn't stay here. Gisela was probably calling up reinforcements right now. I flipped through the phone book and found the lab's address, Alameda Avenue, Glendale. I had been given a street-map with the key of the rental car and quickly found it. Square B7 north of Griffith Drive, somewhere past Universal City and the NBC studios. I could cut up north through Coldwater Canyon and take a right turn on to the Ventura Freeway when I hit North Hollywood. There was a turnoff left for Alameda after about five miles.

I zipped up my trousers, grabbed my jacket and the film. My watch now said 8.05. I ran down the stairs and almost bumped into a man standing in the huge deserted lobby. It was Herb Krein, short, swarthy and smiling in brilliant red t-shirt and light suede blue slacks.

"Dan!" He took hold of my free hand. "*Nice* to see you. Have a good trip?"

"Look—I'll see you in about an hour, OK?"

"Let's make it now. I'm free. I came up for an early swim before breakfast but I'm ready when you are."

"No—have your swim. I have to go somewhere very urgently."

Krein looked bewildered. "Dan, I brought you here, surely you can—"

The desk clerk called, "There's a call for you Mr. Krein."

Over his shoulder I saw, like a slowed-down black-and-white movie shot, a couple of square men come in from the coffee-shop entrance and look round the lobby. I slapped Krein's shoulder, said quickly "See you," and headed for the main entrance.

Outside the sunlight was dazzling. The car valet tried to intercept me but I'd no time to waste having him find the car and bring it up to the door. I walked past as if taking a stroll, then ran down through the bushes to the car park below, hoping the rental was there. There was no one else about. The tab on the key-ring gave me the number; it was right in front of me, a small Chevy. I opened the door and dived in full length, keeping my head down. I sneaked a look back towards the hotel entrace. The two men came out, looked left and right, then down into the car park. I ducked, giving them time to go back into the lobby; when I looked again they'd gone.

I put the key in the lock, started the engine and drove cautiously round into the hotel drive and out on to the boulevard, turning up Beverly Drive for Coldwater. There was no other traffic about. With a shock I suddenly realized that without thinking *I was driving on the left, British-fashion.* I swung over to the right of the road and put my foot down. I soared up the hill through the tree-lined road. On either side were the mansions of ex-moguls: oriental pleasure-domes, Spanish haciendas, way-out modernities, Frank Lloyd Wright gone wrong. This was the Hollywood I'd imagined in my boyhood in rain-soaked Sauchiehall Street, all those way back Saturday nights at the Odean and the old Cosmo—a Hollywood of effortless riches, vast well-kept gardens, personal palaces. But with the old movie grandeur dead who on earth inhabited these studio-induced dreams now?

The road reached a crest and ran out of desirable villas, giving a sudden view of the neat, squared-off sprawl of Hollywood and L.A., and then it descended, running into a tight-knit suburbia of smaller plots and scaled-down architectural flamboyance.

Then I noticed a blue Mustang in my rear-view mirror, following, keeping its distance. As I accelerated it kept pace. At the next traffic lights I swung right on to Ventura Boulevard then left again into a quiet street, braking hard to a sudden stop. The Mustang swung left after me but drove on past, giving me a glimpse of the two figures in the front. I waited a full two minutes, reversed and turned and got back on to the Boulevard. After a couple of U-turns I crossed Moor Park and got myself on to the Ventura Freeway heading east. There was a Sunday morning sprinkling of traffic but no sign of the blue Mustang behind. I pushed the Chevy up to eighty, leaving Burbank and north Hollywood on my left, negotiating a freeway intersection and finally swinging off by the slip road on to Alameda.

The laboratory, square and white painted, was on the left just opposite the Disney plant. I drove up to the barrier. A guard straight out of Highway 77, white-peaked-cap, gun-in-holster, ambled out of his little cabin to come across and lean on the driver's side door.

"Uh?"

"I've got some film for urgent developing."

"From?"

"Er—we're a London company, O'Neill Associates." I couldn't start explaining Hong Kong or Experts now.

"'OK, buster. Drop it in the box over there."

"No, I have to see someone about it—it's rather special."

"You mean dirty? Porno? We don't handle that shit no more."

"It's not like that." But how did I really know?

"Look—just get me to your Processing Manager quickly."

"I'll see who's here. We ain't properly open on Sunday. Park your car over there."

He went back to his box and raised the barrier. As I drove through, the blue Mustang suddenly appeared right behind me and headed me off to a screeching halt by the main entrance. The two men from the Beverly Hills lobby jumped out and came at me fast.

I'd seen this sort of thing so many times that it was like a corny TV playback, but this was real and ugly. In slow motion I saw the first man grab for the door handle. No trained fighter, I desperately tried to remember the exact timing of the Cowcaddens' Crunch. As the man flung the door open I swung my legs around and brought my right knee up hard into his groin, seeing the red sweaty face change down through surprise to pain. The second man pulled him aside. I had the film can in my right hand and tried to slam it like a heavy discus at the man's head. He ducked, his thick hands pulled me out of the car. I felt a sickening blow in the stomach, then another. As the world reeled my last image was of a huge fist tearing the can out of my grasp. . . .

SEVEN

"I promise," O'Neill said thickly. "Nothing's gone wrong. Definitely on its way. No problem."

He held the phone a little way from his aching head as the long distance voice went on and on, petulantly. The call had woken him up. He reached for the glass of Vichy he had put by the bed, found it dry, swore under his breath.

Alone in London he had done the stupidest thing, like some hick had asked the help of the hall-porter, let him fix the girl and the night out. Now, a couple of hundred pounds down, all he had was a bad memory of a sharp boring little female, a disinterested lay, a hangover and a mouth like the original parrot's cage.

The other voice had stopped.

"I know all that," O'Neill said. "Secrecy is, and will continue to be, preserved. You have my word on it."

The other man went on again, then subsided. With infinite relief O'Neill realized the conversation was at an end. "Thank you for calling," he said. "I'll keep you posted."

134

After all, a client was a client.

But as he put the instrument on its rest he remembered. Galloway hadn't called him back from the Caribbean.

I awoke feeling sick and dehydrated. I seemed to be sitting on an upright chair in a plain room with no windows, only a small air-conditioning grill. The door, when I tried it, was predictably locked from the outside. The room had a familiar chemical smell—I was still in the film laboratory. I looked at my watch; ten past eleven. Christ! Whatever happened to Herb Krein?

There was a pitcher of water and a glass on a table beside me; I drank it all straight out of the jug and felt a little better. After a while a key turned in the lock; I stood up and braced myself against the wall for the rough stuff I knew was coming.

The door opened.

A young, very pretty, dark-haired girl with warm and expressive blue eyes stood there. "Feeling better?"

"Listen, before we go into any explanations, I was supposed to see a man at the Beverly Hills two hours ago."

"Mr. Krein? All taken care of—he's expecting you back there for lunch."

"How did you—?"

"Don't worry about a thing. My name's Diane—Diane O'Hara."

She had that superb assurance these Californian girls seem to be born with—a living commercial for the ultimate in wholesome, desirable femininity. She knew she looked good, smelt good, tasted good—and I

135

wondered whether, with one push, I could shove her aisde and go racing down the corridor—but where would that lead?

"They're waiting for you." She stepped back and pointed, "This way."

There was no sign of the two heavies as she led me down the corridor through double doors then across the glaring sunlight of an open yard to a room marked "Projection 7". She looked just as good from the back and she knew it. But I thought I'd detected a certain nervousness as well.

As I entered the darkened room I saw two men watching me from a single row of seats beneath the projection window. The first, a big man in vivid golf shirt and slacks got up. "Good morning. I'm Bob."

"Bob who?"

"Just sit down and watch."

He pressed a button. I took the next vacant seat; the girl Diane sat beside me. She *was* nervous. I noticed her quietly tensing and untensing her hands. Maybe she was aware of what was coming next. I certainly wasn't. The lights dimmed and the "10-9-8-7-6" of a standard leader flashed on to the screen.

There was no sound, just picture; in color, a long shot of a brightly-lit room. A monkey sat on a table, a yellow bird perched in a cage, and below you could just see a couple of rats scurrying about the floor. Smoke suddenly erupted from a box near the table; the monkey caught a whiff and leapt up in a frenzy, turning to silent agony and abrupt collapse. The bird fell from its perch like a leaf and the rats careered madly this way and that trying to escape from the fumes and then they, too, were overcome.

Then, by some amazing feat of special effects, everything in the picture decomposed. The monkey's

136

thick fur fell away from its body, then its flesh crumbled. Finally its bones became nothing more than powder; the bird in the cage disappeared into a small greyish heap of dust, the rats into almost nothing. I felt sick—the cold horror was unbelievable but there. And I was suddenly certain that it wasn't special effects, but some actual, diabolical test.

The lights in the projection room suddenly switched on.

Bob said, "Know what that was?"

"No." I was still dazed, half incredulous, half sick.

"It's on the film you've been carrying."

It meant nothing to me.

The man next to Bob said, "How much do you know?" Surprisingly his voice was English.

"Nothing," I said. "I shot a quick cigarette commercial in the Virgin Islands. The can I had with me contained the rushes, or so I thought. I was taking them back home for processing."

"The film was switched," said Bob. "As I think you've discovered. You were smuggling a stolen film record of a top-secret radiation test which *someone* wants badly enough to set up this whole charade of a cigarette commercial."

"Who are you people?"

"You don't need to know."

"The CIA?"

"Let's say we're on the right side, as far as you're concerned. What I'm going to tell you now is secret and is not, repeat not, to be discussed with anyone."

The Englishman said, "You know the score on official secrets I presume?" His voice echoed the Tower of London.

"I do."

The man called Bob took a deep breath. "A month

ago in the Nevada Desert, about two thousand feet below the surface of the earth, the U.S. Government Nuclear Program made a test, codename 'Dragonfire', a test so dangerous that it might conceivably have destroyed most of life as we know it on this planet."

I began to feel dizzy. I looked at the other people sitting quite normally in the dim, airless room; the young girl, looking fairly shattered by what she had just seen, and the two overweight, worried men. Maybe it *was* all a nightmare.

"No, you're not dreaming," Bob said. "It happened the way you saw it. It's an advanced form of radiation. The destructive process develops as it spreads, breaking down all living substances, consuming all organic matter."

The Englishman said, "The ultimate. The final, infinite, weapon of terror."

Bob breathed out heavily, "The one we were all looking for—the big one."

I tried to think slowly, logically. "But—if it means global annihilation no one can ever use it—surely? Not without risking their own destruction."

"These are limiting factors," Bob said. "Natural barriers, oceans, treeless deserts wide enough to outlast the radition's two or three days' of half-life."

I tried to digest this, to conjure up a mental map of the world in terms of oceans and continents—North and South America, Australia and the Pacific Islands, the huge trunk of Africa with Sinai to the north east, and a massive Europe stretching from southern Spain right up through Russia and Finland, down to the bordering mountains and deserts of India and China. Or did *all* these deserts give a sure guarantee of protection? I gave up. There was something else I found difficult to credit. "If it's totally destructive, how on earth did you manage to film it?"

"The test was made deep in the earth in a specially constructed room, outer-lined with several thicknesses of nuclear resistant material. The lenses of both cameras were built into the walls, and, because of the special protection within the covering glass, not much light came through. So we had to use a superspeed stock which requires unique processing. As far as we know there are only three laboratories in the world that can handle it: one in New York, this one here in California, and one in London."

"But someone else might have the capacity? Somewhere?"

"Possibly. Anyway the test was made and the film was processed. The "A" camera showed what you've just seen, but the film from the "B" camera was blank. We checked the camera—there was no way the film could have been fogged—and the guy who had loaded the magazine simply disappeared; ergo—he'd taken the film from the "B" camera. But whoever had it now had a big problem, how to get it processed. New York and California were obviously too dangerous—"

"Leaving London," I said.

"Unless they'd set up another processing plant elsewhere—expensive but not impossible—leaving them problem number two, how to get the film out of the United States."

"There must be a million ways. A boat—a private plane—?"

"Exactly. The FBI traced him to a place called Winnemucca in Nevada. They got hold of the number and description of a car he'd rented there, and alerted police and border posts with Mexico and Canada. The car was recognized a week later on the other side of the United States near Apalachicola."

"In Florida," said the Englishman. "The South East tip. You know?"

"I've heard of it," I said.

"So—he must have driven right across the country to deliver the film to whoever was buying."

"Not necessarily," I said. "The car could have been a decoy."

"Oh sure. Whichever way it was the Florida police didn't quite catch up with him fast enough. As they were tailing the car had a collision—and the driver disappeared, literally into the swamps. By now we knew it wasn't a mob operation, none of the usual crime syndicates, nor even—as far as we can tell—the official opposition."

"The Russians? What about the Chinese?"

"Unlikely these days. Either it was a guy freelancing on a one-off or it was a totally unknown set-up. We tipped off the Coast Guard along the Florida coast to look for this particular can of film—they're pretty wide-awake down there with all the movement there is in narcotics. Then a man, badly beaten and nearly dead, was washed up near Fort Lauderdale.

"Surprisingly, his attackers hadn't taken his ID card or his driver's license, which were in the name of Jeff Sadler—the guy missing from the experimental nuclear plant in Nevada. The local police Sergeant acted on his own and managed to get the name of a boat he'd been thrown off a few hours before. *The Pasquello.* The Coast Guard had it under surveillance already and were able to pinpoint it and direct a fast cutter to intercept. It was blowing up for a storm, and they were hit by a squall at the time of the contact. The

Pasquello wouldn't stop, and was sunk as instructed. Normally the skipper of the cutter would have carried out a complete search of the surrounding sea area, and checked on any nearby boats for possible pick-ups. But in the foul weather they simply picked up a couple of bodies and headed back to base."

"No other survivors?"

"As far as the skipper knew, no."

"What happened then?"

"The FBI assumed the case closed, and that the secret film had gone down with the other men in the boat. But there was a small element of doubt. There had been another boat in the area, possibly another fast fisherman like the *Pasquello*. If they'd had the inflatable on deck all ready to launch with good strong outboard, and been in radio contact with the other boat, they could—just—have got away at the moment the Coast Guard attacked and the squall struck them. They'd have had a hell of a time keeping upright, but *if* they managed it, with the film perhaps in a waterproof bag strapped to a man's body, and reached the other boat in the darkness, they'd have got away."

My mind was already racing ahead of him, fitting the plot together. "Your theory was that they *had* escaped?"

Bob smiled. "Not mine. But that was the thinking when the President's office handed me the problem. I took it from there. Assume they'd had the luck of the devil and made it to Puerto Rico, say. There they are, holed up, with a roll of hot film they can't even develop in a normal laboratory. If they try to ship it out somehow they risk getting caught. Unless they invent a foolproof method of transporting it all the way to the laboratories in London, carrying it through cus-

141

toms in the normal way, with the film made to look like ordinary unexposed negative for a legitimate shoot."

The Englishman said, "And that's where you came in."

"Me? Why me?"

"You're well known, travel around quite a bit." Bob said.

"Not only that," said the Englishman. "Working for the Corporation you'd have been security cleared by Special Branch. Or didn't you know that?"

"I did. As it happens."

"With your track record, a customs man would accept that any film you were carrying was normal rushes; no question of opening up to have a look, no x-ray, just a friendly wave through."

I said, "You mean they set up the whole complicated business of making a commercial just for this?"

"Just for this, which might be the whole future of mankind."

I had a sudden quick image of Frimley, the bad actor, saying, "It might be for the best," as he shook my hand.

I said, "Why did it have to be me? Why couldn't they just hire an out-of-work freelance?"

"They had to make it look totally respectable, not just a lashed-up one-off."

"Tell me," the Englishman asked, "how exactly did you come to take the job?"

"The Corporation suddenly ended my contract, and my bank manager was leaning on me. I needed the loot."

"The people we're dealing with seem to have extraordinary power in all manner of places."

"Quite."

Bob said, "So that's how it went. You made your shoot in the Caribbean and someone substituted the film of the radiation test for your undeveloped rushes—"

"Haskins."

"Who?"

"A shipping agent, so-called; their contact in the Virgin Islands. Why not pull him in?"

Bob said bluntly, "He's already been taken care of. But their plan nearly worked. Everything would have been fine for them if you'd taken the film straight back to London for processing."

"But I had a call from Herb Krein to come on here." A sudden thought, "He's not mixed up in this too is he?"

"Quite the reverse. He wrecked the whole scheme by asking you to come out west. Your change of plan must have shaken them."

"It certainly shook a girl called Gisela."

"Yeah, we know Gisela," Bob said.

"She's a freelance," said the Englishman. "Worked for the West Germans for a bit, now plays the field. They'd hired her to watch you, see you got back safely to London. The—er—" he took a quick look at the girl Diane, "the other service she rendered wasn't strictly in the contract."

For some ridiculous reason I was shocked. "You bastards. I thought only the Russians played Peeping Tom."

Bob ignored the insult. "When you told her you'd changed your plans and were coming on to L.A. she had to get herself switched to your flight pretty damn quick."

"How could she do that? And so fast?"

"Bribery. How else? Knowing the right guy in the

143

airline to fix something like that would be part of her stock-in-trade."

Something didn't ring true. Then I realized. "How do *you* know what she did? You weren't on to me in the Virgin Islands, were you?"

Bob looked slightly uneasy. "No, not that soon. But we had a little talk with Gisela this morning."

"I see." My mind was racing. Then it all came clear. "So it was the *other* woman, the old one on the plane with the blue rinse, who tumbled to it?"

"Ellen? That's right. She was our only lucky break— one of our best operators. She happened to be on that plane coming back from vacation in San Juan. She knew Gisela from way back, recognized her travelling with you, saw the film when you went through security check, and added two and two."

"She knew about the film?"

"We'd alerted all our principle personnel. Once she'd taken a peek at the can when you went to the john and seen the note about the special developing then we knew for certain what you were carrying."

"So why not take it from me then and there?"

"We were curious. Maybe you knew what you had."

"I didn't—"

"How could we know? We had you followed to the Beverly Hills and watched."

"You told me—"

"Next thing we know is the girl breaking out of your bathroom window this morning."

"I caught her looking for the film."

"Naturally. She'd have needed to check that it hadn't been switched when Ellen handled it on the plane."

"She saw that?"

"Must've."

144

"Still, she got away—"

"Not far."

No of course. They'd had a talk with Gisela this morning, hadn't they? I drew a deep breath. I didn't think much of this particular scenario so far. All I needed was the exit sign. "Very well gentlemen. You have your film back; so that's that. I can go and see my man Krein and get off back to London."

"Not quite."

"How do you mean?"

"You're working for us now—you've been drafted."

I wasn't having *that*. "No way. No bloody way. Accidentally carrying a secret film is one thing but—"

Bob stood up. "Let me introduce myself—General Waldorf."

"Of the CIA?"

"I work for the U.S. Government, and this is Henry Mollinson who's, let's say, loosely attached to the British Embassy."

Mollinson offered me his hand rather primly, like a vicar at a tea party. "I suppose you'd recognize this sort of pass?" he said, flipping open his wallet.

It looked genuine enough.

"Sorry," I said, "I'm not working for you."

Bob sighed. "Shall I spell out your position? Legally? You've been found in possession of a secret film and have violently assaulted two government officers. We have every right to throw the book at you."

"Balls," I said.

The little room was suddenly silent. I caught the girl's eye and thought I saw a look of approval.

Bob said, "We're up against a ruthless organization—we don't know who—who want this roll of film very badly. Why? We don't know. It doesn't show any method of achieving what you've just seen, simply the result; but perhaps that's all they *need* to coax funds out of someone, somewhere, to develop research in the way our people have over here. What frightens me is the fact that the people we're up against can actually contemplate the destruction of all life, *all life*, or at least threaten such a destruction."

"I grasped all that," I said. "I still don't see it as a very persuasive reason for me to risk my own personal destruction. It's your weapon. Your lot made it. I didn't."

"True, and our lot, thank God, want to make sure it's never used, never even considered, strategically. But there's this other lot—the sort of people who can calmly think in terms of so many human beings having to be knocked off like diseased rabbits to ensure their own survival. The sort of people who want more than a reasonable share of the world's resources and who will do anything for grabs. The Master Race." He looked at me straight, with a look I couldn't avoid. "In our lifetime, at the supposed height of human enlightenment, there have been more man-made horrors than in all the other centuries. Yet most of us go on believing and hoping for some sort of peaceful compromise."

I'd heard all this before, I wasn't sure of myself but I said slowly, "Were you a psychologist before you were a general, General? Or just a politician?"

He said, "Maybe I misjudged you. There aren't many people who get the chance to prove which side they're on. And you have it right now."

He didn't look at me again, but simply gazed ahead at the blank screen. He knew he'd hooked me anyway. After a moment or two I said, "What do I have to do?"

Mollinson got up. "First of all we have to find out who set up this theft and why. The film we saw was the "A" camera. The film you were carrying—from the "B" camera—is still undeveloped, still in its can. We've left it untouched in case they've marked it in some way. All you have to do is carry on as normal, finish your business here in California, and carry the film back to London. We take over as soon as you pass the film on."

"To the labs?"

"If that's where they intend it to go, yes."

"You think it could go somewhere else?"

"That's why you have to follow it through. Remember, when the chips are down we do know what you're doing."

"We?"

"The—er—department that answers directly to the Prime Minister; that should give you a certain feeling of security."

"Would you give me a name to drop—if I really get into trouble?"

Mollinson paused and looked anxious. "Only one— Sir Charles Baron, Deputy Secretary on the Prime Minister's own staff. You can reach him through the Home Office."

"The Home Office? But that's hardly—"

"No less that's where you find him. He's been fully briefed to date."

I looked at Mollinson, and at General Waldorf, and at the tense face of the girl. "All right, when do I leave?"

Bob said, "Right now. And Diane will be coming with you as our contact."

She was smiling. "At least," I said, "you've cast great girls in this show."

"You'll need your passport back," Bob said casually, producing it from his pocket. "We had to have it." I took it—the same passport that had taken me to the Far East, the Near East and now the Far West. "Thanks."

A few minutes later I was driving out of Constellation Laboratories, the taped-up can of film on the floor, and the girl called Diane O'Hara beside me. She was going to fix our flight to London while I lunched with Herb Krein.

But as she sat beside me I noticed she was having difficulty stopping her hands from shaking. As we passed under the barrier and turned right on to Alameda she let out a big sigh.

"I didn't enjoy that."

"You work for them."

"The film I mean. It was horrifying. Disgusting."

I said, "Ugly."

She said, "Brings you face to face with what this deal's about." She brought a pack of cigarettes out of her bag, ripped open the top and offered me one.

"No thanks."

"You don't know what you're missing."

She lit up—I recognized the acrid tang. "Pot?"

"Santa Marta Gold no less, straight from Colombia. None of that Chinese horse shit."

"Do they know that you're into it, those guys back there?"

"Oh be your age, Dan." She drew in an expressive lungful, "It's a bad habit, but Saigon was a bad address."

We drove on in silence for a bit. "Saigon?"

"I don't talk about it." Her voice sounded defensive.

"OK." I said easily. I didn't need to hear another girl's reminiscences. Not this week.

The air in the car was sharp with the curious smokey flavor. "I was eighteen," she said almost to herself, "Fresh out of school when I married Jack. He outranked me—he was a general's son, my dad was only a brigadier then. I knew about service life; no one could say I hadn't been warned. He finished his training flying B-52s and we did a tour in Germany. That was great—skiing, parties, trips to Paris, everything a young bride ever dreamed of. And we were in love—you know—not the way people write about it in crazy novels but really living for each other; wild for each other, every moment. Then he got posted to Vietnam. I stuck around home for a time then flew out to Bangkok when Jack had his first furlough. It was steamy heat and all the army wives just sat around the hotel pool bitching their husbands and screaming murder at their kids. And Jack had changed; he'd seen the sort of damage they were doing to those people, seen them in the hospitals, burnt, chopped up. I couldn't help remembering it all when we saw that film just now." She dragged on her joint. "So—don't blame me, Dan. I couldn't stand Bangkok so I used my father to pull a few strings to get me into Saigon with a job of sorts. Christ what we did to that town, those nice people. It's a beautiful place, you know, some parts of it—old French houses like something out of Saratoga Trunk. And we'd made it a whore's town—kid beggars everywhere, sores, flies, ugliness, 'Give us a dollar, Joe'."

We'd reached the freeway. Cars full of Sunday-cheerful Americans were herding down to the beach with surfboards, picnic tables, beach balls, piled aboard, worlds away from the horrors Diane was describing.

"I was into pot by then—wasn't everybody? At parties—'just have a puff', or 'Try it in the fudge, dear'. Then I got the news about Jack. His plane had been

149

seen going down among the paddy fields—no survivors. I dreamt it all in nightmares, flames beating round his face like a great blowtorch—" She broke off. "Sorry, Dan, I don't normally do the true confession stuff, even on Sundays."

We turned off the freeway into the neat roads that led up towards Coldwater Canyon.

"How long have you been doing this sort of work?" I asked.

"Longer than you, baby, but not much. I was sort of attached to CIA in Saigon, then I came back to a kind of widows get-happy group—yuck! Get out the harmoniums and cry a little for the good of your soul, sister. I went home. I tried dating other guys. I might just as well have worn a placard, 'Easy lay, try me', 'cos that's all the guys were after. And then I met Bob and he moved me into his area."

"What do you do?"

"This and that. I'm not a Gisela. I don't hawk my—" she searched for a word then left it—"like most of them." She looked at me with those expressive eyes. "Maybe we'd better get that absolutely straight from the beginning."

"I understand," I said. "I'm not—what's the word? Rapacious?"

"I'm glad. You've got a wife?"

"And three kids."

"You're lucky."

She paused and then said, "But you screwed Gisela?"

"She made me the offer."

"She would." Diane drew hard on her joint, her expression distaste. "I can imagine."

I didn't answer. I didn't need this clean-looking grass-smoking lady to read me a lecture on morality.

"You didn't look that type." I took my eyes off the road for an instant and the oddly-worried blue eyes locked on mine.

"I'm not. Not usually."

"Good." The eyes softened. "You're supposed to watch the road, driver."

We drove on in silence, right through the canyon and up the shrub-bordered drive of the hotel. At the entrance the car-hop took care of the Chevy. In the lobby Diane went off to the travel bureau and the desk clerk called me. "Message for you, Mr. Galloway."

It was a three-line whip to call O'Neill at his London hotel "VERY URGENT". I mounted the stairs slowly. If he'd heard from Gisela I might as well give up. The door of my room was open.

I went in cautiously, in case any friends of Gisela were laying on a reception committee.

"Hi." A cheerful man in light blue overalls called from the bathroom. "Don't know your own strength, huh?"

He was busily tapping a new pane into place.

The bedside phone rang discreetly. I picked it up, and got O'Neill at full volume.

"What the fuck are you playing at? I've been trying to get you for *hours*."

Keep cool, I thought. "What are you on about?"

"You were supposed to get your fat arse right back here after the shoot. What are you doing in Beverly Hills for christsakes?"

"I had a call to come here to see a man about a co-production I'm involved in. It won't waste any time, the labs in London don't process until Monday night and I'll be back by then."

"Just you do that. I need that film."

151

"I know that." How much *did* he know? Had Gisela made contact since leaving St. Thomas? "Who gave you this number, Mike?"

"Your wife, who else?"

I paused. O'Neill shouted, "Are you still there?"

"Of course. Look, I have a meeting with my man Herb Krein at lunchtime and the moment that's over I'll be out of here, on the first available flight this afternoon."

"Fine. Oh, and don't fly direct—fly to New York and take a London connection."

"Why?"

"You imported that raw stock at New York. You'll find it easer to re-export from the same terminal, believe me."

"I believe you."

Click. O'Neill cut off, and knew for sure he hadn't heard from Gisela. And she was in safe hands now, according to Bob.

The carpenter came out of the bathroom. "Good as new, Mac," he said as he closed the door after him.

The phone suddenly shrilled again. Sally's voice, very angry. "Just what are you up to? I've had that madman O'Neill on every five minutes—"

"I've just spoken to him. He didn't understand why I'd come to California and he's worried about getting his film processed in time."

"Have you seen this man Klein?"

"Krein. I'm seeing him for lunch."

"When's that?"

"Any minute now."

"It's bedtime here. When will you be back?"

"Tomorrow evening, for sure."

"You'd better be. I've made another appointment for you to see Sarah's school on Wednesday."

"Good."

We chatted on about the kids and their various doings until the three-minute signal, then Sally said, "Oh, by the way. Did you know they don't show cigarette commercials in Hong Kong? Not on television nor in the cinema."

"Is that so?"

"You did marry a researcher."

I didn't know what to say. I couldn't tell her any more.

"Well, we mustn't push up the phone bill," Sally said. "Bye for now darling."

"See you."

I had no sooner put the phone down than it rang again.

"Hi, Dan. Herb Krein."

"Mr. Krein. I'm sorry I missed our breakfast but—"

Herb cut in. "Don't tell me. I had a call from a guy I knew in Korea. Are you free now?"

"Coming right down."

"I've got Jake Saracen from the Foundation with me. We've got a table by the pool—see you there, OK?"

I placed the receiver gently in the rest, half expecting it to ring yet again. I walked quickly down the green-decorated corridor to the foyer. Diane was there. "We're on the Pan Am direct flight to London right after lunch."

"You'll have to change it. O'Neill wants me to go to New York and clear customs there where I came in."

"Could that be the reason?"

"You tell me—you're the professional."

"Odd."

"Dangerous."

"No choice." She frowned biting her lip nervously.

153

"I'll change the flight to a New York one and come and collect you after your lunch. About two-fifteen, OK?"

The pool was crowded with paunchy men and girls in the briefest bikinis, diving and shimmering pneumatically as sunlit starlets must have done on this very spot for at least fifty years and more.

Herb Krein, sweat-glistening and eager, had a prominent table in the shade. A grey-haired negro in a Palm Beach suit was with him. "This is Jake Saracen."

It was good to sit in the warmth and have an intelligent conversation on a program I cared about, after days of rapid travelling and unreal tension. I tried to put the horrifying image of the putrefying, human-looking monkey I had seen on the screen that morning out of my mind as I started to explain my ideas for the series I wanted to do at the corporation.

I'd written a detailed format, which I assumed they'd read, but I thought it best to spell it out from the beginning, and just hope Jake Saracen was a good listener.

"The question I want to ask is very simple," I said. "Do prisons, so-called 'penitentiaries' for caging convicts, have any useful purpose in an enlightened society?"

"Are you serious?"

"Never more. Look at it. Most, if not all the developed countries still retain an ancient prejudice in favor of punishing criminals rather than trying to correct them. Having found a man or woman guilty, we just lock them up to serve their time, to waste that part of their precious lives. But few people even pretend nowadays that incarceration has any value in reform—it's generally admitted that prisons are breeding

154

grounds for vice, academies for learning the trade of crime. Yet we still go on locking them up."

"What do you suggest instead?"

"Leave out the child murderers, the sub-normal, the psychotics—they'll always have to be held securely, but in special hospitals, geared to their particular problem. Let's consider the other ninety per cent or more of reasonably sane prison inmates. At the moment, all I can say is I want to find out more. There doesn't seem to be nearly enough money or effort going into researching the root and cause of crime. Oh, we've all got our stock answers—bad housing, broken homes, unequal opportunities, and the rest. All very comforting and bland—if you don't happen to be a victim."

Saracen nodded. I wondered for a moment just what sort of prejudice he'd had to live through to get where he was.

"There are so few facilities in our prisons," I said, "for any sort of re-training or genuine re-education. The inmates drag out a sort of half-life of endless boredom, some drifting into the obvious habits, homosexuality, drugs, illicit booze, and the occasional outburst of senseless violence."

"All because society demands vengeance? Is that what you're saying?"

"More or less. But vengeance doesn't seem to pay off. Fear of harsh punishment isn't necessarily a deterrent. Even when Britain had its market places littered with gibbets, murder, rape and sheep-stealing still flourished."

"Then without a convincing punishment as a threat, how do you convince a professional criminal to go straight, when so many of them make a better living at it than if they were honest?"

"There have to be ways. Maybe really heavy fines, confiscation of property. I'm not the expert. That'll be the point of the series, to explore ideas and to see what various countries have already come up with. In Britain we know we haven't found an answer. Our politicians rave on about increasing violence, knowing full well that high unemployment and serious racial problems are partly behind it all. And our prisons are mostly over a century old, crumbling and ugly, the last places you should cram desperate and unbalanced people. But in West Germany, and here in America, where there are usually more modern facilities for containing fit, energetic men and women, and coping with frustration and idleness, they haven't solved the problem either."

"You'll show conditions, emphasize the boredom, and canvas opinions from reformers?"

"Exactly. I also want to look at the various schemes being tried for employing prisoners in useful and interesting work—not the way they do in some States by farming them out as ultra-cheap labor—but by teaching them a skill."

"Making them earn their keep? That's an old idea, too."

"It could still work. They do it in Russia, would you believe? Not only in the labor-camps, but in their regular prisons."

"They would."

"I've found some footage from Russia I want to use, all carefully staged for propaganda no doubt, but still interesting, showing prisoners working in specially set-up factories making cameras, watches, even machine-tools."

"Would they pay them wages in those places?"

"Probably not. But again there's no reason why prisoners shouldn't earn reasonable money, to be able to leave with a decent bit of capital. Too many of our ex-prisoners have grown used to their idleness inside, and remain poverty-stricken 'ex-cons' long after their release, half-starving on the spiritual gruel of welfare for the rest of their lives."

I answered more questions; Saracen didn't miss a point. We sat there in the effortless warm sunshine toying with superb seafood and thousand-islands-drenched salad, backed by the laughter from the pool, surface-noise of leisure and wealth, thousands of miles away from the harsh realities of stone walls and iron bars we were discussing.

I explained the physical construction of each episode of the series; how much would be specially staged, how much straight-to-camera interview, how much we'd shoot in the States, in Britain, and in Germany. Herb Krein, who had been sitting quietly listening, or maybe dozing off, came to life suddenly at the mention of Germany; he was sure, he said, he could make a tie-in with one of their networks.

Coffee arrived, and Saracen suddenly leant towards me and smiled. "Dan, you've got yourself a deal."

"The whole series?"

"Just the way you told it. Make it with your set-up back in England. We'll put up fifty per cent of the above-the-line. OK?"

OK, but maybe it was all a little too fast. "I can say yes and glad to, but I'm afraid I can't answer for the Corporation. Not till they've had a chance to consider it again."

"I thought they wanted to make it."

"They do. That is—I have a problem with the guy I work with." I turned to Krein. "Did you have a chance to talk to Frimley?"

157

Krein made a face. "That stuffed paprika? Not yet."

Saracen asked, "Who's Frimley?"

"Head of Vital Features."

"How vital is Vital Features?"

"Very. We can't make the program unless he agrees it."

"OK." Krien heaved a theatrical sigh. "If I have to talk to him, I have to."

"You do. I can't finalize anything unless Frimley says so."

"I see that," Saracen said. "We'll have to leave the persuading to you. But as far as the Foundation's concerned we want to make the program at the figure we discussed, with you, the Corporation, and with Herb here." He held out his hand. I took it.

Herb said, "I'll have a letter sent to you confirming all this."

"Thanks. And thank you, Mr. Saracen." I could see Diane hovering at the other end of the pool. "Nice meeting you."

"Off back to foggy old London?" Herb said.

"Yes."

"Why not stay a couple of days? Be my guest?"

It was tempting to tell O'Neill to go stuff himself, his film and his boring intrigue, and to tell Bob I wasn't having any. It would be so much easier to stay among the glamor, the sunshine, the easy living. . . .

"Dan." Diane was right behind me. "We have to go."

I smiled at Herb. "Some other time maybe."

The Chevy was waiting at the entrance, my bag already neatly packed and the film-can in my briefcase.

Diane said, "We're flying the American Airways two-forty p.m. to New York. What with the change to

Eastern Time it'll be nearly eleven when we get there."

"And after that?"

"It's a different terminal. Good old British Airways, old fruit."

I gunned the Chevy down San Diego Freeway, enjoying the warmth that all too soon would be left behind. Tomorrow I'd be back in the cold; but at least I had something concrete on *Gateway* to confound Frimley.

Diane jumped out at the terminal, I drove on round the block to deposit the rented car, then found a Western Union office to cable Sally, and O'Neill, giving the flight number. Diane was already checking us in. As I passed a bunch of passengers watching a portable television tuned to a news program I stopped. It was a moment or two before it made sense, then the words came clear. "Air Hostess Death Riddle." I switched in and concentrated on the tiny screen. "Police have no clue to the identity of the air hostess apparently killed in a road accident at Santa Monica early this morning."

A black-and-white still flashed quickly on to the screen and off again—a smudgy image of a girl's body being lifted aboard an ambulance. Just another accident victim. But did I imagine it or did I really see, dangling from limp wrist, a familiar bracelet pendant with two crosses merging together?

The newscaster was already off into pony trotting. I headed for the check-in to find Diane.

"Diane. What's happened to Gisela?"

"Your girlfriend? Oh, she's OK."

"Where is she?"

"How would I know? They'll hold her for a day or two then let her go, I guess."

I told her what I'd seen on the tube, what I thought I might have seen. "You promise me she's safe?"

"How can I? I simply don't *know*. She ought to be—she's always been a great survivor. But she's also a whore—and whores in this game are usually expendable."

I looked at her, feeling sick.

She sighed. "Dan. Try to remember what this is all about—maybe the murder of millions and millions of quite innocent people."

"Murder. You said it."

"Stop worrying. She's nothing to you." The blue eyes looked honest enough but I still had that awful doubt. . . .

"They're calling our flight," Diane said, thrusting a boarding card into my hand.

I stood still for a moment, then followed.

We'd agreed to sit apart for the flight. I had a book but couldn't take in a word. What sort of people was I involved with, and who on earth was this mysterious group opposing us? A group, Bob had said, ruthless enough to contemplate the destrutcion of all life on earth. But judging from what Diane had said, his home team didn't seem to balk at cold-blooded murder, either. Sitting there at thirty thousand feet, sun streaming through the windows, warm and well-fed hearing the comforting throb of the engines speeding me effortlessly eastwards didn't seem possible. Not here. Not nowadays.

Yet what sort of world was it we *really* lived in? A world of hatred between super-rich and ultra-poor, threatened by racism, over-population, political inertia, famine, wastage of resources, environmental pollution and nuclear abuse. What right had I to start con-

160

demning violent action as irrational? Given our self-created circumstances it was not difficult to imagine men mad enough or desperate enough to threaten total annihilation of the rest of the world to try and buy their personal survival.

Within the pressurized metal womb, hurtling through air, I found little comfort. . . .

"O'Neill here."

O'Neill surveyed himself in the mirror. Not bad for his age. Tonight, he promised himself, he'd go to bed good and early. After the shock of finding out that fool had flown to California sleep might be welcome.

"I thought I'd better call you," he said smoothly into the phone. "Our man was delayed in America on some private business he was hustling, which he didn't have the courtesy to tell me about. But he's on his way home now. The film will definitely be processed tomorrow night."

The voice at the other end rapped a negative, and rasped out a couple more short sentences.

O'Neill was surprised. "Have you got the processing facilities? You know the technical problem."

The voice reassured him they had.

"OK you're the boss. I'll fix a re-routing. What shall I tell him?"

A curt suggestion from the other end.

"I like it. Goodbye." O'Neill put the phone down and caught another glimpse of his reflection, pulling his stomach in as an automatic reflex. Not bad at all. Maybe he'd give the old night-life another whirl after all. . . .

* * *

The plane bumped to land. New York's JFK, night-cold, was bleak and unwelcoming as Diane and I stood separately to claim our bags and trundle them all the way to the British Airways terminal.

As I handed my ticket to the girl on the check-in she said, "Galloway—are you Mr. Galloway?" I admitted it. She left her perch and returned a minute or so later with a written message, "We've had instructions from London to re-route you to Johannesburg."

"*Johannesburg?*"

"That's right. South Africa. BA 178 at twenty-three forty. You've got thirty-five minutes. Check in at Desk 3."

I saw Diane in the check-in queue. "I've got to phone O'Neill urgently," I whispered as I passed. O'Neill was asleep but I made the hotel ring him until he answered.

"Wha—*Christ*, it's four in the morning."

"Not here it isn't. What's all this Johannesburg stuff?"

"Oh yeah. We've got a film laboratory strike here in London."

"I didn't hear about it."

"Well we've got one. I have to get that film of ours processed in a hurry."

"Why not process it here in the States?"

"No credit. Expert has a big account in South Africa." And as he said it I realized his accent wasn't Australian at all—he was from Jo'burg, S.A.

"OK Mike. I'll send it on by freight."

"*No.*" A touch of panic in his voice. "Take it yourself, *please* Dan. It's very important. Listen, I'll double your shooting fee if you go."

I waited a full five seconds. "Hullo," he said.

"Where do I take it?"

"You'll be met—at Jo'burg Airport."

"Very well, Mike, I'll do it."

I heard the phone disconnect that end, then dialled Sally. It rang for a long time then a lovely, sleepy voice said, "Hallo."

"Darling, I'm in New York."

"What time is it?"

"Getting on for midnight. I said I'd be home tomorrow—"

"Oh come on—"

"I have to go to Johannesburg."

"*Where?*"

"South Africa."

"What on earth for?"

"There's a lab strike in London so the film's got to be processed over there."

"That's not true."

"No?"

"There's no lab strike."

"There must be. O'Neill said so."

"Then he lied. He must have some other reason for wanting the film in Jo'burg. So what is it?"

"Don't ask me. You're the researcher."

"Don't make corny jokes, Dan. If he wants it there so desperately why can't someone esle take it?"

"Because *I've* got it. And there's no one else around."

"I don't believe it. You're not a messenger."

"O'Neill upped my fee—doubled it."

"Dan, this is getting ridiculous. You said you'd be home on Saturday, then it was Hollywood, now it's Africa. Where to next—the moon?"

"Darling—"

"You were coming back to see Sarah's school. Dammit, you *do* have a family—"

I put more money in the slot; three lots of pips later

I'd finished apologizing. Then I left the booth, found Diane waiting, and brought her up to date. She frowned.

"South Africa?"

"The Republic government? Is that the opposition?"

"Could be. Or it could be just a bunch of business-men who want something to scare their government with. Something that'll get a big vote of research money from their politicians. Who do you contact when you get there?"

"O'Neill simply said I'd be met."

"I'll call Bob. We'll need a set-up out there. Fast."

"We?"

"I'm coming with you."

"Christ—" I felt angry and belligerent. "You don't want to end up like Gisela."

Her look was pure ice. "*You're* going.

"Maybe I don't need to."

"You've no choice."

"Diane," I said, "don't try the old 'England expects' routine on me, please. There's no power on earth that can force me to go against my will."

Very gently, very quietly she said, "Dan, don't you understand? You're *in* this thing now. There's no way you're going to walk out on to a plane for London, not knowing what you know. No way at all."

No threat, just a simple realistic statement, and I felt very cold. The memory of that flashed image of a body that might have been Gisela's on its way to the morgue endorsed my fears. I knew we were being watched, all the way. And that was why Diane was still so very nervous.

I picked up my briefcase, weighted down with the film-can, and walked over to check-in at Desk Three. Diane watched me go then headed for the phone. I showed the sealed film-can once again to the customs, the man stamped the last page but one of the carnet, and I passed on, through the barrier. Later I saw Diane queueing behind me as we were boarding the plane, but again we sat well apart through the long flight over the South Atlantic.

The dawn seemed to come up after only three hours or so; we were moving back into the time zone I was used to. I managed to sleep through most of the journey—broken sleep, colored by vivid dreams of that monkey that had changed from bright life to dust. In my dream it reversed the process and re-formed itself from the grey heap, coming alive and mad with violence, smashing the window to come out and claw at the eyes of its tormentors—

"Orange juice, sir?" The trim hostess, sexless and straight off a Kensington poster, smiled down at me.

"Was I—?"

"Talking in your sleep? A little." She was so goddammed pure and superior. For a moment I wondered what she'd say if I told her that on the film in my bag I had proof of a means of tatally destroying all humanity as we, or even she, knew it. But what would be her reaction? To give me a tranquillizer, or just another meaningless smile?

"I've been flying a lot too much lately," I mumbled. She smiled again, quite uninterested, and moved on. I undid my seat belt to strtch out my aching limbs. This was all it seemed to have been for a week; strapping in, unfastening, sitting supine like a lump of pressurized human freight to be catapulted from one end of the globe to the other, head muzzy, mouth like an Egyptian wadi in high summer, only partly-living.

The captain was yapping over the p.a.; some mountain range would be clearly visible as soon as we crossed the west coast of Africa. I looked below through the window. Glowing white, the shores of Namibia looked nothing like the burning white sands of the Skeleton Coast of feverish boys' fiction, where diamonds lay in heaps waiting to be pocketed by bearded desperados. . . .

Another hour, another plastic trayful, another hour on top, and sharp pains in the ear warned of descent before the captain's confident prediction of landing. And here it was now three o'clock in the afternoon so it must be Jo'burg.

I felt very nervous; but it would soon all be over, I told myself. Deliver the film into someone's hands and climb back on the first flight for good old London, then no more planes—not for some time.

I shuffled out of the plane feeling the momentary heat as we crossed the tarmac to the airport building. By the immigration desk there was a great blond young man in a white tunic, like some sort of appollonian symbol, glaring searchingly at everyone as they shuffled past, blacks to the left, whites to the right, coloreds in between. The policeman in his little box stared at my passport photo—taken in a do-it-yourself on a hot day in Stanmore post office years ago—then nodded me on.

A customs man grabbed my briefcase, won it after a brief tussle and was about to put it in an x-ray machine when I stopped him. "There's undeveloped film in there."

"Got the papers?"

I showed him the forms that had been rubber-stamped in and out of New York. He looked up at me, "This all?"

I nodded.

He moved away, and found a grey-haired man with

a few more stripes on his epaulettes and Second World War medal ribbons on his chest.

"Mr. Galloway?"

"Yes."

No smile. No "Welcome to our beautiful country". Just a curt "This way."

I was led to a small detention room with bars on its single high window. The officer closed the door. He placed the briefcase on the table between us, flicked the catches, opened it and lifted out the film-can. "This it?"

"That's the film, yes."

"Wait here." He left me in the room, shutting the door behind him. After a few moments I went to the door and opened it, watching the crocodile of passengers from the plane drifting about between the two great rubber luggage conveyors. Diane was among them looking tired and wary; she registered where I was but made no sign. As the luggage started to appear out of the cavemouth she moved forward suddenly and dropped the magazine she was holding. As she bent to pick it up I recognized the red cover of *Time*. I watched her as she waited then suddenly darted forward to claim her overnight bag. The customs man appeared beside me. "Did you have a bag?" he asked.

"Yes," I said, "a brown leather holdall." I started to move forward but he checked me.

"Stay there. Give me the tab."

Diane had seen my bag being lifted off the conveyor by a porter. In the crowd she drifted up to it, putting her own bag down for a second near it. As she left I could see the *Time* magazine was now wedged into the top strap of my holdall. The customs man moved round the heaps of luggage, found the bag and brought it over. "Inside," he indicated.

I went into the room, took the bag from him, set it down beside the chair and sat down. The customs man left. I pulled the *Time* from the top of the bag and opened it. Above the editorial Diane had written: "Get out of there fast. Film in can you gave them *not the right one.*"

My heart almost stopped pumping.

The words swam in front of me. Fool, trusting idiot that I was, I'd been sold right up the river. If the film was a dummy and I was the only person available to the South Africans to answer questions I was in for a re-run on the receiving end of every torture scene I'd ever imagined.

Mouth sour with the bile of fright, I could almost feel the sharp pain from the electrodes just where they'd hurt most. The door opened. It was the grey-haired officer with the medal ribbons with another man—a swarthy thirty-year-old in a tropical suit.

"We're sending your film for processing," he said. His eyes were curiously dark and very cold.

"You're from Mike O'Neill's company?" I asked, keeping my voice as calm as I could.

"Something like that." I could already picture him asking me very nasty questions.

"Shouldn't I have some sort of receipt? I've come a long way with that film."

"Here." The man handed me an envelope. "All typed out."

I was thinking desperately; ask for something—anything.

"I'd like to see the film when you've processed it. It was an interesting shoot but I didn't know the cameraman; I've no idea what his work's like."

168

"That won't be necessary," the swarthy man said. He was very sure of himself.

"Directors usually see their **rushes**," I said.

"Not in this case."

"How long will your lab take to process it?"

"Four to five hours."

"Maybe I'd better see if I can get a plane to London then."

"You're already booked—at eleven tonight."

"Not before?"

"We'd like you to stay around just until we've viewed this film."

I said, "I don't relish sitting in an airport for eight hours—"

"We thought you'd prefer it."

"What, in here?"

"Yes."

"In this?" I almost called it a cell.

"It's private. You could have a meal sent in if you wanted."

"Listen—if I've got to wait I'd like to do some sightseeing. I've never been to Jo'burg before."

The man hesitated. "There's not much to see in a few hours."

"There must be something—a museum, an art exhibition—something."

The customs officer said, "There's the gallery at Joubert Park."

The dark man looked dubious. "That'll be closing soon."

The customs man said, "Not till five."

"I'll go there," I said quickly. I knew that if I made a fuss they wouldn't hold me, not without doing a lot of explaining.

"You won't see much in an hour or two."

"I'll risk that. Shall I get a taxi?"

The dark man suddenly made up his mind. "My chauffeur will take you. Then when you're through he can bring you on to my office to wait there." I saw the briefest suggestion of an exchange of looks between the dark man and the customs officer.

"You can leave your luggage here," the customs officer said, "Ready for check-in when you come back."

"Thanks." I picked up my briefcase—that at least I wasn't parting with—and turned to follow the dark man out of the claustrophobic little room.

In the main concourse Diane stood like a stranded tourist, part of the scenery, slim and innocent—my only hope. She made no move of recognition as we approached. As we passed her I said to the customs man loudly, "How far away is this art gallery, this Joubert Park?"

"Not far," 'he said, "Right in town."

Diane didn't react, but I knew she'd heard.

We made our way outside to a large black Mercedes parked right by a "No Parking" sign. A chauffeur built like a gorilla opened the front door.

"Piet," the dark man said, "You're to take Mr. Galloway to the art gallery and stay with him."

The driver looked blank; his voice was thick. "What about you, Mr. Brouger?"

"I'll take a taxi back to the office. Keep the car and bring Mr. Galloway straight on when he's through."

"Very good sir."

Brouger's eyes fixed on mine without warmth. "See you later."

I sat in the car and the chauffeur heaved his huge body into the driver's seat beside me. He grinned and shot out a fist, "My name's Piet van Straat—call me Piet."

The great knuckles crushed mine. If I'd had any doubt about his being my jailer I had none any more. He swung the car clear of the curb and headed away from the terminal. Brouger watched us out of sight.

"Bad traffic this time of the day," Piet said.

"We'll live with it," I was trying to think of some plan of escape. Short of hurling myself out of the car at fifty miles an hour I was bereft of ideas. I looked at my watch. I'd corrected it, yet again, to South African time in the plane. "When does the museum shut?"

Piet thought about it, "About five. But the gardens—you know—all that sculpture, they don't close until later."

He negotiated a gap in the traffic and forced his way ahead into the fast lane. "First time in Jo'burg?"

"Yes."

"You don't wanna believe all that crap you read in your British papers; you know—all that stuff about the blacks having a hard time. It's propaganda, communist propaganda."

"Then why do the papers print it? They're not all communist."

"Must be commies in there somewhere. Take it from me, in S.A. if a black is prepared to work he can get along all right. Some of them get to be millionaires, you know."

"Oh come on—"

"It's the truth. They set up shop in one of these Bantustan townships, the only shop, no competition for miles, charge what they like—their own people mind—and end up rolling." He hooted as an ancient Fairlane swerved out ahead, its broken muffler hitting the ground every few yards with showers of sparks like a firework. Piet kept his fist on the horn as he swept past, the negro driver ignored him.

171

"See that," Piet said. "Driving around in that old banger and probably got more dough than I have."

We were running into the suburbs now. Piet cut off right, drove through a couple of sets of traffic lights on the amber, and presently pulled up outside an Edwardian-looking pile with an orderly garden behind. The gallery.

He followed me up the steps and through the heavy glass doors. I had no South African money on me. "Can you buy me a catalogue?"

"Sure thing." Piet returned with a glossy booklet. A plan was slowly forming in my head. I flipped through the pages and saw they had the odd Van Gogh, Degas and a Renoir.

"Know anything about Impressionist paintings?" I asked.

Piet mumbled, "Can't say I do."

We found our way to a long, cool room with a Monet and a Pissarro at one end. My only hope was to bore Piet stupid so that he couldn't bear the inaction and had to move on away from me. I went up to the first painting and stared at it hard, going close and examining each single brush stroke intently. I stood motionless, concentrating on the solitary points of colored paint.

Behind me, Piet stood first on one foot then on the other. He looked all round the room, wandered over to a picture that briefly interested him, glanced at it, then strolled back to where I was still minutely inspecting pointilliste detail. I stood there motionless for a full five minutes and let him fidget, then slowly and reluctantly moved to the next picture to commence the whole process again. "Extraordinary," I muttered.

Piet said, "I'm dying for a smoke."

I looked up at one of the "No Smoking" signs dotted around the room and shrugged. I began to wonder for how many endless minutes he would be able to stand it. I hadn't too long to wait. As I finally moved to the third picture to commence a close scrutiny of the bottom left-hand corner he broke.

"Just going down to the doorway for a drag," he said. "Five minutes, all right?"

"I'll be here," I said.

"You planning to look at pictures till closing?"

"Certainly."

He walked out of the room, his rubber-soled shoes squeaking on the parquet. I tried to rehearse in my mind the time he would take walking down the main staircase. I imagined him strolling through the door, settling himself comfortably and lighting up on the steps outside. Then I moved as fast as I could without attracting attention.

There was a corridor at the end of the gallery leading off to the right with a small barrier marked "Private." A sign above pointed "Fire Exit." In front of it, watching me, was a uniformed attendant. I turned round again, trying to make it look natural, and walked the full length of the room, heading for the main stairs. I was just in time to see Piet's huge form going out of the big glass doors below. In the concourse, by the postcard stand, was Diane. I couldn't understand why my saviour looked so vulnerable.

I ran down the stairs and gripped her arm tightly. I was suddenly so angry with her I could scarcely form words. "What the fuck are you people at?"

She was very calm. "I've got the real film in my luggage. The film of the Nevada test, that is. The film

173

you had was the negative you brought from London with the shoot of the Caribbean commercial on it—we got it back when we arrested Haskins."

"So—technically—I was carrying the film I ought to have?"

"Yeah, but I doubt if that will satisfy this mob."

"But for God's sake—why couldn't you just have told me—? I mean they have to suspect I know what's going on now."

"That's true. But Waldorf wants to find out who's *really* after this test film. We couldn't tell *you* any more because we weren't sure you could manage the whole scene."

"Why not?"

"Because, old chum, you're not a pro."

"And you are?"

"I passed out in Basic."

"Explain then."

"We don't think this South African group—if it is a South African group—are working on their own. There has to be someone in Britain—someone very high up—organizing the whole thing."

"Very interesting. And what about me? I suppose I'm expendable? Like Gisela?"

"No Dan. Believe me, please. I'm here to get you away. I've got a car right outside."

"And I've got Guy the Gorilla right outside." I nodded towards the glass doors.

I could just see the outline of Piet resting on the sunny stone balustrade wreathed in smoke, his back towards us. "I've got to get past him to get to your car."

"Oh. Difficult. Any ideas?"

"I thought that was your department."

"It should be, but—"

"I've just *one* idea, and not very good at that—as you said, I'm not a pro."

"Tell me."

"There's a fire exit upstairs. If you could chat up the attendant I'll get out of the back and meet you."

We walked back up the stairs to the Impressionist Room. I watched as Diane approached the attendant, asked him a question. He took her by the arm and walked down the length of the gallery, past me, to start pointing out another room on the floor above. But by then I'd hopped over the wooden barrier and turned another corner. At the end of the corridor was a door with a window marked "Fire Exit" leading to an iron staircase outside. I hurled myself the last few yards and turned the handle.

It was locked.

EIGHT

I stood looking at the door for a moment, baffled, then turned and knocked at the nearest office door. A sour-faced secretary looked up. "Yes?"

I managed what I hoped was a winning smile. "My name's Muller, Fire Department." I flipped out my wallet and flashed my Corporation ID card quickly. "Do you happen to have a key to the fire exit?"

She frowned, then said, "I'll have to ask Mr. Herman." She rose from her desk and came through the door, shutting it after her, to leave me in the corridor. I watched her walk away and turn fully out of sight at the end.

I waited, imagining everything she might be doing. A quick call to the Fire Department? Then with relief I saw her coming back, a bunch of keys in her hands. "Shouldn't be locked really," she said. "But we have a security problem. Anyone could get in from the park."

"Yes. Trouble is if there were a fire—"

She unlocked the door and I stepped onto the iron platform as if checking it. "When was it last painted?"

"Last year, I think," she said.

"Fireproof paint, of course?"

"I've no idea." She started to look uncertain. "Shall I get Mr. Herman? He can tell you."

"Don't bother." I held on to the balustrade and looked down the stairs—just two flights to the park and freedom. "I'll go down this way. You can lock up behind me."

She smiled in a wintry sort of way and went back inside. I walked thoughtfully down the stairs.

There were plenty of people moving round among the open-air sculpture; mothers and children and office-workers on their way home. I found a path round to a gate where I could take a look at the entrance of the gallery.

Piet was still sitting on the steps, dreaming. As I watched he took a long, last drag on his cigarette and threw it across the road. I waited, expecting him to go into the gallery but after a moment he reached for his cigarette pack, selected another and lit up.

Behind him I saw a grey Cortina with Diane waiting beside it. To reach it I'd have to walk back through the park, round the back of the gallery and approach fast from the other end, hoping Piet was looking the other way.

I ran quickly through the strolling crowd, my anger evaporating. If Diane knew about the film then she obviously knew the rest of the story. They'd be able to identify the swarthy man, Brouger. They'd obviously have another plan to get me out of South Africa to carry out the last bit.

I hoped.

And where would the last bit happen? London, Diane had said.

I came round the north side of the building, down a

tree-lined path and saw the Cortina parked a few yards away. Diane saw me and whipped the passenger door open; in four steps I was inside with my head well down. She ran round and jumped into the driver's seat and started off. Crouching towards the dashboard I watched her glance towards where Piet must have been sitting, unconcerned, on the gallery steps as we passed.

"OK, you can come up now."

I straightened up to sit normally. The car reeked of pot. Diane, pausing at an amber light, reached for her cigarette pack. "Reefer?"

"I don't. And neither should you." I suddenly realized I must sound very prim.

She threw the pack down. "Sorry."

"Where are we going?"

"Back to the airport."

"The *airport*? Are you mad?"

"Not really. It's the quickest way to get you out. There's a local flight to Durban at six. The deal is for us to get aboard a tanker tonight and sail before midnight. We get off at Mombasa and fly on to London from there."

"And then what?"

"Then you wait with the film in London until someone contacts you."

"You're sure someone will?"

"Sure."

She was driving fast, weaving her way through the traffic like an ace commuter on the Great West Road. I said, "Slow down. No need to get picked up for traffic violation."

She smiled. "Good thinking chum."

By now Piet must surely have walked back through those doors, up those stairs to the Impressionist Room.

Maybe he'd spend another five minutes trying other galleries; then, with luck, he'd walk right through the museum once more for a final check. . . . Call it ten minutes. And then he'd phone. . . .

I said, "What makes you think we'll get away on the Durban flight?"

"I told you. These people aren't government. They can't just order police and customs to arrest people."

"But they've got influence?"

"Oh sure. But they have to ask for, and buy, every bit of co-operation they need. That means delay, so we may just get through."

I wasn't convinced. "Who was the dark man who took the film? His name is Brouger."

"No idea. I managed to get a polaroid as you came out of the office, but I haven't had time to wire it to Bob yet. I must do that the moment we hit the airport."

"How?"

"Through the ordinary cable office. We have ways, my friend."

We were coming out of the suburbs now towards the flat, dry land approaching the airfield. Diane was more relaxed, long fingers gently touching the wheel, her eyes shining, mouth slightly open as she held the car to a level fifty on the fast lane. She took a left fork as indicated and we swung down the access road in a wide loop that led to the terminal. Around the International Departures, cars and taxis were jammed two abreast, but further on Domestic Departures was quiet and relatively deserted.

Diane found a parking space and switched off. She pulled the key from the ignition. "I'll let Hertz have their car back."

"No," I said, "hang on to the keys. You never know."

She nodded. "You're some thinker, Dan." She fished an envelope out of her bag. "Everything you need should be in there."

I took it and opened it. There was a newish green U.S. passport in the name of Ian Taylor, born Lexington, Mass., with a copy of my old photo taken in Stanmore post office staring up at me from the crisp page—they must have made a quick copy when they took away my passport in California—a South African Airways ticket one-way to Durban and a couple of hundred rands. "Everything," I said, "except my luggage."

She frowned, "Customs are holding on to that. There's no way we can get it. The film's in here." She handed me a canvas Pan Am airbag.

"I'm to take it?"

"Who else? Just in case they try to make contact somewhere en route. I'll see you on the plane but we're travelling separately like before. Otherwise—see you in Durban. Good luck—as they say."

She started to get out of the car then sat back into her seat and looked at me seriously. "Dan, thanks for being so—"

"Cooperative?"

"Just—*British.*' She leant across and kissed my cheek for a second and was suddenly away, slamming the car door after her.

I watched her neat young figure as she walked across to Departure, confident and—I had to admit—highly attractive even in this mess. For a moment as she entered the tall glass doors I enjoyed watching her, then I gathered up the flight bag heavy with the film, put the new passport, ticket and money in my inside pocket, and thought for a moment what I'd need for the voyage. I'd been travelling light but I

180

had a washbag in my briefcase. I transferred this to the canvas bag. All that was left in the briefcase were a few papers and the Expert commercial script. And a lot of use that was to me now.

Half expecting the simian Piet to roar up in the Mercedes any minute, I got out of the Cortina and walked cautiously across the tarmac road to the Departure building. Inside there weren't many people about, just the usual collection of porters, groundhostesses and travellers, all caught up in that semipetrified limbo preceding rapid flight. I got some change, found a block of left-luggage lockers, put in a couple of coins and locked the briefcase safely away. Who knew when I might ever see it again?

The Durban flight was prominently displayed on a large board. It was now ten to six but they hadn't announced boarding yet. I went over to the S.A.A. desk, showed my ticket and was given a boarding pass. Then I found a small gift shop and picked up a couple of florid sports shirts and half a dozen brightly-patterned Y-fronts. I moved over to the book shop and chose a couple of maps of South Africa and an illustrated tourists' guide to Jo'burg. As I collected my change the P.A. speaker suddenly chimed and crackled, prelude to an announcement. I looked up, half afraid of what I knew must be coming. The voice said it in Afrikaans first, but my German was just about good enough to tell me the worst before it was repeated in English.

"South African Airways regret to announce that their flight 101 to Durban will be delayed for up to one hour due to technical trouble."

I found my way to a seat in a corner behind a pillar. It was all over. Piet must have discovered my disappearance faster than I'd imagined and somehow they already knew I was on the Durban flight. Any minute now I'd see the gross figure of the chauffeur and an angry Brouger come charging through the plate glass doors, maybe with a couple of police heavies in tow, looking for me.

I couldn't think of anything but this inescapable climax. There was no sign of Diane; presumably she was still cabling General Waldorf. I wandered across to the Cable Office and looked in but she wasn't there. I went back to my seat by the pillar where I could see everyone who came in through the doors, wondering what to do. The plane to Durban had been our best chance of getting away but waiting for it now was the big risk. But what else could I do? Minutes passed. Odd people entered with luggage, families. Safe people, secure in a friendly environment, not fugitives waiting for the inevitable.

Maybe if I could find Diane I could get the keys of the car and drive back to Jo'burg. And what then? Find the British Consul? I was sure Brouger was quite capable of trumping up some charge to get me back into his custody. Or just drive? I had a map. I opened it out; the colors and words blurred in front of me. I reached for my reading glasses; the comfort of familiar thick black rims, the lenses that brought the names and shapes into focus. The words on the map were meaningless—Krugersdorp, Benoni, Verwoerdburg— where in these hard-sounding places was there likely to be any help?

And what help did I need? I was a British subject who had brought a can of film into South Africa. I had committed no crime; all the rest was panic—sheer irrational fear, a crude interpretation of the unmistakable messages of violence I'd received from Brouger's first look.

182

Still more minutes had passed with no eruption through the doors. Suppose there really was technical trouble on the plane. . . . The P.A. pinged like a Ruislip door-chime. The Afrikaans got mixed up in a scream of howl-round then started again. Could it . . . ?

"South African Airways announce the departure of flight 101 to Durban. All passengers please board at gate 2."

One last look at the doors and suddenly Diane was beside me. "Keep the glasses on," she said, "It's a sort of disguise. For the odd mug-shot." And she was gone.

Of course I should have thought of it myself, but as she'd said before, I wasn't a pro. At Schipol in Amsterdam, they have this system that instantly photographs every single passenger who checks through. The friendly South Africans probably had it too, so I kept my reading-glasses on, even though they threw everything into soft-focus, making me semi-blind.

I picked up the flight bag and followed the queue. Diane was three or four passengers ahead. The security check was pretty perfunctory. I merely opened up the flight bag, explained that I was carrying a can of film, got a nod and passed through.

The sun was setting as we emerged onto the tarmac, bronzing the DC9 with a warming light. Diane was ahead in the smoking section, I chose a window seat at the back. The doors were slammed shut, the engines started and with a sense of unbelief I felt the aircraft taxi to the runway and take off, leaving Brouger and Johannesburg behind. Somewhere down there among those packed buildings a red-faced chauffeur was trying to explain how he'd let his charge slip away. . . .

A hostess came round with coffee and a smile, the

engines purred, the captain's voice did all the welcome aboard and flight-time number, apologizing for the delay.

I shut my eyes. It had been a tiring day. What day? Was it really only a week since Frimley had jingled his coins in his trouser pocket and dropped his bombshell? I was past caring.

The pictures came on to the screen at five-second intervals, each one a face—tired women, fat men, balding middle-age, youth. They seemed to embrace the entire spectrum of human features—blue eyes, hazel eyes, pale skin and black, cheerful or depressed, old and hopeful.

"Hold it." The grey-haired man with the Second World War ribbons on his tunic snapped his fingers. "Go back two, no—three."

The faces flicked up in reverse and stopped. The man inspected a black and white image, then, satisfied, said, "Carry on."

The photographs clicked on, blinking, staring, unaware, happy. . . .

"Hold it. Go back two."

The faces changed again. A man with glasses stared unwinkingly from the screen. The grey-haired man reached for the telephone and dialled quickly.

"Mr. Brouger, please."

Within the narrow cabin the noise of the jets seemed unnaturally loud. A voice seemed to be trying to penetrate the haze of sleep. ". . . owing to pressurization problems I regret that we have to return to Johannesburg where further arrangements for passengers to Durban will be made. . . ."

I was awake, dry mouthed. I glimpsed Diane's face several seats ahead as she looked round anxiously. The plane banked as it made its 180 degree turn back to where we'd come from.

Outside it was getting dark. I was thinking fast. Obviously I couldn't get off the plane with all the other passengers and go back into the departure hall into the arms of Piet and Brouger. For this time it couldn't be coincidence. I knew they must have checked out the polaroids of all departing passengers and glasses or no glasses I'd been spotted. I rose and moved into the aisle; ahead I saw Diane get up too. Good girl.

I headed for the rear toilet, my Jo'burg guide book in hand. I went in and clicked the bolt on the door behind me and wrote a swift message on page thirty of the guide, right by a map of Jan Smuts Airport: "Get car and meet me here," with an arrow to the south-east corner of the airfield where a minor road ran fairly close outside the perimeter fence. I left the book open in the sink and undid the door. Diane was waiting outside; our eyes met for an instant, our hands touched, then she moved inside and I went back to my seat to wait. A few moments later I saw Diane take her place up front again.

Shortly, the engines changed pitch and I felt the plane start to descend. The "No Smoking" and "Seat Belt" lights flicked on but I picked up the flight bag and headed for the rear john again. In the gangway a hostess hissed, "The seat belt sign's on, sir. Return to your seat."

"Urgent call," I said, hoping she wouldn't notice I was weighted down with a flight bag, and went on

185

into the toilet, which was as near as possible as I could get to the rear door. The captain's voice was already announcing the landing and apologizing yet again for the delay and inconvenience.

I left the door unlatched so that I could peer through a crack. The little compartment wasn't insulated for sound and I got the full force of the hydraulic wheeljacks in stereo. Then the wind noise increased as we approached land and finally with a bump and a screaming skid, the wheels hit tarmac. The engines thumped into reverse and brakes slammed on, bringing the plane to a taxiing speed in seconds.

For what seemed an age, the plane taxied on round the end of the runway until it must have reached the terminal buildings and came to a final halt. I heard one engine die, then another, then the other two. I glimpsed the light blue of the hostess's uniform as she took up position by the rear door then heard the electric gear lowering the staircase.

It was now or never.

With the flight bag in my hand I flung back the toilet door and pushed the startled hostess away with the other, then hurled myself down the steps past a couple of surprised men in dark uniforms, out of the small lit area around the plane, striking towards darkness and the far perimeter fence.

I heard confused shouts behind me—questions nobody bothered to answer. Then I heard a Land Rover starting up near the main building. I looked round to see a pair of headlights coming on fast. On my right was a low concrete gulley, shining with greasy liquid. I dived and landed in four inches of slime just as the Land Rover's headlights swept towards me over and on past into the darkness.

A siren sounded from the control tower; lights snapped on all along the wire fence. If their radar was any good they'd have me pinpointed anyway—knee deep in mud and slime. It was only fifty yards to the nearest section of fence at the darkest point between two lights. The Land Rover was away in the distance. I staggered to my feet and ran. As I neared the fence I made a running jump that took me three feet up, then scrambled up the rest, thanking God for National Service that gave you these skills gratis.

At the top were four tight strands of barbed wire. Laying the flight bag across I swung my body up and over, feeling the knee of my left trouser leg rip as I went. Then, hanging, I freed the impaled flight bag from the top of the barbed wire, hung on for a second and jumped, hoping the earth beneath was soft.

It was, but my knees took the shock badly and for a moment I lay there gasping in pain. I looked back towards the terminal. Incredibly no one seemed to have seen my Douglas Fairbanks acrobatics, but I wasn't going back for Take Two. I rose groggily to my feet, picked up the bag and tottered over the rough ground away from the fence. Keeping a distance of twenty or so yards from the wire, I began to follow its circumference, aiming away from the terminal building towards the point where I said I'd meet Diane.

The Land Rover came roaring back, giving me ample warning to duck out of the light of its headlamps before it passed. I plodded on, leaving the terminal well behind.

I was free, and if Diane could do her stuff quickly enough I'd soon be back in the car, travelling fast. But where would we go? In the last few minutes in the plane I'd had a look at the map. To the north and the west of Jo'burg were five of the belts of territory that make up the independent territory of Bophuta Tswana—one of the "Bantustans" set up by the South African government as part of apartheid. If we could make it that far. . . .

I tried to imagine Diane at that moment, probably going through another security check—a more searching one than we'd had on departure. There was nothing to connect us and I'd got the film; sooner or later she'd come driving up in the grey Cortina. I hoped.

From the right behind me I saw headlights approaching along a road that converged towards the fence. I sank to my knees behind a bush and saw an open truckload of troops drive past. So Brouger had that much influence. I waited for another but that was all. The road now closed in on the fence. I must be somewhere near the south east corner I'd marked on the map for Diane. I crossed the tarmac road quickly and sat in a clump of bushes to wait.

Half an hour must have gone by. Occasional cars or trucks, and once an overcrowded ancient bus, sped past either way. Then I saw the lights of a car coming, slow down, hesitate, and turn off the road to park in a small copse just ahead. The headlights went out. I moved quickly through the darkness towards it.

"Diane?"

As I reached the car I suddenly saw there were two figures in the front, two figures interlocked in a familiar embrace, now disturbed by the sound of my voice. I dived back towards the shadows, hearing the click of the car door opening behind me.

"Whozatt?" A beery voice called from the car.

Safe in the bushes I saw a middle-aged man get out of the car and peer all round. Behind him a suggestion of tousled blond hair, the girl putting herself to rights. Grumbling, the man got back into the car and some sort of argument started between them. Then abruptly the headlights were switched on, the car jerked back on to the road and drove off.

The motor noise tailed off into infinity. Now there were only the renewed sounds of secret night life, the busying of crickets, the rasp of frogs, the rustle of small furry movement suddenly loud in the darkness.

Where was Diane? Even allowing for extreme delay she should have been here by now. She had the car keys still—what sixth sense of mine had prompted that suggestion? She only had to drive a mile or so. . . . And yet I knew she'd come, because in the few breathless exchanges we'd had I'd come to know her as well as I knew anybody. At that moment I wasn't thinking about the danger but of her, her face, her eyes, the warmth of that young, live body beneath her dress. When we'd touched briefly in the aircraft by the toilet the effect had been electric. I suddenly realized that she was as sexually aware of me as I now knew I was of her. It became clear to me that my impatience over her absence had very little to do with fear, and quite a lot to do with lust—and a desire to be close to her again with no more separations.

And that, I knew, was madness.

NINE

"We can't hold him." Superintendent van Harten preferred to stand, even in his own office—sitting down spoiled the smart hang of your uniform. There was too much slovenliness about, even among his own junior officers. "Not unless you make a formal charge. I've gone farther than I should already—diverting an aircraft—"

"We still lost him," Brouger said.

"He won't get far. We've put a ring round the immediate area of the airport. But when we catch him—what the devil do we charge him with?"

Brouger didn't answer. He wondered how much he could really trust this solid policeman; he'd have to tell him something. "Listen," he said, "I can't reveal too much but—let's say my firm's involved with someone very high up in the Defense Ministry. Very high up."

Van Harten looked uneasy. He didn't like being party to this sort of information. "Careful what you're saying Mr. Brouger."

"I won't name anyone. Galloway was bringing a secret film from the States; it's a vital part of our negotiations. He wasn't supposed to know what it was, but obviously he found out and got clever. The can he brought was the right one, but when we developed the film it was simply a cigarette commercial."

"A—what?"

"He'd been set up to shoot a fake advertisement in the Caribbean. But we'd switched the film he was carrying for the undeveloped roll of the secret test. He must know the film had been switched back."

"So he'll also know who's got the real test film now?"

"Right. All I'll need is ten minutes—say fifteen at the most—alone with Mr. Galloway, to find out where the hell it is." Brouger's fists clenched involuntarily at the thought.

"That's why you want your hands on him?"

"Of course."

"This—er—interrogation. It couldn't happen anywhere near police property, you know that. We've had too many lies written about us overseas already."

"I accept that."

Van Harten had a thought. "Could this bloke be 'political'?"

"Terrorist you mean? No, he's just some video producer from London."

"If he was even suspected of terrorism we could issue a warrant under the Act."

Brouger looked up. This policeman wasn't so stupid. "Why not?"

"Then if we arrest him, and somehow he escapes into the bush, what happens to him after that wouldn't be our problem."

Brouger smiled. "Good thinking."

The superintendent said, "Fancy a cold beer?"

191

"Thanks."

Van Harten walked over to a refrigerator in the corner and dug out a couple of frosted cans. "I'll set that business up right away."

Brouger took the cold can and pulled the ring from the top. It sprang open with a sharp click, like the sound of a safety catch being released.

"Cheers," he said.

The car appeared at last, approaching slowly from the direction of the airport. I broke from the shadows and into the brightness of the headlamps. The lights flashed and the car stopped; thankfully I saw that it was Diane and she was alone. I slipped into the passenger seat, pressing her hand for an instant.

"Dan—"

"What's wrong?"

"When I saw you haring away down those steps I thought I'd lost you—" I could see her eyes glistening.

"Let's get moving—I'd better drive." Without a word she changed seats. I put the car into gear and put my foot down.

I said, "What happened?"

"We were all shepherded off the plane back into the terminal. Your friend Brouger and the driver were there looking at everybody."

"So they did check the departure polaroids?"

"Must have. Don't underestimate these Afrikaaners."

"I don't. But what kept you after that?"

"I had to call Bob."

"Why? Calling America from a call-box in a country like this where the wires are certainly tapped—"

"I had to get new instructions. Don't worry—he'd set

up a special number and it was a "Hallo Dad, how's Mum?" sort of conversation in code."

"Why bother? I've thought of a plan—we aim for Bophuta Tswana, sixty miles away."

"That's where we *don't* go—the obvious, where they're *sure to* be looking. Anyway it's full of white South Africans who go up there for the gambling—it's a sort of tacky Vegas."

The road now joined the main highway. Without asking I turned left. "So where *do* we go?"

"Swaziland, three hundred miles to the east."

"As far as that? There'll be police all the way."

"Bob says no. It's a big tourist area; so long as we play it as tourists they won't crowd us too much. And we stick to back roads, OK?"

I took the road map from under the dashboard, "How good's your map reading?"

"Passed out at Langley—the rush course."

"Full marks."

"Yes—but you'd better slow down right now. Look at what's ahead."

About half a mile in front of us I could just see a queue of cars and bright lights. "An accident?"

"A roadblock."

I braked hard.

Diane said, "On foot, soldier. I'll meet you about a mile on."

"Right." I glimpsed her face for an instant, white and strained, before I got out into the night and she slipped into the driving seat and sped off. I looked around in the darkness; it was a sort of rich residential area with large houses in two or three acres, all equipped, I was sure, with burglar alarms and trip wires for your common marauder. Like me.

I walked along the road for a while until I found a

gap between two fences, which led me uphill to a small wood of firs and rhododendrons. Through the trees I could look down on the road and see the queue of cars as they waited to be checked.

This roadblock must have been set up by the truck-load of soldiers who had passed earlier. They looked very tough, though their search was perfunctory—just a quick glance into each car and a look in the trunk then a wave on. As I watched, Diane's grey Cortina went through.

Now all I had to do was to get back to her. The path, such as it was, led steeply through fern and brambles, pulling at the bottom of my trousers. From somewhere ahead a dog starting barking, the effort-less mechanical noise sounding loud through the tall trees. A loud voice suddenly shouted; the dog stopped for a moment then started again. I could see the lights of a house ahead of me. I back-tracked, looking for some other path that would still lead back onto the main road. The sound of barking receded and then stopped. But then I heard other noises, voices of men—at least a couple—approaching the way I'd come first.

Now I saw them more closely. One of them had a flashlamp which he occasionally shone ahead then swung from side to side, not with any particular pur-pose, it seemed, except to see the immediate way ahead.

I pushed into the thick undergrowth and lay down, watching the men as they came level—a couple of strong-looking negroes, gardeners possibly, finding their way back to their sleeping quarters after the day's work. Using their sound and the occasional flash of their lamp as a guide I was able to follow stealthily as they trod a path well-known to them, skirting the

194

house and coming at last to a group of small huts. Over to the right I could see the lights of cars on the road speeding away from the roadblock. With unspoken thanks to the two unwitting guides I made off in that direction.

The road when I reached it was skirted by a low post-and-rail fence. Keeping inside it, away from the passing traffic, I walked a further half mile before seing the grey Cortina parked ahead. I ran up. As I opened the door the smoky aroma of pot hit me. Diane's head was a misty mass in a cloud as she drew in on the butt. I jumped into the driver's seat and drove off, suddenly angry at her need for toxic relaxation. "Didn't anyone tell you those things are bad for you?"

"So's this kind of work bad for you too." I glanced at her; she was just as tense as I was. "Dan, I *was* worried about you. Honest."

"You wouldn't lose me so easily. Let's hope we don't have to separate any more."

"I'll smoke to that."

We drove on for a mile or so in silence.

"Shouldn't we be turning off fairly soon? You said 'back roads'."

Diane reached for the map and flicked on the interior light.

"Yes. We take a right in about a mile. Should be sign-posted 'Welgedacht' or 'Randklip'."

We found the turning and took it. We'd left prosperous suburbia behind now and were driving through more wooded mountainous country. It was beginning to be, as Diane had said, a tourist area. Signs briefly announced various scenic attractions as we passed—caves, waterfalls, nature reserves.

"Pity it's too dark to see it," Diane said suddenly.

"Let's just keep moving."

The road was now winding up between the steep walls of a huge gorge.

"Hungry?"

"*Am* I?"

Diane produced a plastic bag full of pies and sausage rolls she'd bought at the airport. For a while we muched in silence, then she said, "Tell me about her."

"Who?"

"Your wife. What's her name?"

"Sally."

Diane frowned suddenly and looked at the map, "I think you have to go left here."

"OK."

"You were telling me—"

I told her—as far as anyone can ever tell a third party the odd details and facts of a life shared together. I'd no idea why she'd suddenly brought the subject up, whether it was as a primitive form of mental defense against feelings she—or I—possibly couldn't control. I didn't know. I didn't ask, for some hours I simply told her all I could about Sally and the children. Sheltered by thick trees speeding by on either side in a dark confessional, words came easily as I spoke of mutual jokes, a special sort of vital language two people can discover as they explore the joint possibilities of living. If I'd been asked in any other place I couldn't have spoken so fully. Here, with scope and time, the precise and vivid meaning of Sally and me seemed to emerge clearly from my words.

"But what about Gisela?" Diane said flatly.

"I told you." I found myself angry with her again. Why on earth did I have to convince her of all people that the bedroom bounce with Gisela had been nothing important? I'd tell Sally about it in my own time,

196

making it as insignificant as it really was. It was nothing to do with Diane. . . .

We drove on. The journey was not exactly unmarred with mistakes in navigation. For one thing, the map wasn't all that detailed and twice Diane misread it, leading us into sudden hairpin turns under great rocky overhangs or brief areas of open scrubland where the road abruptly ended. Once we followed a promising track right into the middle of a huge, brightly-lit lumber-camp working round the clock, before retreating again fast.

As the first red fingers of dawn began to streak the horizon, we were passing close to some caves called Sudwala and heading across the high road to Mount Anderson with a town named Sabie lying beneath it. Below, on our right, the early sun slowly crept across an amazing panorama of pine forest, tree fern and every sort of exotic flower.

Diane gasped, "What a fantastic country this is."

"No wonder the whites don't want to give it up in a hurry."

We drove on into a great wooden cathedral of many-scented succulents, of beobab and jacaranda and acacia, so dense as to shut out the pervading sunlight.

"Where now?" I asked.

"We're nearly there." Diane pulled a notebook out of her bag. "Graskop. We stop at the Welcome Inn."

"Why?"

"We have a man there."

"Do we need him?"

"We won't get out of this country without help."

Gorges rose high and sharply beside us, broken up by waterfalls glittering in the glancing early sunlight.

197

Soon we were running down the main street of Sabie, still sleeping. I spotted a phone box.

"Why don't we phone? Warn him."

"Good thinking."

Diane slipped out of her seat and I fumbled for coins. "What's his name?"

"Stevens. Known as 'Steve'."

"You don't say. What does he do?"

"He's a night porter."

Diane dialled and got through quickly, but Steve was off-duty until six. "There's no point in going there before."

"So what do we do?"

An ancient black woman was passing on her way to market, her barrow loaded with paw-paws, mangoes and oranges. We bought a huge bagfull and got back into the car to look for somewhere to breakfast.

We drove back towards Mount Anderson and then up a promising track through thickly growing pines. Quite abruptly we were facing a vast amphitheater with a massive waterfall spreading itself in the shape of a rainbow-glittering fan, to sprinkle the surface of a crystal blue lake. On one side the waterfall, on the other side another great view of the veldt, flowers, lake and forest. We left the car and found a small dell. The sun was much warmer now and the fruit delicious.

Diane wandered off towards the other side of the lake. I lay back and enjoyed the heat, the lazy luxury of not having to hide, or run, or think my way out of some new bad situation.

I heard a splash. Diane had slipped off her clothes and dived in, an effortless bronzed fish in the azure clarity of the lake. I pulled off my shirt and trousers and followed.

The cold of the water was a literal shock. I struck out in search of Diane, envying the streamlined ease of her Californian-tanned body scything through the water. After a few lengths I turned to lie on my back to float and let the sun take over, suddenly realizing how very tiring the night and the day before had been.

I was distantly aware of Diane, nimble as a nymph, clambering ashore near the car, a momentary Venus as she ran round to the back to get a towel from her bag.

Some minutes later, when I hauled myself lazily out of the water, she was already dressed in a crisp fresh top and slacks, rubbing her long dark hair dry. She threw me the other towel and I wrapped it around me and lay down on the turf. Sleep came easily in the voluptuous heat.

When I awoke, thirst raging, the sun was already low in the trees. A delicious smell of cooking aroused my appetite. Diane had made a fire and was cooking some of her airport hamburgers over a twig grill.

"How are you feeling?"

"Never better." I rose, grabbing at the towel wrapped around my waist as it nearly fell. I found the least garish of the shirts I'd bought at the gift shop and looked around for my trousers.

"Oh I did a sort of cleaning job," Diane said.

They were neatly folded over a tree root, the mud and slime all washed off, the tear from the airport perimeter fence neatly darned.

"Thank you," I said, putting them on, "you'd make someone a wonderful wife."

Her face clouded, "I didn't."

"But you told me—"

"It wasn't true. I was a lousy wife in what became a

199

lousy marriage. Jack and I just didn't get near the sort of warmth and tenderness and understanding you were telling me about last night—you and your Sally and your babies. At the end we were just—angry rivals, accidentally partnered off for an aggressive sex game, griping and picking on each other just to score cheap points."

"I'm sorry."

"Don't be. He's dead. The marriage was dead long before."

She turned away to pick the hot slabs of meat on to flat, broad leaves. I wondered whether I should go to her and put my arms around her.

She turned and saw me hesitating. "No demonstrations, thanks."

She came up to me and rubbed my face, "Anyway you need a shave."

"I'll soon fix that."

"Have your dinner first, or lunch or whatever it is."

In the late afternoon sunshine the hamburgers looked and tasted rich and ambrosially rare. We finished the fruit and I cleaned up and shaved in the car's rear-view mirror. Diane was far away—a tiny figure sitting on a rock looking out over the amazing golden valley. I went across to her; she didn't turn. As I came close I saw she was crying.

Very gently I took her hand. "What's wrong?"

She turned to me, almost fiercely. "How can they think of doing it?"

"What?"

"Destroying all this. Reducing it all to dust—like that poor little monkey—in that test."

I put my arm firmly around her shoulder. "They won't. It's unthinkable."

"Unthinkable?" she said angrily. "Don't you believe

it. They think of it all the time! And *do* it too! You don't know. I saw places in Vietnam just as lovely as this—and saw what they looked like after defoliation or napalm. My people did that—Americans—ordinary, decent Americans. And given the right sort of push those same people would do the same sort of thing right here—or anywhere."

"Sure they *could*. Madness is always a possibility, but sane people have to try and make sure the lunatics don't get power."

"You saw those guys back in California—all theoretically perfectly sane. Yet they live with the knowledge of that terrible destruction—and a whole lot more I can tell you—and they still go home to their wives and families and pretend they're normal human beings."

"If they didn't pretend they'd surely go mad."

It was the old argument that must have echoed everywhere from inside Hitler's Germany to the outposts of Suleimein the Magnificent's Moorish Empire. Who is responsible enough to possess the power of life or death over his fellow humans? And like those earlier questioners we too had no answer.

All around us the birds sang, the sun felt full and warm on our heads, the air was rich with the delicate scent of dozens of exotic flowers. Ahead, the view across the vast river canyon stretched endlessly into a golden haze.

I looked down to the girl's worried young face. She seemed suddenly very close, very attainable, memorable from that moment when she was a slim, naked sylph running out of the water. . . .

Gently I made the small move towards her to kiss her. Just as gently and neatly she disengaged.

"I told you, Dan, I'm not playing 'relationships'. Maybe it's time we looked for the 'Welcome Inn.'"

We got back into the Cortina and drove down the rocky track, joining a green-lined avenue through the pines and shapely tree ferns. The low sun slanted gold through the foliage as we passed under, turning each leaf dazzling light green in succession. I only hoped I'd remember the pleasure this day had brought. . . .

"Any news?"

Brouger had put off making this call for some hours, telling himself repeatedly that van Harten was bound to come through to him soon. But there had been no word from the big policeman all day.

"No sign." Van Harten moved to sit cautiously on the edge of his desk, carefully adjusting the knees of his trousers to avoid disturbing the knife-like crease. "He must have had help if he got clear of Jan Smuts airport. Or maybe he's still there, holed up in a warehouse somewhere. We're working on the assumption he got out, though."

"What now?" Brouger asked, trying to keep the impatience out of his voice.

"I got the approval for the warrant, from the Minister's own office, just after lunch," van Harten added, with a certain pride. "Not bad going considering the speed they normally work. We're issuing descriptions to the radio and television, so they can get it on the news tonight."

"Good." Brouger felt his confidence returning.

"I said before," the big policeman said as he rose from the desk, ready to replace the phone. "He can't get far."

Graskop, as we drove along its main street, turned out to be a pleasant little town of Edwardian-looking timber bungalows, marred here and there by lumber-works and chemical factories. I could imagine the place about a century ago, with gold-prospectors in wide-brimmed hats and flowing moustaches crowding the sandy main street. Now there were sharp, shiny shops, ice-cream bars and tall office blocks jostling progress even into this quiet retreat.

The "Welcome Inn" was on a hillside at the far end of town, a series of pleasant bungalows grouped around a main dining and reception complex of stone and stucco and blue tiles. A couple of tourist buses dominated the car park and quite a few of the tourists were wandering around, almost all white with the occasional smartly-dressed black couple keeping determinedly to themselves.

Diane said, "My passport says Mrs. Taylor. We'll be booking in as a married couple but it stops there, OK?"

"Whatever you say."

Inside the main building the warm sun was banished; air-conditioning granted us frigid admission. I followed Diane to reception and produced the Taylor passport. We registered and were allotted a bungalow.

Diane said loudly, "Let's find out about tours darling," and moved over to the hall porter's counter. A young, alert-looking black was in charge. Diane began asking him about bus excursions to local beauty spots and he started making recommendations. Somewhere within the conversation must have been the password and the correct answer.

The hall porter turned away to get some leaflets. Diane said quickly, "This is our man."

He spread the leaflets in bewildering array in front of us. God's Window, Mac Mac Falls, Klinkraad Pools, Kruger National Game Park, Bourkes Luck Potholes.

It was impossible to make a choice without help. The young man began to expound the features of each.

"You speak like an American," I said suddenly, aware as I spoke that my own assumed accent mightn't be too convincing.

"I was there three years at college in Utah."

"Unusual for a South African, surely, Mr.—er—"

"Stevens. Very unusual for a Zulu."

He looked at me for a moment with something like a request for recognition. He didn't say any more but looked towards Diane as if expecting her to make the next move. I realized my presence embarrassed them and upset his finely-tuned sense of security.

I said to Diane, "I'll go and sort out the rooms. Your Mr. Stevens can surprise me with a trip for tomorrow."

I crossed the hall and found a porter. The place was getting quite crowded as tourists drifted in towards the bar. Most of the accents were American with here and there the clipped, rasping tones of Afrikaaners, the occasional guttural Swede or German.

Outside, the friendly sun was welcome. I gave the porter the key and he got into the car beside me and directed me up the hill to our bungalow set among young pine trees and carefully cultivated prickly pears. As he opened the door he reached up to switch on the air conditioner. "Forget it," I said.

He lifted Diane's two cases and holdall out of the trunk. I picked up the flight bag, now a little worse for wear. "That all, sir?"

"That's all, thank you."

The bungalow was pleasant, a roomy lounge opening to a veranda, a bedroom with two single beds, a bathroom and a mini kitchen. I paid off the porter and took a quick shower, enjoying the refreshing bombardment of sharp watery needles. As I was dressing I saw Diane coming up the path, the setting sun flaming roseate behind her, walking like a girl without a care in the world, in a land that had confidently given itself to her for the asking. The crumbling, dying, glassy-eyed monkey, first of many victims, belonged in another time, another universe.

She came in the door and stopped. "They've already given out your name and description on the radio. 'Suspected terrorist wanted for questioning. Last seen running away at Jo'burg Airport.' And we know who Brouger is. Bob's run his photo through the Langley computer. He's in charge of research and development out here for Gerondo Chemical."

"Gerondo? So that's who." They were a big name, possibly the biggest, in everything from garden fertilizer to North Sea oil, with tie-ups in Sweden, Germany, France, and of course the Republic of South Africa.

"This radiation weapon must be part of their survival plan. South Africa *matters*. They need the film to convince the one or two remaining doves out here that they have to fight back. Let us alone or—pfft!—goodbye the rest of the world."

"Has Gerondo the capacity to develop a weapon like this?"

"They'd find it, make no mistake. We're up against deadly, utterly unfeeling and ruthless people."

"Just you—and me?"

"And Bob's organization. We just have to keep our cool. Steve's set it all up with the local net. We're to join the bus party that goes up to look at the view from a place called God's Window first thing in the morning. From there they drive on to Kruger Park. In the car park by the main entrance, where they leave the cars that are for rent, there'll be a Land-Rover, keys in the ignition, with a couple of day passes for Swaziland. We take the main road south, straight down through the frontier post to Pigg's Peak and on to Mbabane. Then it's simply a local flight to Nairobi and a jumbo to London.

"Great." It all seemed an anti-climax.

Diane had wandered into the bedroom surveying the two beds.

"Do you mind being near the window?"

"No."

She plumped down on the nearer one. "I'll take this."

I said, "If you're fussy, I could sleep out here on the sofa."

She smiled. "Dan." She knew how much I wanted her but she was in no mood to tease. "Look, you go and set up a couple of drinks, I'll take a bath and join you."

"OK."

I wandered out into the evening light. The crickets had already started; there was no wind, just a delicious fragrance from the pines. It was the sort of night that in the days of the good old British Empire made ex-patriots forget the heat and dust and grind of the day and thank their stars for whatever it was that made Britons greater than their fellows. All gone now.

I reached the reception building, cold as a freezer, and pushed into the crowded bar. The shirt I was wearing from Jo'burg Airport was pretty jazzy but sartorially I was quite restrained in this smoky rainbow's end. Violent reds and purples clashed with greens and sharp yellows, all featured in full on the gross distended bodies of middle-age on the holiday of a lifetime—something to tell the folks back home.

Voices raised to fever pitch as they argued about the size and fierceness of the animals they'd bagged with Nikon and Olympus, or whether the rugged grandeur of Blyde River stood a chance alongside their own Grand Canyon.

Someone had had the bright idea of decorating the bar with miner's picks, safety helmets, carbide lamps and making it look like Siegfried's grotto, increasing the bizarre effect of all the soft, unworried faces.

I was well enough trained in edging towards bar counters. Swimming through a veritable sea of sweating, nylon-covered blubber I made it at last. "Whiskey Collins please, the big one."

"Yassah, coming right up sah." In this last bastion of Stepin-Fetchit-land the barman played the lead in a sort of *Uncle Tom's Farewell.*

An ice-steamed glass appeared before me. The noise seemed to be getting louder—shouts, laughter, screams that might be fear in any other place.

Suddenly a voice said, "Hold it folks! The news!"

In Israel, after the Yom Kippur war, I'd heard silence descend in seconds after such an announcement. News—the holy mass of the late twentieth-century; but here only a few bothered to lower their loud voices. I craned my head near to the radio set to decipher the message. The other people in the bar, mainly Americans, couldn't give a perfumed fig for South Africa's problems, although even the most hedonistic must have realized they were playing tourist in a beleaguered fortress; but silence was too high a price, not included in the tour rate.

The time signal familiar as Droitwich, pipped out loud and clear, then an Anglicized voice began the main points of the news.

There'd been another resolution in the United Nations condemning apartheid, an aircrash near Khartoum with South Africans among the passengers, coal prices were going up again and petrol stations were going to shut from Friday midday to Monday noon. And at the end, bottom billing, "Dan Galloway, the London man suspected of terrorist affiliations, is still at large after breaking out of a domestic plane at Jan Smuts Airport last night". The description that followed was fair but unflattering. I looked cautiously round the room; it would have fitted five or six of the less bloated men standing there just as well as it fitted me.

Then with relief I saw Diane at the door, the radio was turned down and noise returned.

"What can I get you to drink?"

"Let's eat."

The dining room was cool and uncrowded compared with the bar, but by the time we'd had the iced turtle soup the mob had moved in. It was someone called Henry's birthday, an event that needed celebrating it seemed by a battle of beercans, which, shaken up to explosive point then ripped open, successively showered Henry, Mrs. Henry and friends in boozy compliment. The manager, in a grey safari suit, appeared to quieten the festivities then moved from table to table.

As our Veal Holsteins appeared so did he. "Sonny Vandervell," a beefy hand appeared under my nose. "And if no one's said it before, welcome to the 'Welcome Inn.'"

Diane and I both managed the correct tourist's embarrassed acknowledgement.

"Mr. and Mrs. Taylor," the man said. "I couldn't help noticing you're from Lexington."

"That's right."

"Nice little place. You been away long?"

"On holiday you mean?"

"No, from the States?"

Desperately I tried to remember the occupation I'd seen written in my passport. "Heating engineer", that was it. "About five years isn't it darling?"

"All of that," Diane said.

"Fitting heating systems—and air conditioning—"

"Where?"

"All over the Middle East. Saudi Arabia—"

"Tell me, did they ever put up that statue to the mayor?"

"Statue?"

"In Lexington, your home town. I was over in Boston about ten years ago and all I remember was the papers being full of this argument about the mayor of Lexington's statue."

"You remember, honey," Diane said smoothly, "There *was* a hell of a fuss at the time. He was run in for corruption a year or so later. What was his name—Ryan, Murphy?"

"No, it wasn't an Irish name," Vandervell said, "more like Polish. Kowalski, or some such."

"Could be," I said.

"So he was done for corruption? God, you can't trust any politician these days, particularly the ones you seem to get in America, but they're nothing compared to the Brits. Did you hear the news just now? Some other bloody terrorist's been let loose. Bastard commie—I'd shoot the lot of them."

"Hi Sonny!" Another guest was hailing him. "Come on over."

"Excuse me," Vandervell said, getting up, "we must have another talk about Lexington sometime."

"Sure," I said, "I look forward to that."

209

The big man moved away.

"Why the hell did Bob have to pick Lexington?" I whispered to Diane.

"Probably seemed a good idea. Don't worry, Vandervell has no means of checking."

"Unless he meets another guest from Massachusetts."

"Unlikely,"

The dessert arrived and with it a desire for sleep.

"Coming, Diane?"

"You go on up, I'll just have a quick word with Steve."

The bungalow was warm and relaxing. I washed quickly, brushed my teeth and got undressed. Having no luggage solved the problem of whether or not I should wear pajamas. I checked the film was still in its can in the flight bag, then pulled back the sheets and turned in, rolling over on to one elbow to read the paperback I'd started on the way out from London.

Diane appeared a moment or so later. "All calm," she said, "Steve's on duty all night."

She unzipped her holdall, pulled out a nightdress, bathrobe, and washbag and disappeared into the bathroom.

I tried to concentrate on the words on the page in front of me, but they made no sense. I heard every sound from the bathroom, the fizz of the shower and the silence after it was turned off. I was within a few feet of this lovely and desirable young girl, alone with her, and yet I knew I would make no move. Call it what you like, respect, loyalty, she was as safe with me in this apparently married state as a vestal virgin. She came back into the room decently covered in filmy silk and slipped off her bathrobe and slid into the other bed.

Her bedside light snapped off. "Goodnight Dan."

"Goodnight." I tried to read further, but after a few pointless minutes gave up the attempt and put the book down, switching off the remaining light. I knew that after the long rest I'd had during the day sleep might be difficult. In the gloom I listened to the distant laughter from the bar down-valley and the animal sounds from the wooded hills all round us.

This was Tuesday night, just a week from the first flight from London—a week of incredible change and upset—and I thought: "I've got to get word to Sally. . . ."

A match rasped from the bed beside me. The unmistakable aroma of marijuana filled the warm air. As Diane drew in the smoke I saw a pale glitter in her eyes.

Then she spoke, almost inaudibly.

"I can't do it, Dan."

"What?"

"Just go along with the plan. Deliver you and the film back to London, find out whatever it is Bob and Langley want to find out."

"Whyever not?"

"I just can't, that's all."

"But surely this is what you have to do. That's what the whole bloody performance has been for—finding Mr. Big in London?"

"I know but—look, we know the sort of set-up behind it—influence, capital, probably a politician or two, no surprise. OK we discover one man in London and close one loophole, but there'll be another and another—a secret like this isn't ever going to be kept. So—you get the Russians and the Cubans and Uncle Tom Cobley into the act and the whole boring thing

211

starts all over. Another Vietnam. All for what? People like—Sonny Vandervell and your Mr. Brouger?"

"Diane, you're overtired."

"I'm overtired of the whole damn business."

"If you feel like that you shouldn't have joined."

"You're right—I shouldn't."

"But you're in it now."

"You said it. I'm *in*."

The end of the joint glowed near her mouth in the dimly-lit room. Shafts of moonlight began to filter through the curtains. I heard her stub out the butt and settle between the sheets.

But sleep still eluded me. Diane, the one and only person on whom I could rely, beginning to have doubts? I began to feel very lonely in a vast undeveloped land. . . .

"Dan."

I opened my eyes. Diane was out of bed, very close, on her knees looking at me. "Mm?"

Her voice was very soft. "Love me."

"Uh?"

"Now."

"But you said—"

"Forget what I said, just do."

She stood up and now I saw she was naked, her young full breasts and narrow hips cross-lit with soft blue. She held out her arms to me, I took her hands and rose up towards her, taking her in my arms. She kissed my lips in short, gentle bursts, breaking away each time I tried to invade. Her mouth was smoky and soft, perfumed and rough, slowly urging.

I lifted her on to the bed. Her breasts tingled and glowed under my touch, her firm loins were soft and yielding as we joined. I tasted the salt tears on her cheek and felt a kind of shared anger at the whole

212

absurd charade we were enacting, an anger that cas-
caded into a torrent of desire and quieter pleasure
that could only end in sweet delight. . . .

I rolled on to my back into the cool wonder of relaxation, drowsy bliss, uttering small my only question. "Diane?"

"Mmm?"

"Why?"

A moment then, "Need."

"Only that?" Silence. I wanted to know. "Was that
all?"

"You guess."

I paused. "Love?"

"Something very like it."

"Darling." I tried to roll over to face her but she
turned away. I put my arms around her waist; softly
she firmly removed them.

"No more. Have your sleep. You'll need that more
than anything."

"Maybe." I couldn't tell what I needed. At a time
like this I had to get involved, deeply it seemed, with
the very girl I required to be cool and unemotional if
we were to be extricated from the whole bloody mess.

I clambered dimly into my own bed, now grown
cold, but soon a bower of dreamless quiescence, total
slumber. . . .

And suddenly I was being shaken violently. "What
the—?"

Diane, face close, urgently. "It's after three. Steve's
just called. Vandervell saw the late News on TV and
they showed your airport mug-shot."

"With glasses?"

"Recognizable enough. He seems to have mulled it
over for a bit then he started talking to one of those
drunks from the east coast. It wasn't Lexington where

they had all the fuss about the mayor's statue—it was *Arlington*. Bang goes our credibility. Anyway, he called the police a few moments ago and they're on their way up from Graskop."

I grabbed my clothes and put them on fast. Diane was already dressed. She opened the door a couple of inches and pointed. Outside, among the prickly pears, one of the porters was hanging about, obviously set on guard by Vandervell.

Diane handed me a hefty vase, "I'll call him, you slug him."

I got behind the door and Diane called in a tough, Auntie Mame voice, "Hey boy! Come here at once! Someone's broken into this goddammed place."

Through the crack I watched the man turn and respond to authority like a reflex. He was young and thickset, his shiny black face dark against the trees as he moved slowly up the path.

Diane shouted, "Come in, boy. Don't hang about."

The man came on, Diane stepped back and as he entered the room I brought the vase down hard, smashing it across his curly head. In a TV show it would have knocked him cold but life isn't like that, alas.

He simply uttered a low grunt of pain and aimed a hefty fist just where my jaw would have been if I hadn't managed to deflect the blow with a fast upperthrust with my elbow. Diane waded in with a low kick that doubled him up and I followed through with a hard chop on the back of the neck that nearly broke all the bones in my hand. He crumpled at last.

"Poor man," Diane said, "It's not his battle."

In a minute we had him trussed and gagged with bedsheets and locked into the bathroom. Picking up our bags we ran into the darkness towards the Cortina. I'd parked facing uphill; sweating, we had to push her round in a three-point turn, then get in and release the handbrake. Silently the car rolled down the hill, past the reception block where the faithful Steve sat over a solitary lamp. There was no sign of Vandervell; he may have been in the bar sustaining himself.

As the road flattened out near the entrance gates, I let in the clutch very gently and felt the engine fire, slowly increasing power to take it through the gate and round on to the road where I could put my foot down to speed towards the town below. After a moment Diane said, "Here they come."

Headlights were flashing through the trees. I swung the car right up a handy track, scattering leaves and earth as the wheels spun then gripped and surged us up between the protective undergrowth. I switched off the engine and looked out. Lights came racing urgently up the road towards us and soon a police van groaned its way past. Scarcely breathing we waited. It didn't stop but swung up through the gates towards the hotel.

"Five minutes, ten at the most," I said, starting the engine and backing fast on to the road. "What was the name of the place the tour was going tomorrow?"

"God's Window."

"Find it on the map. We get there, dump this car and wait for the bus trip to arrive and join them as planned."

Diane flopped the map open on her knee. "Right, you head north-east on this main road for—let's see— about five miles, then there's a right turn, a corkscrew sort of road, probably unpaved, leading straight up."

215

"Thanks."

"I love you."

I looked at her for an instant. "What a time to tell me."

"What a time to find out."

In less than ten minutes we'd found the turning and followed the hairpin bends to the top. Before dawn there was nothing as yet to see when we arrived at the summit, just an asphalt park and a precipitous edge with telescopes standing like deserted artillery. Having found our objective, we returned about a mile down the hill again and drove the car up a track for a further half mile into a clearing made some time ago by the forestry people and now deserted. Heaps of cut branches lay around. I ran the car as close into the trees as I could and grabbed the precious flight bag and helped Diane out. She started to lift her bags out of the back but I stopped her.

"We'll have to bury those."

"Why?"

"If we're going to join that bus looking like day-trippers. . . ."

"Yes, of course. I wasn't thinking."

Quickly she picked out a few essentials to stow into her shoulder-bag. I dug a hole in a heap of under-brush and thrust the cases in, covering them over, then began to lay cut branches over the car, not con-cealing it completely but making it less visible from the road.

"Come on." I held out my hand to Diane, she took it and came towards me. For a moment I held her close, feeling her heart beating rapidly against my chest. Then, my arm round her waist, we walked out of the forest on to the road. There was enough moonlight to help us find our way and we were in no hurry. As we reached the summit the sky, which a moment before had been greenish-lilac with a long purple brush-stroke of cloud lazily marking the horizon, changed to pink and slowly faded to ochre, banishing the great shadows with a gold light that became more and more brilliant. It spread like genesis across the epic view of forests and mountains below us, Blyde River Canyon to the north, the open long veldt and then Kruger Park to the east.

We sat on a rock, watching the magic happen, like children, holding hands, like lovers. . . .

And Diane suddenly said, "Shall I ever see you again?"

The very question I didn't want to answer.

She said, "You'll go back to Sally and your children. All this—" she waved at the incredible vista below, "— will seem quite unreal. As though you'd never even seen it."

"I won't forget it. I'll remember it exactly the way it was."

She said, "I've got to see you."

I turned to face her. "Diane, don't let's make any plans, not till we're through this last bit."

I knew it wasn't what she wanted, but it wouldn't have been honest to pretend. Much as I loved her—and I did at that moment—I couldn't imagine any sort of future for us.

"Suppose I resign from Bob's set-up?"

"Would they let you?"

"America's still a free country. Suppose I came to London—got a job there. . . ."

"Diane," I said, "You know that wouldn't work."

She got up, fumbling in her bag for a packet of

weeds, lit one almost angrily and walked away. Perhaps I should have followed her, gone to her, taken her in my arms and told her that I'd never leave her. That was certainly what she wanted but I missed that opportunity.

She looked back. "Listen."

From the distance came the low growl of a diesel in bottom gear, the first of the day's tourist buses. It arrived around the corner, brakes squeaking to a halt, disgorging its brightly-colored, polyester-clad cargo of eager spectators. Where there had been a vast silence was now a parrot-house in stereo, volume set at "loud". Women called to their mates, urging them to snap this, take that, just look at this—wow! Men returned the call, cried out, laughed and gasped at the wonder of it all.

Another bus arrived and another to treble the multitude. I had become separated from Diane. Through the busy movement of peeling arms and oversized polaroid sunglasses I saw her drawing on her joint with deep breaths—like a victim before execution. I walked over to her; she looked at me strangely, examining me as if I was some curious newfound biological species. Her gaze, neither friendly nor hostile, was simply curious and slightly surprised.

Then she spoke. "The bus."

I looked behind. Two more buses had parked behind the others. Diane had recognized them from the Welcome Inn. People began stepping down and enacting the surprise and wonder bit, faces I half-recognized from the bar and the night before.

Suddenly I had doubts. "Do you think Vandervell will have told any of them?"

"I doubt it. When the police went to the bungalow

and found us gone, he'd have got them away pretty damn quick. He wouldn't want to alarm these sort of people with stories about a suspected terrorist on the premises. It would be bad for trade."

I hoped she was right. The birthday celebrant, Henry, was aiming his Mamiyaflex at Mrs. Henry. If anyone would know about me he would. I wandered past as he clicked the shutter for posterity. "Great view," I said.

He looked round and grinned. "Makes me wish I was an artist. Y'know, a painter like Grandma Moses or that guy Roosso."

To which there was no answer. I grinned aimlessly and sauntered back to Diane. "All clear, I think."

We waited the full fifteen minutes promised by the itinerary and watched the hotel guests piling back on to the buses. The first bus, full, drove off. Diane and I joined the queue for the second and climbed aboard to be counted by an avid young Indian girl courier. As the last person came up she frowned and began to walk down the aisle, counting more anxiously now. She looked at us. "Were you on this bus coming up?"

I looked up at the worried brown eyes as she paused by our row. Diane said, "Were we, darling?"

"I don't remember."

"Did I see your tickets?"

Diane opened her bag and produced the necessary vouchers—luckily she'd had the sense to pick them up from Steve the night before. "Here."

The girl took them, frowned once more then tore a corner off the top of each. "I'm sorry. It must be Marianne, the other courier—she's just plain stupid."

I smiled, Diane smiled, the girl smiled, then grabbed a handle suddenly to keep her balance as the

219

bus came to life and moved off. The courier walked forward to begin a sing-song monologue into a microphone.

"So that, ladies and gentlemen, was God's Window, one of the most famous views in the whole continent of Africa. We now resume our journey to the Kruger National Park, considered by many experts to be the outstandingly beautiful reserve for wild game in the whole world. On the way I shall be pointing out items of scenic interest and places of historical note. Shortly we shall be passing Pinnacle Rock, a huge natural column of granite towering from a densely wooded gorge at the southern end of the canyon—"

I caught Diane's eye. She smiled warmly and reached for my hand. Whatever thoughts had troubled her seemed to have been forgotten.

The bus ambled down to Graskop. At the end of the town a police car and a motorcycle patrol-man lounged under trees, waving the coach driver on with a friendly salute. Diane's hand pressed mine for a moment. The sun felt hot through the window and it grew steadily hotter as we turned east away from the river and climbed on and up through more thickly wooded hills.

"Let's go through it again, Mr. Vandervell."

The young white police sergeant paced around the spacious hotel office. The air-conditioning was over-running, making curious clicking noises that interrupted the otherwise almost inaudible hum. He didn't care for Vandervell There'd been a minor burglary at the Welcome Inn a few months back that they hadn't managed to clear up. Vandervell had written a stiff complaint to headquarters and there'd been the usual rocket.

The sergeant picked up the photograph, a grainy black and white polaroid taken from the TV tube last night, of a nondescript man with glasses. "You're sure this Taylor's the same man?"

"As far as I can judge, yes." Vandervell was becoming irritable.

He'd tried to be a good citizen, promptly reported a wanted man, and this halfwit of a country copper, who couldn't even catch a thief on his own doorstep, started questioning his memory.

"As far as you can judge?"

"That is definitely Mr. Taylor."

"Your night porter, Steve, isn't so sure. He had as much chance of getting a good look at this man as you did."

"Maybe he's just stupid. Or frightened of police. They usually are."

"I didn't hear that, Mr. Vandervell."

"Listen, the Taylors left in the middle of the night without paying their bill—"

"Steve says they made arrangements the night before. Signed a blank bill with a credit card. He's got no reason for saying that if it isn't true."

"They knocked out one of my porters and left him tied up in their bungalow. Is that the action of innocent people? At least you can get them on an assault charge."

"If we prove it. You want that sort of publicity for your hotel?"

Vandervell fell silent. If this was helping the police, he'd keep quiet in future.

The sergeant said quietly, "We have the number of

221

*their car. Our road patrols are bound to pick them up
wherever they try to go."*

"Bound to?"

"That's what I said, Mr. Vandervell."

The bus ground its way upwards through the forest in
low gear, high branches towering above us, dense
green on either side. We began to see signs on either
side of the road announcing the park and soon we
were entering Paul Kruger Gate.

The courier began shepherding her charges towards
the restaurant. Diane stopped at a postcard stand. Behind us were a couple of orderly rows of Land-Rovers
with rental stickers on the windscreens. As the last of
our party entered the dining room we moved casually
towards the vehicles. The first one had an ignition key
in place and on the front seat a rental form correctly
filled in in the name of Taylor, with a couple of day-
passes for Swaziland. I pocketed the papers, jumped
up into the driver's seat and pressed the starter.

The engine turned over but didn't fire.

I tried again. No.

Again. Nothing.

Sweating, I jumped down and ran round to the
front of the car. As I was about to heave the bonnet
open I heard a cry from the direction of the restaurant.

"Sir!" The young girl courier came hurrying towards
us.

"Sir—you're supposed to have lunch with us now—"

"Yeah—well—we thought we'd rent ourselves one of
these things—"

"But sir—the bus trip takes you through all the best
parts of the park—"

"Ah—but my—er—wife got kind of sick on the bus. We'd rather take one of these Land-Rovers."

The girl was puzzled, almost frightened. "But, sir—how will you get back?"

"We'll meet you—right here when you come by. What time, say?"

"About six, but—" She faltered, "You know where the car rent office is?"

"Yeah—right there." I jerked my head.

"Well—you can please yourself, I suppose, but don't be late."

"We won't." I smiled at her, poor, mystified and lovely young creature. I knew why she was so nervous. So-called "coloreds" have just as hard a time getting and keeping reasonable jobs as blacks. I couldn't reassure her by telling her we were up against some of the very people that oppressed her in this beautiful country where everybody should have a right to live an equal and full life. I couldn't tell her anything; I just went on smiling.

She gave up. "See you about six then."

"Sure." We watched her walk back to the restaurant to cope with her other, less eccentric, charges. The moment she was inside the door I pulled the bonnet open. I could see the main spark lead dangling loose from the distributor head. I screwed it in quickly. Diane had moved over to the driver's seat, "Try now," I said.

She did and the engine roared. "Jump in," she called. I piled into the passenger seat and she drove on to the tarmac road leading into the park. I picked up the map and worked out a simple route. "We need to make our way through the park to a place called Skukuza. Then, if we can find this small track on the right, double back through the back of the park on to

223

the main N4. The next turning left takes us down south all the way to Swaziland."

"We have to cross the frontier by a place called Pigg's Peak, that's what Steve said."

"Bang on. That's right where we're heading."

She drove on for a bit, then said, "I'm hungry."

"I wish you hadn't mentioned that, I'm starving."

We found a rough sort of tea shanty a bit further along the road and filled up on thick sandwiches and beer. As I was about to get into the driving seat Diane said, "Let me drive some more, I was enjoying myself."

"Be my guest." She started up and we drove on through the forest. In the trees that almost linked branches above us, monkeys chattered and chased high through the dazzling green, gazelles treated us to an occasional glimpse of pounding grace and from the distance came the thunderous bull-roar of elephants, while every sort and color of bird swooped and soared through the foliage, brilliant and black by turns in the broken-up shafts of sunlight.

Diane pulled out her crumpled cigarette pack, selected the last of her reefers, screwed the empty package into a ball and threw it away and lit up. The curiously unattractive reek tickled my nostrils.

"Bob was right, you know," she said, "when he talked back in California about getting a chance to change history."

"He didn't exactly say that—"

"He meant it. I know him better than you do. He's a very serious guy, Bob. Serious, dedicated, and kind of—wrong."

"How do you mean—wrong?"

"Why should he trust a guy like you to do the right thing with that film?" Her eyes had that curious brightness I'd seen in the projection room—almost a madness.

"God knows."

"I suppose you've got a track record as a TV producer but suppose—just suppose—you took it into your head to take off and pass it on—elsewhere?"

"I don't follow you—"

"To pass it to the official opposition—the Russians—or our new friends the Chinese?" She drew in on the joint and exhaled a dry cloud of brownish smoke.

"There's no way I could," I said.

"No? Look at that map again Dan." She jabbed at it vaguely with her finger. "There's a track there after Tshokwane that runs you straight to Nwandedzi."

"Yes—another fifty miles or so."

"And beyond that?"

"It goes right up to the border."

"With Mozambique. That's where we ought to go."

"*Mozambique*? But they're—"

"Right. When they threw the Portuguese out they got a new left-wing government."

"Communist—"

"Nationalist—liberationist—or *screw* it—What do these words *mean*?" She drew hard on the joint again. Whatever smokey junk was going into her lungs was making her higher than Kilimanjaro. "We go through to Mozambique and give ourselves up."

I stared at her. "You're mad."

"No. Eminently sane and rational." Her face was like a fox—wild and cunning.

"You can go. Not me." I said.

"You're on your way, brother." She swung the Land Rover round a bend flat out. I had to grab hold hard to stay upright.

"When did you think all this up?"

225

"I'd already decided before we made love last night."

"So that was your reason?"

"Or the other way round."

"You're talking in riddles."

The road ahead curved sharply. Without slackening speed Diane took the corner almost on two wheels, throwing up clouds of sand and stones in her wake. "Wow!" She laughed in an uncontrolled sort of way.

I tried to restrain her. "Diane—"

"My mind's made up."

"You're crazy—"

"No Dan, just listen to what I have to say and think about it. You saw that poor monkey, the bird, the rats. They're you, buster, and your wife and your children—"

"Not if the secret is kept."

"It *won't* be. If the South Africans don't get it from us they'll get it some other way. The only hope is a power that really believes in peace."

"Like who?"

"The Chinese, of course. You don't know them, I do. We saw enough of them in the Far East. If there's going to be peace anywhere it'll be through the Chinese." She blew out smoke like an opium cloud. Her eyes were glazed as she kept her foot down hard on the throttle, her hands swinging the driving wheel around like a small boy let loose at Monza.

"What's all this to do with Mozambique?"

"It's our only hope of getting through to the Chinese, stupid. If you go back to London you'll be watched all the way, but if we can cross the border to Mozambique we can aim straight for the Chinese Embassy. . . ."

"If they have one out here—"

"They do—we could hand *them* the film."

"It's undeveloped—"

"So we tell them that—"

"It's new stock. Maybe they can't develop it, they don't have the know-how—"

"So we tell them what's on it. Oh Dan—the film's not important. It's the *act—our act* in going over, declaring ourselves wholeheartedly for *peace*."

"We'll get shot as we approach the border—"

"We'll have to find a local and send him through with a message—"

She aimed the car at another hair-raising bend with a precipitous drop on the right and skidded through with inches to spare.

I gasped, "If we even get there. Please Diane—*slow down*."

She took no notice. I could see the sweat glistening on her face and forehead, adding radiance to insanity. We were heading uphill, straight again for a few hundred yeards. Diane pushed her throttle foot hard down to the floorboards. The protesting Land-Rover bumped us about even more violently in the cramped hot metal cab.

"I want to keep hold of you," Diane said in a quiet, calm voice. "Not let you run back to wife and kids. My father used to tell me that whenever you've got a choice of action you should always take the bravest course. So—at last—I want to *commit* myself somewhere I can believe again, and I want you with me, Dan."

We hit another gravel-and-dust corner at top speed. The Rover broke away right towards the awful edge, skidded, then came back round on course as Diane swung the wheel back and forth like a veteran.

I caught breath and shouted, "Let's talk all this out calmly somewhere—" grabbing hard as she made another incedible fast turn that smashed my shoulder roughly against the door. "*For God's sake!*" I roared. "*Slow down!*"

She glanced at me with a half-mad, half-cunning look. "So that you can grab the wheel and take over? No, old chum—just hang on for dear life, for that's what we're saving—dear life."

The wheels spun wildly as the car hit a patch of loose gravel then got a grip and shot us forward fast. Diane's eyes were sparkling, her cheeks aflame, as she swung the Land-Rover through the rough country.

"Diane," I said, "Aren't you even frightened for your own safety? We could be shot at, beaten up, tortured—"

"Raped? Is that what you're worried about?"

"I worry for *you.*"

"God, you're so British, Dan. Can't let the little woman face a fate worse than death. They'll be *human beings* at that border post for god's sake—not gorillas."

Neither of us saw the concrete pillar until it was too late, a post cemented into the middle of the track to stop vehicles going any further. At the last moment Diane swung the wheel hard over right, desperately trying to avoid it. The out-side wheel struck a hard rending noise, the Rover spun round, tilted and rolled over the cliff edge. I was flung hard against the passenger door, remembered in a split second that Land Rover door handles pull upwards, heaved hard, and was flung out on to turf and rock, landing heavily. I was just in time to see the little truck spinning away, plunging down through scrub and stony outcrop tearing off lumps of wing and canvas roof, spinning over once more, finally coming to rest on all four wheels again in a cloud of steam and exhaust smoke.

TEN

"Diane!" I ran down through the thick treacherous scrub, thorn bushes tearing at my clothes, calling her name.

I reached the wreck and tried to pull open the smashed door. Diane was slumped back away from the wheel, blood pumping regularly from a deep wound on her forehead. I heaved at the door and finally lifted it bodily off its hinges and got to her. Thick blood was pouring down her face. I tore off my shirt and made a rough kind of bandage that quickly became a red sodden mass.

I didn't know what else you did for a wound like that. I propped her up as comfortably as possible but the red surge went on. Her face as I wiped it was deadly white; she seemed quite unconscious, but still breathing. Where, how, could I get help? We hadn't seen any vehicles on this track. But there had to be someone.

I started to scramble up the track away from the

gully and heard a movement somewhere behind me. I turned and called, "Help!"

A pair of eyes was watching me from the shade of a thornbush. I stared and the creature moved into the light—a full-grown leopard, lithe and beautiful. I looked into the animal's angry eyes, its fierce snarling jaws, a representative at that moment of all the creatures who had ever been hunted or tormented by man, turned savage by the scent of blood, Diane's blood.

I stood there hypnotized, petrified, naked scapegoat for all mankind's cruelty to other species, awaiting the inevitable moment when the leopard would suddenly take the few strides that separated us and start to rend me apart.

But the beast made no move.

Cautiously I edged back to the wreck. The leopard took a step forward towards me.

I shouted violently, "Get away!" The animal froze for an instant, long enough to give me time to scramble back down the scrub and scree to the crashed vehicle. I couldn't look at the bloody heap in the driver's seat but ferretted desperately for her handbag, her lighter. There were a couple of old newspapers on the floor; I ripped them up and held the lighter to them. They were oily enought to burn with a bright flame. I held the wad of paper up like a torch and turned to face the leopard as it started towards me.

He was only five yards away, yellow eyes gleaming, breath coming in short gasps. I could almost feel the closeness of his body, the deadly heat of his hunting instinct, his appetite for the fresh blood he had sensed from afar.

I edged towards the fallen car door and grabbed it

up like a shield even as the leopard hurled itself towards me. I lifted the door and its forepaws smashed hard against the metal, the weight pushing me over. I smelt the sour fierceness of its breath as I thrust my flaming newspaper torch right between its eyes. As the fire bit, singeing the fur above its nose, it gave a great roar and fell away, clawing my left arm from shoulder to wrist with an angry forepaw—then it retreated towards the bush out of sight.

I dropped the torch; the dry grass on the ground began to catch fire. Of course, this was the way—the only way—I'd get help here quickly.

Rapidly I gathered dry brush and leaves and piled them on the burning paper where it lay. I found a rag in the back of the truck, dipped it in the petrol tank and threw it on to the blaze. It ignited with a roar. Now a plume of smoke ascended above the trees that was bound to be seen soon.

Diane made a small movement and groaned. I went over to her, holding her poor bloodied head against my chest.

"Dan," she whispered, "I—I want you to be with me. Always."

"I'm here, Diane."

I crouched there beside her in the cramped front seat until, after some time, I heard the noise of an approaching truck on the road above. I got out and waved—a couple of African forest rangers clambered out and scrambled down the rockface towards me.

"An accident—" I said, unnecessarily.

One of them had a first-aid kit and began to do what he could for Diane, the other reached for the two-way radio strapped to his belt to call an ambulance.

Then I remembered—I'd lost all chance of getting

out of this country, and I didn't much care. . . . All that mattered was that Diane should stay alive. . . .

The Indian girl's immediate look of fear as she entered the small interrogation room saddened the young sergeant; too many of these people expected violence, and only violence, from the police. "Sit down please," he said politely. "Miss—?"

"Dulipsinghi." Her voice was the merest whisper, her eyes wide and terrified.

"We're not going to hurt you. I can promise you that. You'll be leaving in about ten minutes. My officer here will drive you home." He nodded towards the friendly-faced Basuto in uniform standing beside him. "All I want you to do is tell me exactly what you told Mr. Vandervell at the hotel about the two people who disappeared from your coach trip this afternoon."

Haltingly, the girl began. She had first noticed them after the stop at God's Window, when they got on the wrong bus—her bus.

"They hadn't been on it when you started from the hotel?"

"I don't think so. And Marianne, the other girl, doesn't remember them starting on hers either."

"But they had the right tickets?"

"Oh yes. I checked that out at once, sure thing."

"And what happened next?"

"When we stopped in the Kruger Park for lunch, I saw them getting into a Land-Rover—one of the ones they have for rent there—so I said, "You must have lunch first." But the man said his wife was sick from the bus-ride, and they wanted to get off and see the animals. So I told them to be sure and be back at the entrance at six to catch the bus home."

"And they didn't show up?"

"No. I went to the car-hire office to see if they had rented the car properly, and that was all in order. But they hadn't seen the car come back yet. I waited for nearly half an hour more, but all the other passengers started to get mad at me, and I had to leave without the two people. Then I told Mr. Vandervell, because I didn't want to get into any trouble for leaving people in the Game Park."

"You did right," The sergeant said. He picked up the polaroid from the desk. "Have you seen this man before?"

The girl inspected it carefully. "I think that must be the man who took the Land Rover."

"Thank you Miss—er—Dulip—"

"Singhi."

"Yes. That's all for now. My officer will take you home." The girl smiled relief. The sergeant rose and watched her leave with the Basuto constable. Then he moved quickly to the radio in the next room.

The blood-dripper, ubiquitous prop of so many television hospital series, attached above Diane's spotless bed, was the first symbol of confidence that helped me recover from the delayed shock of the accident. She lay white-faced but peaceful, her head bandaged, sleeping a tranquillized sleep.

I had no idea where the small hospital was; the ambulance had had opaque windows. We'd bumped down the track and later a smoother road for a couple of hours, as I held her hand under the gentle eyes of the African medical orderly who'd arrived, taken charge effortlessly, stopped the bleeding and organized the two forest rangers as a stretcher party before binding up my gashed left arm.

Before leaving, I'd shown my American passport to the two rangers for their report. The car had been properly hired; there was nothing to show we weren't just a couple of ordinary tourists in trouble. But I could scarcely think ahead. At the last moment before boarding the ambulance I'd remembered the can of undeveloped film and had run back down the hill to rescue the flight bag out of the wreck.

Now I sat, watching Diane's face, her gentle breathing, waiting for the next chapter.

A sandy-haired doctor of about forty appeared from the end of the ward, followed by a nurse. Ignoring me he went to Diane, gently and quickly checked her pulse and heartbeat and made a note on his pad.

"That's all, thanks," he said to the nurse dismissing her, "I'll just have a word with Mr.—er—"

"Taylor."

"That's not the name they said on television."

I didn't answer.

"Galloway, wasn't it? I was interested in the name because I'd taken a couple of holidays just by Galloway when I was a lad."

His accent was Scottish. "Where are you from?" I asked.

"I was born just north of Peebles—a borderer—but I've been out here eleven years. My name's McCabe, by the way. Donald McCabe. Where do you come from?"

I told him.

"Hard town, Glasgow."

"The people aren't."

"No, I'll give you that. Now—what am I to do with

235

you? You're supposed to be some sort of terrorist wanted by the authorities. You don't look like it, I must say."

"I'm not." I started to tell him the whole story. How I'd been squeezed out of the Corporation and into making the bogus commercial, the meeting I'd set up in California with Herb Krein, of Gisela and how I'd found out what was really on the film. I didn't give him too many details, just said it was a nuclear test.

"Radiation? It couldn't be simply radiation," he said seriously.

"Whatever it is, it's a deadly weapon, one that can kill off all life on this planet in time."

His eyes widened. "You're not having me on?"

"I saw the test film."

"And someone down here wants it?"

I told him the rest, the switch of destinations to Johannesburg, Diane's revelation that I'd handed over a dummy film, our attempts to leave, ending in the final crash.

He sat thinking for a good two minutes. "You know the sort of country this is?"

I nodded.

"It's not so bad for whites but—any suggestion of terrorism gets the full security treatment."

"I know."

"You understand that anyone helping you will be subject to the same sort of pressures too?"

"Quite."

"So, my clear duty as a citizen is to hand you over to the authorities? And the only safe thing to do in all conscience." He paused. "But if what you tell me is true—and if it's not, then you're an extraordinary story-teller—there'll be all sorts of pressures from the people you're involved with—that General in California and so on. Whatever happened to you in the end there'd be more bad publicity for South Africa, more stirring up of all this black/white hatred."

He looked at me kindly. "I love this country. You haven't seen much of it but it truly is the most beautiful country in the world—a land flowing with milk and honey—"

"For whites only."

"It could be for us all, given time. I believe in gradual improvement. It will come. It's the only hope for any of us. If I didn't believe that I wouldn't stay here another five minutes. I've no desire to be filthy rich like those people in Jo'burg—I just want to live here, do my job—and I certainly want no truck with the sort of people looking for some quick solution by blackmailing the rest of the world with some ghastly new weapon."

He rose. "So really I've no choice. I'll mark your file, 'Left hospital after treatment' and see you're put on your way."

"Where?"

"Swaziland. That's where you were heading wasn't it? You can get a plane out of there easily enough."

"Can you do that—safely?"

His blue eyes smiled. "I've had a wee bit of experience now and again."

"Then all I can say is, thanks." I looked over at Diane. She seemed to be sleeping, "About—er—Mrs. Taylor. There's a man called Stevens, a hall porter at the Welcome Inn in Graskop. Just tell him she's here; he should be able to do the rest."

"Good." He offered his hand, I took it. "Good luck for the rest of the journey."

I crossed to Diane; her sleep seemed untroubled. I held her hand tight for what may have been the last time—poor lovely, worried, adorable, unhappy, pot-headed Californian girl.

"Goodbye Diane."

She slept on.

"*What's this?*"

The sergeant looked over the shoulder of the black constable as he typed slowly and methodically.

"*Accident report. Couple of Americans rented a car and crashed it.*"

"*What car?*"

"*A Land-Rover.*"

"*Where was this?*"

"*Kruger Park. On the track leading up to Nwandedzi. The woman was driving—she's badly hurt—but it doesn't say nothing about the man.*"

"*The name of the people?*"

"*Taylor.*"

"*Where are they now?*"

"*Up in that new hospital between Legogote and Gutshwa.*"

The sergeant grabbed a map and made a quick calculation, feeling the sort of excitement he'd known as a boy out with his father, stalking buck. He could be there in less than two hours. . . .

"*I want a car, quickly.*"

I waited for half an hour in the pitch darkness outside the hospital before McCabe's wife appeared to pick me up in their car. She was a gaunt, unhappy-looking woman with eyes as cold as a wet night in Sauchiehall Street. As we drove away I tried to make conversation, asking the name of the place we were in.

"It's best we don't talk," she said dourly. "And best you don't know where you've been. I don't approve of my husband's action in this but he's my husband and he's given you his word. Let be."

So that was that. She drove in tight-lipped silence for about an hour, through small roads and the occasional cattle track, until we arrived at what seemed to be a missionary settlement.

"Wait here," she said, taking the ignition key and entering the main building. After what seemed like hours, but what was probably only ten minutes, she reappeared with a harrassed-looking black priest. There were no introductions.

Mrs. McCabe simply said, "Have you got fifty rands?"

"Yes."

"Give it to him." I reached for my wallet and selected the notes. Mrs. McCabe took them and gave them to the African. He took my arm and shepherded me to the back of the building, into a small room with an old army cot and a couple of blankets, and left. I heard Mrs. McCabe drive away; no one came back so I settled down to sleep.

"I cannot help you.

Still in pajamas, apparently roused from deep sleep, Dr. McCabe spoke as if still in a half-daze. "The man simply saw that his wife was comfortable, had his own superificial wound treated, then left."

"By what means?" the sergeant asked. "Did he have a taxi waiting, or a car?"

"Visitors transport arrangements are scarcely my concern,"

"You're not being very helpful, Dr. McCabe."

"I'm far more concerned with the condition of the girl, Mrs. Taylor. With rest and care she will recover, but her injuries are grievous."

"I'd like to talk to her. . . ."

"There's no question of your doing that, sergeant." McCabe's eyes hardened. "She's under heavy sedation. Even if I were to permit you to see her there's not the slightest chance she'd be able to make sense of any of your questions."

"Let me be the judge of that."

"I'm the only judge of what's best for people placed in my care."

"This is an important case—to the Republic."

"All life is equally important, sergeant."

"The woman isn't so special. But the man Taylor—or Galloway—that's his real name—is a suspected terrorist, wanted for questioning in Jo'burg. They had his picture on the News last night. Didn't you see it?"

"I don't have time for much television. He'll have made his way from here fast enough I'm sure."

The sergeant looked into the pale blue eyes and saw nothing but quiet determination. "You can't suggest anywhere he might be heading?"

"I said before—I cannot help you."

I'd worried myself awake even before the dawn filtered into the small back room at the mission house, fretting about Sally, all those miles away, with no word from me, no idea where I was. Our last contact had been the call I'd made from JFK whole days ago. The interlude with Diane already seemed like some episode from another lifetime. Now all I could remember was a wife expecting me home, a child's special school to look at.

The priest came in with a crude sort of porridge and unsweetened tea for breakfast. I asked him if there was any way he could get a cable through to England, but he refused to discuss it. "You'll be leaving tonight," he said shortly. "Just lie low until then."

Without a book or even a scrap of paper to write on, I discovered how long a day can appear to last, learning the total boredom that real prisoners must endure for every day of their internment. I'd theorized enough about prisoners in my series format; now I tasted the crude reality.

I did most of the things people of "strong moral fiber" have ever written about—paced the length and breadth of my room to work out its exact measurement, watched the sun move from the left side of a high tree to its right and timed it with my watch, thought of all the places I'd rather be, and waited. Lunch arrived—stringy slices of dead goat with a sort of gravy like brown custard, and half-cooked plantains that tasted like rotten parsnips—and then I faced the long afternoon. I emptied the contents of the flight bag; my shaving gear and wash bag and the surviving sports shirt I'd bought in Jo'burg, the "Taylor" American passport, my own British one, and the can of undeveloped film. None of the equipment of a super-spy, able to karate and kill and fly off out of trouble. I must wait—I knew not even where—attendant to the gratuitous aid of perfect strangers.

Dialling London from Johannesburg is easy, in theory, providing the main connection isn't busy. Seven times Brouger dialled, and seven times an oh-so-polite lady's voice, informed him, with perfectly recorded modula-

tion, that the lines to London were engaged. "Please try later."

At last he dialled the operator, waiting for minutes as the ringing tone sounded rhythmically in his ear; then he was suddenly answered. He gave the number carefully—getting through had become a major operation.

"Have you tried direct dialling?"

"Yes. Seven times. The lines are always busy." Brouger tried to hold down his mounting impatience.

"It's a busy time. People often try for hours. I had one lady just now who—"

"Could you cut the backchat and get the number?"

"Certainly, sir." Brouger almost felt the icy blast down the line. "Hold on." He heard each click as she dialled out the whole number, then, as clearly as next-door, the number ringing.

The voice that answered simply repeated the number.

"Brouger here."

"Hold on."

A moment's pause and then another voice, "Brouger?"

"The man's been sighted. Somewhere up near Kruger Park."

"Arrested?"

"Not yet. The police are still searching."

"Don't ring again until you've questioned him."

"Understood."

"And Brouger. No violence."

There was a single click in the earpiece as the other man cut off.

Thoughtfully Brouger replaced the instrument on its rest. No violence. Coming from the author of this little adventure that was rich. Really rich.

At last night came again; another meal of stew-fat and gristle, and then the reappearance of the black priest.

"Come quickly." I gathered up the flight bag, put on my jacket and followed him outside to an old British Army-type three-tonner, Second World War vintage. He shook my hand formally and helped me up into the back, banging on the tailboard to signal the driver to jerk into motion. As the truck bumped its way over the uneven track and my eyes became accustomed to the dark, I could see the two other occupants more clearly. They were both black, one with spectacles, sitting apart from each other, not speaking with that frozen hopeless look of people who still have a long way to go. There was no point in even trying to talk. All I could do would be to ask questions which I had no right to ask and they need scarcely bother to answer. They were on their way out like I was, but unlike me they were presumably intending to continue whatever struggle they were involved in, and were conserving and renewing the cold courage they would need for that task. There was a sad, sour smell about them, a mixture of real poverty and fear, fouling the close air in the back of the truck. The ultimate stinking odor of the denial of human dignity with which they had lived for too long. . . .

More than an hour passed, an hour of metallic pounding and crashing, and then we heard the truck slow down and stop. My two companions got up and clambered over the tailboard on to the ground. I followed. "Where now?" I whispered.

The man with the spectacles banged on the tailboard and the truck drew off into the night. "Follow me."

I followed. Into the bush, dark, clinging and thorny, tearing at my face and clothes with sharp fingers, down a dark, rock-strewn path into utter blackness. Once I fell, calling softly ahead. A rough hand pulled me to my feet and urged me on. The man in spectacles obviously knew his way and led at a cruel pace. Bruised, tired and out of breath, I had the greatest difficulty keeping up with them.

Then it started to rain, quite heavily. Large sticky drops that soaked right through my jacket and shirt, mingling with runnels of hot sweat down my back.

We came to the edge of a small river. The man in front turned to grab my hand and guide me down through the slippery mud; as we forded the water poured into my cracked shoes, giving small comfort to my suffering feet. Then we were on land again, the forest less thick, and soon, as the rain stopped and early sunlight streaked the sky, we arrived at a flat dusty plain and a tarmac road.

The man with the spectacles said, "Kadaki and Mbabane that way," and disappeared with his companion in the same direction. Too tired to go on, I sat by the roadside and rested.

"I think you should see this." The Basuto constable handed the young sergeant the message he had carefully transcribed from the patrol radio.

"What is it?"

"One of the road patrols. Picked up a truck driver with a puncture near the Swazi border."

"Why'd they pick him up?"

"His annual licence was three months out of date. They thought he was acting nervous."

Nervous, the sergeant repeated the word to himself.

I'll be more than nervous myself when the inspector finds out we've spent a whole night and a day looking for this bloody terrorist and come up with nothing. "Did they ask him if he'd seen this Taylor?"

"They didn't say. They suspect he could have been running terrorists over the border, but he's not saying nothing."

The sergeant snapped, "Get back on the radio. Tell them to bring the driver in here for proper questioning."

The Basuto's eyes widened. "Questioning?"

"The old one-two." The sergeant's voice was suddenly hard. "Maybe he was running Taylor out of the country with the others. That's why he's nervous. Go on, move."

"Yes sergeant." The Basuto moved back to the radio, troubled.

"No marks. No bruises," the sergeant said. "That's policy." He sat down, not wanting to meet the Basuto constable's eyes again, tiredness overcoming him.

He hated violence. But he had to have whatever information he could get, from this driver or anyone else. And violence, in the end, was the only thing these blacks understood.

I wandered along the road until I heard a bus approaching from behind. I held up my hand, it stopped, and I was crammed in as an object of curiosity among the frayed duffle coats and woolly hats of early workers. The bus drove on through the flat countryside in the early sunlight and then began to thread its way past a huddle of patched-up shacks on the outskirts of a small town, to arrive in time in a dusty square. Here the buildings were two-story, peeling and sad, shutters down for the coming heat.

Already the square was fairly crowded, market set up, with goats, scrawny-looking cows, a few sheep in hastily erected pens, dead chickens trussed by their claws and hung for inspection.

I didn't see the policeman as I first stepped off the bus; he must have been beckoning to me but I didn't notice.

"Hey!" I turned to look at him. He was well-built, youngish and very black, with three stripes on his uniform sleeve.

"Where have you come from?"

My blood turned to ice. I had no convincing cover story, no friends, not even the name of a hotel to give as an address, nothing. Images of further detention in some flea-infested police cell, waiting, begging to explain, waiting more—sped through my brain like some all-too likely nightmare. . . .

The policeman just looked at me as I struggled to concoct a story. Minutes seemed to pass. "I've been for a walk," I said.

"Where are you staying?"

"Haven't decided yet."

"When did you arrive in Swaziland?"

"Last night."

"By train?"

"No. By car. I was—given a lift."

"Who by?"

"A couple of people I met."

"Where?"

"On the road. I—er—decided to come here on impulse. I'm on holiday down here—and had a row with my wife. I wanted to get away—so I hitched a lift."

"In South Africa? Don't you know it's illegal?"

I tried to smile. "No I didn't. We do it all the time back home." I wondered how convincing my American accent must sound to an African.

"So where did you spend the night?"

"By the roadside, I guess. The folks that gave me the lift took me to a couple of bars. I guess I must have had too many and passed out. I was under a kind of strain, you know." It all sounded horribly unlikely. "First thing I remember was the dawn breaking—and there I was, by the road."

At least I looked the part. Unshaven, torn clothes, dried mud up to my knees. . . .

The policeman said flatly. "Entry pass?" holding out his hand, whitish palm uppermost.

I brought the pass I'd found waiting in the Land Rover—so long ago—out of my inside pocket and handed it to him. He turned it over and inspected the back. "Where did you enter?"

I tried to remember the name of the place Diane had mentioned. "Was it—Pigg's Peak?"

"You could have come in that way," the policeman said slowly. "But they don't seem to have stamped your pass on entry."

"Is that unusual?" I said, trying to keep my voice casual.

"Depends on who was on duty. Sometimes they do forget." He paused. Around us a small crowd had collected to watch. Though I could hear shouts and animal noises from the market beyond, the assembled faces surrounding me were rapt.

"British, are you?"

"American." My accent gave the lie.

"May I see your passport?"

I reached for my Taylor passport and gave it to him. Then I remembered. Like a fool, I'd put a hundred dollar bill between the cover and the first page—the old pressman's trick for an easy ride through Immigration, particularly in Africa. It works one of two ways; either the man inspecting your passport ceremoniously hands you back your money, and you mumble an apology, or you get just the passport back, and smiles all round.

The policeman opened the passport, saw the note, and looked up at me. "Careless with your money, aren't you?"

He picked up the hundred between finger and thumb as if it were diseased and passed it towards me. I took it in absolute silence.

Carefully and slowly he worked his way through the green booklet, studying the photo and physical description, and checking each detail with a quick glance up at me. The little crowd, growing larger now, with nothing better to do than enjoy the show, watched the policeman's every move, expecting any minute the big climax, the arrest of this scruffy white man.

I stood there wretchedly, awaiting the pleasure of an earnest policeman in the middle of an unknown town in a small dusty state.

A few days ago I'd been a welcome guest in the Caribbean, lazing, as they say, in the sunshine. Now, under the same hot sun, but in a different continent, sweaty, unkempt and frightened, I waited for a local policeman to pass judgement on me, and with it, probably, if only he knew, the fate of himself and millions of others.

As he deliberated I began to assess the odds against me. This was independent Swaziland, not the Republic of South Africa. Foreigners still had rights here, surely? Would it really be worth his while to arrest an

American citizen, clearly not a vagrant, with a legal passport, just on instinct. . . ?

He suddenly snapped the passport shut and held it out towards me. I reached out and took it, resisting a sort of paralysis. He looked me straight in the eye. "If I were you my friend, I'd move on. Fast."

He turned on his heel abruptly and marched away through the busy market like an officer on a parade ground, short black baton tucked under his left arm at the approved Sandhurst angle.

Carefully I put the green passport back into my inside jacket pocket. The little crowd started to melt away, though odd people stopped and turned to stare at me again before they drifted off.

Sour bile filled my mouth. I tried to conquer the over-whelming feeling of sickness, failed, and stood helplessly as a sudden gusher of vomit poured out on to the dusty earth by my feet. Dizzily I reached for a handkerchief to wipe my face. From nowhere a couple of mangy sore-encrusted dogs appeared to inspect the sodden mess on the ground.

Nearly fainting, I breathed in deeply, inhaling the sharp mixture of animal and human debris enlivened by the added condiment of my own foul contribution, and gazed weakly around me at the sad commerce of the seedy square.

The Basuto constable came in from the back with a mug of tea; the white sergeant felt he needed it. The interrogation of the truck driver had taken longer than expected.

"He confessed," the sergeant said. "There was a white man with the other two he slipped over the border."

249

The Basuto made no reaction.

The sergeant said, "Tell HQ to alert the Swazis."

"They don't return terrorists."

"He's wanted for assault as well."

The ancient telex machine, installed some time ago in the old British Army barracks that now served as Police Headquarters in Mbabane, clattered out its message, reluctantly on to the brownish sheet. The Swazi lieutenant mechanically tore it from the machine. The end of the paper ripped and jammed leaving a streamer trailing.

"Time they bought us a new machine," he grunted. The other policeman in the room didn't answer. The complaint was so old it didn't merit acknowledgement.

Slowly the lieutenant puzzled out the text, misspellings and all, transmitted from the Police Department of the Republic. Another suspected criminal, extradition requested. These weren't so many these days now they'd given up asking for politicals; a few years back the telex had chattered out whole directories of wanted names. Now they could only claim people who'd committed a statutory crime.

"Assault" it said on the sheet. "Using American passport." But the name was unfamiliar. "Taxlom." Didn't sound right.

The lieutenant pressed the necessary keys for a rerun. After the usual delay the machine tapped out its message again. This time the name showed as "Taylor."

The lieutenant reached for the telephone. First the border posts, then Immigration at the airport.

"Passport please."

I held it out. The black hand took it and opened it. I watched him reading through it, as calmly as I could. The encounter with the policeman in the square had shaken my confidence. I'd found a cafe and ordered tea, all they had to offer, and thought out my situation very carefully.

As Dan Galloway I'd enterd South Africa legally and done nothing against the law. But as "Taylor" I'd thumped an African porter, so the least I could expect would be an assault charge. Was simple assault extraditable from Swaziland? I didn't know—or care to put it to the test. But if stopped again it wouldn't do to be found carrying two passports.

I paid for the tea and asked the barman for a box of matches. I walked out of the square and found my way up a stinking alley where I found a corner out of the wind to crouch in; by the smell others had made use before me. Lighting matches one after another I destroyed the Taylor passport page by page, scattering the ashes. Then I went out to look for a taxi, somehow found a broken-down Austin Cambridge that passed as one, and asked the driver for the airport, using the last of my South African rands as fare.

There was a morning flight to Zambia, I was told, a Fokker Friendship. The ticket absorbed most of my remaining U.S. dollars, but from thereon, the clerk told me, I'd be able to use my Jo'burg return ticket to London. When the flight was called, I offered the immigration officer my genuine blue British passport, Dan Galloway version. . . .

He consulted a list, found no name that corresponded, and handed it back with a smile. I walked out to the sunlight and boarded.

A bumpy low-level trip finally landed me in Zambia. A better connection took me to Nairobi Airport and a telephone that actually worked and the warm reassurance of Sally's voice at last.

"Dan! Where on earth have you been? I've been out of my mind with worry."

"On the run, sort of. I told you I had to deliver the film to someone in Jo'burg—but it wasn't just a cigarette commercial, as you probably guessed."

"What was it then?"

"I can't tell you now. It's"—I tried to find the right word that wouldn't scare her—"security."

"Whose security?"

"I can't tell you—"

"I don't understand any of it. I tried to call that man O'Neill at his hotel but he'd checked out. And there was this dreadful bit in the paper about you being wanted as a terrorist in South Africa—"

"All a case of mistaken identity. I'll explain—when I see you—"

"Explain now."

"It's all too complicated."

"But listen—it's *Thursday* night. You were supposed to be home on Monday."

"I'll be home tomorrow. How is everybody?"

"Sarah's got a stinking cold and we still haven't done anything about her new school."

"Next week—we'll do it all *next week*, I promise.—"

"That's what you promised last week."

"What's a week?" A week—only a week? Was it really only a week? A lifetime.

"Dan, you sound so peculiar. What's wrong, really?"

"Darling, I told you I'd explain everything when I see you. That's tomorrow. I'm arriving on BA720 from Nairobi about eleven at Heathrow. Oh, and can you do something?"

252

"What?"

I tried to cast my mind back to Sunday morning in that projection room in California. The Englishman called Henry Mollinson had given me a name. . . .

"*Baron*, Sir Charles Baron, that's it. You have to ring the Home Office. Ask for Sir Charles Baron. Tell him—just tell him I'll be arriving on that flight."

"You're being awfully mysterious."

"It's all very simple darling, but please do it."

The pips went. Sally said, "Please come home," and the line went blank.

"On his way?" The voice, usually cool, had an uncommon trace of excitement.

The ground floor Albany living room was elegantly furnished with artefacts from ancient Egypt. But only he knew which were genuine eighteenth dynasty and which carefully-made reproductions. One nearly-complete cartouche, one scarab, a single alabaster vitrine, the rest street-market rubbish. . . .

"BA720 from Nairobi."

"Covered?" The unyielding stone gaze of Ramesses II held his for a moment.

"Naturally."

"You're sure?" Anubis, black and canine-sleek, crouched at his elbow.

"Phone-tap on his home line when he rang his wife."

"Sensitive area." The god Horus, bird-beaked and bright of eye, glared down from a wall relief. "Don't use it again."

"No other way, sir."

A pause. "Anything else?"

"Nothing sir."
"Keep me informed then."

In the cool of Nairobi airport the London flight was called, and within a few short steps I was back in the maternal arms of British Airways. Sterilized comforts administered by stewardesses straight out of the deep-freeze. In my torn muddy trousers, dirty shirt and one-day growth of beard I couldn't have looked exactly jet set, but I was soon settled out of harm's way at the back.

Just before the doors closed, a florid man in a straw hat and a tropical suit came stumping down the aisle and lowered his weight into the seat beside me. He said, "Good afternoon," but I only grunted. I wanted two things—sleep and a chance to think.

They were both denied by the man beside me. He insisted on telling me that his name was Goldsmith and that he was an estate agent from Port Elizabeth. He bemoaned the drop in real estate values in Cape Province due to events in Zimbabwe and the general uncertainty all over Africa. The odd noise of assent I gave him can't have been conversationally encouraging, but he droned on and on as night fell at thirty-five thousand feet, and until at last the lights dimmed.

I finally nodded off, trying to remember what precisely I wanted to think about. My mind was too woozy to assemble the facts in any sort of order and yet somewhere I knew there was something within the whole story that I'd missed. . . .

I remembered the leopard, the vile living smell of his hot breath, the vivid eyes . . . and I suddenly realized I'd never killed before.

Why? For survival? I felt a terrible feeling of guilt.

254

The guilt of my own blood and breed. I was part of the only species known to use up and destroy, cruelly and wastefully—like the monkey forced to die in that chamber—any other animal in a determined search for new ways of tormenting and killing mankind itself. And all with an arrogant assumption of utter superiority.

But were we, are we, will we always be the finest form of life? Have we any right to assume that *our* brains, such as they are, our music, our art, our so-called souls, are the pinnacle of evolution? I glanced at the overweight self-satisfied South African snoring beside me and found no reassurance.

"Orange juice." The air stewardess was suddenly very near, very important. The air seemed colder, pink light creeping through the plastic shades on the windows.

"Where are we?"

"In twenty minutes we'll be landing at Zurich."

"Thank you."

My hefty neighbor was still soundly asleep. I sipped the sour juice and tried to clear my brain of morbidity. Where did I really stand?

One, I still had the film. Whoever was after it would seek me out as soon as they found out I was home. Two, there must be a way of knowing who was behind it all. I must think it out from the beginning, from Frimley jingling the loose coins in his trouser pocket in his office at the Corporation. . . .

"Arrggh!" Goldsmith suddenly awoke. "Whassa time?"

"About eight o'clock European time, in the morning."

The plane was making its descent through grey,

greasy clouds like frozen washing-up water, then there was a break and a view of the cold, white snow below.

"Zurich," I said.

"Oh yah." He stood up and reached for his coat. "Going to be bloody cold—don't know why I come to Europe in winter, except I've got to keep up my old contacts in U.K. Never know when I might need them if the balloon goes up in the Cape."

I didn't bother to leave the aircraft at Zurich. My appetite for gift-wrapped milk chocolate and over-priced digital clocks was minimal. I was beginning to get the idea. Frimley, then Patrick Timothy. . . .

Goldsmith was back with a bottle of pflümliwasser. "Try some."

I took a mouthful from the plastic bottle cap. Cheap raw schnapps with blackcurrant juice hit me right in the throat. "Delicious," I coughed.

The engines were revving again and soon we were clear into the blue. And I was clear in my head, too; it all suddenly made sense. . . . And they'd be in London, ready, waiting for me. . . .

Sleet lashed the windows as we landed in dark-grey Heathrow. As we taxied to the terminal. Goldsmith rose and reached for his coat from the locker above. The aircraft lurched momentarily and the flight bag by my feet fell against his. He bent, picked it up and put it on his seat.

"Christ, that's heavy. What have you got in there, gold bars?"

"Just the week's takings."

He grinned and moved off up the cabin. I took hold of my bag and followed. At the open door the air was fresh and freezing; the ground at the foot of the

256

steps felt secure. Into the crowded heat of a bus, to be driven breakneck round the redbrick terminal, juddering to a violent stop, decanted to the foot of a yellow escalator that someone had thoughtfully switched off.

The same old musak, stuck in the groove of perpetual nostalgia, greeted us in the wide assembly area. I mumbled a goodbye to Goldsmith as he headed for Exit B—non-UK passports—while I queued behind a line of returning citizens, idly watching him flip open his passport and beetle off towards a payphone.

"Passport please?"

I handed it over mechanically, expecting the usual quick glance and tired smile. But not this time. The officer opened the passport, held it very still for a moment, then gave a short nod to a man in a brown suit standing behind him.

"Mr. Galloway?" Brown suit said. "Would you mind coming this way?"

I thought, if Sally has made the call to Baron at the Home Office I could be getting the old VIP deal. Or not. . . .

"Of course."

I followed him past the queue of haggard travellers through a small door into a narrow corridor. A few people sat on a couple of long forms, mainly Indians and Pakistanis, waiting for interview in the fullness of bureaucratic time. The man opened another door. "Wait in here please."

He closed the door on me and left. The room was bare but for a cheap desk and a pair of chairs, reminding me suddenly of that other bare room where the monkey and the rats had met their horrifying end. A last year's calendar hung askew on the far wall—a picture of Sydney Opera House by night, carved chunks of yellow cheese reflected in a black glass mirror. Then I heard the door open behind me. I turned to see the last person I needed.

"Patrick."

"Dan. Are you—all right?" He didn't look particularly right himself, his fat agent's face sickly pale under what must have been make-up, lightly applied. "I've got to whisk you off this very minute."

"No way. I'm meeting my wife. She'll be waiting outside."

"Er—no, Dan. I had her paged and spoke to her, told her you had this meeting—"

"What meeting?"

"She's gone back home."

"What the hell for?" Sally was the one person I wanted right then, not this old fart.

"It's—hard to explain, Dan."

"Try. For a start, how did you know I'd be on this flight?"

"I telephoned your wife this morning. She told me."

All unknowing, she'd delivered me up. "All right," I said. "Let's have a few facts shall we? For a start there was no bloody commercial at all, was there?"

"Well—"

"You knew it was a fake set-up all the time. Didn't you?"

"Perhaps. Er—you still have the film?"

I tapped the flight bag. "Right here."

"I'd better take that." He reached out for it but I held on. He started to struggle but I pushed him away, hard. "I'll keep it. After what I've been through. . . ."

He didn't like that. "We'd better be going. The car's outside."

"Where?"

"You'll see."

"I asked you a question, Patrick. Where are we going?"

"A meeting." His anguished face creased like cracked distemper.

"Top secret, old man. *Please* don't make it more difficult for me—"

I was about to do just that when the door opened and another man came in; thick-set figure, nondescript tweed jacket, furry flannel trousers, black tie and police-issue blue shirt. He stood passively just inside, awaiting orders.

"Who's this?"

Patrick simply looked even more unhappy.

"Who's your friend?"

"My name is Ruddock," the man said.

"Sergeant, or just plain constable?"

"Mister will do."

Patrick said, "Please come."

I noticed Ruddock flex slightly, ready for trouble. He was too heavy for me to have stood a chance.

"Let's get out by the main exit," I said. "Just in case Sally's still there."

Patrick hesitated a second, then said, "Very well."

I followed him out, Ruddock two steps behind, down Islamabad Alley again, huge eyes framed in brown watching fearfully as the three of us passed. Prisoner and escort.

We went through "Nothing To Declare" to the outer area and the rail dividing bona fide travellers from those whey-faced mothers and irritable children anxiously searching each passing face for smiling recognition. Sally wasn't there.

I went up and down the line twice to make sure, then Patrick gently steered me out through the far door into the leather comfort of a hired Daimler. Ruddock squeezed into the back seat beside me to make a tight three. For the moment they were playing it politely. The engine was already running and the chauffeur swung us out into the main traffic stream, fast-lane down to the tunnel.

I realized how hard I was gripping the flight bag, balanced on my knees. I said to Patrick, "That Mike O'Neill. What was he supposed to be?"

"What he *is*," Patrick said stuffily. "A regular advertising agent in the Far East. Exactly as I told you."

"But you brought him in to this? He didn't come to you with the offer, did he?"

Patrick pursed his lips and pointedly looked away. We emerged from the tunnel into the thick pearly mist of the M4, part of the heavy traffic sludging to London. Ruddock had sunk into a gloomy trance, gazing out at the passing murky suburbs.

I felt a sudden spurt of anger at the ridiculous Patrick, limousine-squatting like the Queen Mother, trying to appear as if everything was perfectly normal. I said, "You might have made your joke commercial a bit more credible by organizing it better."

Patrick looked even paler. "I'd rather you waited for—for a proper explanation from the man we're seeing—"

"And who's that? Where are we going?"

A pause and then, "My office." And I knew he was lying.

"Not that old party political stuff again?"

"I told you—wait and see." Patrick sounded petulant, involved in something quite beyond him and not liking it at all.

We were heading into Knightsbridge and crawling

traffic. Ahead of us a man suddenly left the pavement, launching himself through moving cars, just managing to jump aboard the back of a bus as it lurched forward again. There was something about his frantic movement that reminded me of the suffering dying monkey clawing desperately at the unremitting wall before falling back at last and expiring, all unknowing, finally disintegrating into dust.

My secret knowledge. Terrible and final destruction. And at that moment I knew I had about as much chance of surviving as that poor little monkey. . . .

We had turned right down Beauchamp Place and were now in Pont Street. The chauffeur drew up beside one of the tall redstone blocks.

"Where's this?"

"My club," Patrick said easily. "Thought you'd like a wash—"

I got out of the car and followed him through double doors. The entrance hall was deserted; an empty desk with no porter, a war memorial covering one wall with crowded names, a staircase.

"This way." Patrick led me through to a cloakroom; rows of numbered hooks for members' coats, a couple of wash-basins and a mirror. "Help yourself. Must go upstairs to 'phone."

A new razor, shaving cream, and a clean towel were already laid out. In the mirror I watched Patrick leave and Ruddock sit down on a chair behind me. I put the flight bag down under the basin, squeezed the shaving cream onto my hand and spread it cool across my face. The razor sliced cleanly through the night's growth, just like in the commercials. I bathed my face, enjoying the luxury of the water's delicious warmth and reached for the towel.

Ruddock had risen and was right beside me. His hand rested lightly on my elbow. "If you'd care for a shower, sir, there's time."

The showers, a pleasant prospect, were off left. But Ruddock wasn't quite a good enough actor. The grip on my elbow was suddenly too strong; his eyes spoke of holocaust, mass-murder. . . .

"Good idea," I said.

There was a big red fire extinguisher standing by the door. My only chance. I bent quickly and grabbed it up. Before Ruddock knew what was on, the thin stream of chemical hit him right between the eyes. He screamed—surprise, pain—then lunged at me, but I was ready. An upward thrust with the heavy base and a strong push and he tottered, still blinded by stinging foam, as I followed through with a hefty shove. He fell back, head making a satisfactory cracking noise on the porcelain as he went down. I grabbed up the flight bag and headed for the entrance. As I went through I glimpsed Patrick at the top of the stairs with another man.

Piers Gaveston. No surprise.

"*Dan!*" Patrick screamed, but I didn't stop, pushing through the swing doors into the street. The chauffeur was dozing in the Daimler, and beyond him a taxi was passing, slowing down for the traffic light on the corner. In two steps I'd reached it, flung open the door and piled in.

An elderly clerk looked up in alarm. "This cab's taken."

"It's all right," I gasped. "Desperate hurry. Go wherever you're going. I'll pay. And a fiver over the odds," I called to the driver.

"What's the rush, mate?"

"Her husband caught me." I flopped down on the

262

seat next to the startled passenger and looked back through the window. As the cab swung right at the lights I saw Patrick, Gaveston, and a battered Ruddock come running out of the club and pile into the Daimler, four cars behind us as they edged into the traffic stream.

Gaveston. The smooth-talker I'd met that night in Patrick's flat. He was behind it all. Of course. With access to the Cabinet he'd have known about the test, and known the right people in South Africa. And I'd passed the audition as messenger. . . .

"I want to get off at Sloane Square," the little man beside me said suddenly.

"Fine," I said. "And I'm most grateful for your help."

The taxi turned into the Square, squealed to a stop opposite the Royal Court. The man started to get up. I pulled open the door and propelled him rapidly onto the pavement. Behind, I could see the Daimler just turning the corner.

"Where now, guv?"

I had to think of somewhere, somewhere safe. "Victoria Station. And step on it." In a station there'd be crowds, and a chance of throwing off the pursuit.

But the Daimler was now right behind us. "Can you lose our friend?"

The cabby checked his mirror. "Dodgy—"

"For a tenner?"

A grin. "Have a go, shall we?"

The first set of lights in Eaton Square glowed green, then the next, then the third. As we reached the final crossing at Grosvenor Place the signals turned orange; the cabby swung right into the empty outer lane and we sailed through on the red. The Daimler tried to follow, but he was wider, and a Rover suddenly swerved out in front and blocked him off before he could get through.

We were away. Down Lower Grosvenor Place, across into Bressenden Place, hard right into the station entrance. I jumped out, slapped a ten into the cabby's hand, saw no sign of the Daimler following, and ran into the station to look for a phone. There was a row of boxes just before the main concourse, all occupied with long-players. But someone was coming out of one at the end. I sprinted for it, pushing past a girl who'd been waiting. "Sorry love. Emergency."

She glared. I slammed the door in her face and felt in my pocket for change. But though I'd a couple of notes left in my wallet I had no English coins handy. I dialled 100. Ages seemed to pass before the operator answered.

"Transfer charge please." I asked for my home number, heard the clicks as she dialled it out, then a ringing tone. On and on. No reply. So Sally must still be on her way back from the airport. And I couldn't risk going home—not till I'd delivered the film into safe hands.

But to whom? I had the one name from California. "Sir Charles Baron of the Home Office." And by now Sally should have alerted him.

I came cautiously out of the box, said "Thanks" to the girl, was rewarded by another glare as she pushed inside. I looked carefully right and left. No sign of pursuit. Flight bag in hand I walked on into the concourse and headed right to the small exit on to Buckingham Palace Road. A taxi was waiting.

"Home Office, please."

"The old one in Whitehall, or the new one?"

Which? "The new one I suppose."

The cabby took a U-turn and headed towards St. James'. As it repassed the station entrance I saw the Daimler parked outside, chauffeur standing beside it. Did his eye catch mine? As my cab drove on into anonymous traffic I simply couldn't be sure. But I wasn't sure of anything at that moment. I was in London, friendly old London, running like a fugitive for my very life. . . .

Traffic was heavier around Buckingham Palace. They change the guard at eleven-thirty—it was now nearly twelve and bunches of tourists were still ambling about, despite the cold. We shunted right of Queen Victoria's hefty white monument and round left into Birdcage Walk, abruptly shuttling right again at Queen Anne Gate to arrive at a curious large sandstone block in Petty France.

"Home Office." I handed the driver my last couple of quid and got out. Within minutes I ought to be safe. I pushed through the glass doors. A bench had been set up just inside and a security man grabbed the flight bag and pulled it open. He was about to take the film can when I said, "It's undeveloped."

He still took hold of it and was rippling off the tape round the edge when I stopped him. "It mustn't be opened."

"You can't bring it in then, sir."

"I'm seeing Sir Charles Baron."

"Who?"

A uniformed messenger was passing. "Who did you say, sir?"

"Sir Charles Baron."

"No one of that name here."

"There has to be." Surely after all this—

"What's *your* name, sir?"

"Galloway."

"Take a seat sir. I'll see if I can find someone to attend to you."

I was allowed to pass the bench, trying to replace the tape round the can as best I could, to sit on a padded seat by the window overlooking the street.

No approaching Daimler. Not so far. But if the chauffeur had alerted Gaveston and Co. it wouldn't take them long to deduce where I'd headed. I looked around the foyer again; it was airy and open. Facing the entrance were three glassed-in booths where visitors stated their names and business. Maybe if I saw the Daimler coming I might step up to one of them and hunch myself into back-view anonymity. Forlorn hope. . . .

"Sir." The messenger was beside me again. "Mr. Ryder will see you now sir."

"Ryder? Who's he?"

"He's offered to deal with you sir."

"Where's Sir Charles Baron?"

"I told you, sir. There's no one here of that name."

What could I say, except, "I'll see Mr. Ryder then."

I followed the man to the elevators, noticing how he neatly stopped me from entering one that was half-full and about to ascend, to wait for the next, empty one. As I got in I took one last look at the entrance. No pursuers. I was safe.

The messenger pressed the seventh floor button and we went up. As the doors opened again he led me along a clean corridor still smelling of fresh paint, through double firedoors into what must have been a conference room, with a long table and perhaps half a dozen chairs, each place laid with a new scribbling pad and freshly sharpened pencil.

"Mr. Galloway?"

A man I'd never seen before, blue-blazered and fresh-faced, more like a rugger-playing parson than a civil servant, came in.

"My name is Ryder. Do sit down."

"Where's Sir Charles Baron?"

"Sorry—I don't think we have—"

"Don't give me that 'not here' routine. I was definitely told to contact Sir Charles Baron by a man called Henry Mollinson in Los Angeles."

"Mollinson? Ah yes—"

"At least you've heard of him—"

"Naturally." He was too avuncular—headmaster's study, nice teatime chat. "Suppose you tell me a little of what exactly you've been up to?"

I told him, as rapidly as I could, though I suspect he knew already. I laid the film-can on the table, not taking my hand off it. Ryder listened carefully. At the end, on cue, he produced a pipe and tobacco pouch. "Er—you don't mind if I—"

"*Mind?*" I wouldn't have cared if he'd sniffed coke. "All I want to do is deliver the film into safe hands."

"Mm. Yes. I suppose I'd better take it off you."

"*No.*" My voice sounded unnaturally loud in the huge room. "It's the only bargaining counter I've got."

"Bargaining counter?"

"For my life. Knowing what I do I could so easily be. . . ."

"Done away with? Oh come." Pipe-smoking parson blew out a cloud of incredulous smoke. "Isn't that rather. . . . ?"

"Melodramatic? Not at all. I nearly copped a fatal heart-attack in a shower-bath in Pont Street. I need a cast-iron assurance."

"Hm." Ryder's blue eyes, quite extraordinarily hard

all of a sudden, rested on mine for a moment. "Who do you suppose might give you that assurance?"

"The Head of Security Services?"

"The Head of Security in this country happens to be the Prime Minister."

I thought quickly. Who else? I could think of no one better. "Very well. I'll deliver the film into his hands and his hands only."

"But my dear chap—that's hardly possible—"

"It's the only deal I'm offering."

The blue eyes fixed on mine. Then he rose, snuffed out the pipe with a long brown-stained finger, and put it back in his pocket. "Wait."

I didn't have much choice. As he left the room I got up from the hard chair and wandered over to the window. Below, the street was filling with office-workers on their way to lunch. Singles, couples arm-in-arm, laughing groups, all carelessly heading for food and warmth, basic necessities in a cold country. I watched them and envied each one, my destructive secret lying canned-up on the table behind me, my life entrusted to a man called Ryder. . . .

I heard the click of the door opening and swung round. But Ryder was alone. "I've made the appointment."

"The Prime Minister?"

"At Number Ten."

"When?"

"Now."

I could scarcely believe it.

Ryder said, "Shall we go?"

I stuffed my precious can in the flight bag and followed him down the corridor into the elevator and down seven floors to a small back exit leading to an enclosed quadrangle. An official black Rover was waiting.

We were driven in silence through busy grey streets the half mile or so to Horse Guards, turning in between the rows of parked cars on the old Parade Ground towards a small wooden sentry box on the far right. A commissionaire appeared from within, checked Ryder's name off on a clipboard, and we were allowed to drive into a small reserved area, to park just below the steps leading up through the gap in the railings at the closed-off end of Downing Street. The moment the car stopped, Ryder said, "Come quickly." He opened the car door. I picked up the flight bag and followed him.

The policeman on duty at Number 10 looked, as they always do, absurdly young. Ryder spoke to him briefly. He turned and rang the bell of the familiar black door; a footman in knee breeches opened it, took our names, consulted a list and admitted us.

The entrance hall was bare except for a few chipped gilt chairs like remnants from a Conservative fete. Not that I had time to notice much. A security man expertly wrestled the flight bag out of my hand, pulled out the can of film, and was tearing at the outer tape when Ryder stopped him.

"Leave it," he said quietly. The security man slapped the tape back on, none too carefully, and handed me the can and bag.

The footman, who'd been speaking into a housephone, must have received some sort of confirmation. He summoned an attendant, who led us up a flight of stairs to a first-floor landing running round three sides of the foyer. Oiled and idealized portraits of past prime ministers gazed down benevolent and unreal from the walls.

Through another room, bright with the yellowish paper I recognized from televised prime ministers' homely chats and on into a drawing room done out in Harrods' best chintz, with a few decent eighteenth-century landscapes and a grand piano, and a view of the cramped wall-garden, sodden with winter outside.

Silhouetted against the farthest window a man stood motionless; as he turned and moved towards us into the light I recognized him.

Piers Gaveston.

I made a fast move to the door but Ryder was there, ready.

"It's time this farce was ended," Gaveston said. "Give me the film."

I looked at Ryder. "You know what he is, don't you?"

"Hand it over," Ryder said.

"Now."

Was Gaveston acting on his own or for the prime minister? Surely not the PM? But he was here—smooth bastard, used to treating people like so many counters in a politicians' game, injuring them like Diane, perhaps even killing them like Gisela. . . . Gaveston the party fixer, developing his own special relationship with top dogs in South Africa. *Who else?* Who else could have used his influence, his old gays' network? Patrick Timothy, Frimley, maybe even poor old Misery Martin. . . .

"Here."

I slowly lifted the film can. Gaveston came forward, hand outstretched to take it—and I suddenly jerked my arm upward in the approved Cowcaddens Junior style, smashing the side of the can very hard into his neck just below the ear. He staggered back, starting to bleed as I hit him on the head again with the flat side and followed through with a knee-up fast to the groin. This time it all worked. He collapsed with a shout of pain.

"For God's sake!" Ryder suddenly came to life rushing at me aiming a low rabbit-punch, catching the film can on the upbeat, grabbing for it with clumsy fingers, fingernails connecting with the protective tape so that it burst open as it flew through the air, smashing through the window, the film, released at last, sailing in black shining coils down to the lawn below, as Ryder came for me looking murder. . . .

"What exactly is going on?"

Ryder's sledgehammer fist slammed into the side of my head as I swung round—to see an all-too-well-known face in the doorway.

John-Henry Baskomb, Her Britannic Majesty's Principal Minister of State, glaring at this extraordinary scene of violence inside his very drawing-room.

Ryder suddenly dropped his fists like a guardsman called to attention. I shouted, "You've lost the film— *ruined it!"*

Then a grey-haired military-looking man stepped from behind the premier. "My name is Charles Baron. Your wife telephoned my office." By now a couple of security men had appeared and effectively pinioned my arms.

"What *is* all this, Charles?" John-Henry complained.

Baron took him by the shoulder. " 'Dragonfire,' sir. The film of the American test that went missing, sir. All over your garden."

271

John-Henry surveyed the scene. Gaveston, partially recovered, raised himself groggily to a sitting position. "The leak?"

"Gaveston," Baron said. "As suspected."

John-Henry suddenly focussed on me. "And this is—?"

"The runner, sir. Expendable, in their book."

"But not in ours." John-Henry took a couple of steps towards me; now I could smell the whiskey on his breath. "You've heard of Official Secrets?"

"Yes." I wondered if he expected me to call him sir.

"You're into one. One word and I'll have your head."

"I understand."

"You'd better. Can't risk any more security scandals, can we, Charles?"

"No sir."

No sir, I thought. Not in election year.

ELEVEN

I was allowed to telephone home, to reassure a worried Sally that I was safe and hadn't ended up in clink, then debriefing—as Sir Charles Baron called it—took up the whole of the rest of the afternoon in one of those underground rooms under the ivy-clad orange sandstone monstrosity by the Admiralty Arch. They were interested in Stevens the CIA night-porter at the Welcome Inn at Graskop—"the Matabele connection", as one of the interrogators put it—but more inquisitive about just what Diane and I had been doing motoring on that particular road heading north east for Mozambique when we should have been pointing south to Swaziland.

My excuse of a map-reading error sounded thin enough, but I could let Diane herself explain—if she ever had to. At last it ended, with smiles and handshakes, then it was the Corporation's turn. I was informed the Commissioner-General himself wanted to see me back at the Fun Factory.

An official car took me swiftly to Wembley. The C.G. had his office on the sixth floor of Video City. Needless to say, in all my years at the Corporation I'd never penetrated so high before.

He was waiting for me, smiling, in a velvet dinner jacket, obviously interrupted on his way to some grand social occasion.

I entered the sound-proofed, well carpeted, softly-lit room, safe, conscious of my scruffy appearance, the none-too-close shave from the Pont St. loo, my torn trousers and crumpled jacket.

"Sit down, Galloway. Make yourself at home." The C.G. poured me a cut-glass flower vase half-full of whiskey. "Ice?"

"No, just water, thanks." He added water gravely, like a scientist in a laboratory, took a ginger ale for himself and spoke.

"The feeling in Whitehall is—that you did rather well in what was—what had to be—an *ad hoc* situation."

I took a drink. The good stuff went down like lemonade in high summer, with as little effect.

"I—er—knew nothing of it, of course. Frimley had unfortunately been persuaded to—engineer—the whole thing himself, prompted by—er—certain friends of his in, well, certain places. He moves in, what shall I say, rather *special* circles."

Special, yes, but it'll never make headlines in *Gay News* now.

"May I ask, sir, what's become of Frimley?"

Pause. "He's on—ah—sick leave. He won't be back for some time, and not—as Head of Vital Features in any case." The C.G. looked at me carefully. "It's early days yet but—I suppose you—er—wouldn't be—"

"Interested?"

"In becoming Head of Vital Features?"

I breathed in. "I don't think so. I'd rather stay producing, thanks."

The C.G.'s eyes clouded slightly. Forget it, said the whole establishment. Stay in the ranks, sucker. "As you please. Now, I've given some thought to your—er—current position. I think it will be best if we continue your contract for a further twelve months, subject, of course, to any pay rises, etcetera, the Corporation and the union may agree—"

"Subject to special negotiation," I said. "I'd like to see my personnel officer next week to improve my whole deal."

The C.G. didn't enjoy that one. "If you insist."

"I do. I've discovered how much I need the money."

He nodded.

I said, "You know what I've been doing in the last few days? All of it?"

"I had the gist—but as, technically, you've been under contract to the Corporation throughout that period, we'll treat it as official Corporation business, bound as usual, by the Security Clause. . . ."

"I've already been warned. But I'll have to tell some of it to my wife—I mean, I've been flying about from the Caribbean to California and down to Africa. . . ."

"Least said—"

"I see."

"Memory can be misleading." The dull eyes gleamed for a moment then became dull again.

I drained my glass. Two lovely girls—Gisela, who had offered love and warmth in a trade not worthy of her and probably died for it, and Diane—muddled, courageous, original, Diane. Instinctively I knew I'd never hear from her again. Already, as the C.G. had said, the whole episode was disappearing into a sort of photo album, confused, fading, soft-focus—an old man's fantasy kit to be turned up with some surprise in my declining years.

The C.G. rose, smiled, said no more. He didn't, of course, need to—the message was clear enough.

That's it, Dan. No reward, no George Cross, not even a "thank you" for saving the whole of humanity—(but who would ever believe that?), just a pat on the head, "Good dog, Rover."

The C.G. said, "I hope—er—*Doorway—is* a success."

"*Gateway.*"

"Of course. *Gateway.* Prison reform. Splendid stuff."

He gave me a final nod, meaning, "Get lost."

I'd reached the door and had my hand on the handle when he spoke again.

"*You shouldn't have interfered.*"

I looked at him. The eyes weren't dull any more. The voice was suddenly very hard.

"Interfered?" what could he possibly mean? "I simply went along with the CIA—or whoever those Americans really were. . . ."

"You should have considered your real interests. British interests."

"What is this? I don't understand."

"Once they'd detained you in Johannesburg you should have told them the American girl had the real film."

"And let them take it?"

"Naturally."

"But—" My mind was spinning. I was trying to make some sense of all this. "You mean—you think

South Africa has a right to possess a totally lethal weapon?"

"It's not what *I* think."

"The Prime Minister doesn't think that way. Otherwise he wouldn't have intervened."

"Prime Ministers come and go." His voice was pure Drambuie and honey. "The people who really run this country—whichever party happens to be in power—feel that a stable South African government must be preferable to—well, *chaos.*"

I couldn't find an answer.

"You've learnt something," the C.G. said. "I hope." And this time it did mean, "Go."

The chauffeur-driven car from Whitehall took me back to Stanmore. I stepped out at the gate and walked up the path. From inside I could hear Sarah coughing quietly but not too badly. I paused before putting my key in the lock. The black car drove silently away into the darkness.

It was over. Caribbean, California, chasing about the Cape, the lot. I'd had my outing, a fling with Gisela, my moment of infatuation for Diane, but it had never been more than Dreamsville. All past.

Sally and the kids were the real present, what I had, what I'd always wanted. If you're lucky enough to find someone, just one, who really cares deeply for you, and hold on, it should be enough. Let the General Waldorfs, the Sir Charles Barons, the Gavestons and the Frimleys play their little games of tinkering with the global future and welcome. I was too tired.

I turned the key.

Sally was in the hall, in the dark. My arms were around her and it was best. Her cheeks were wet.

I took a deep breath.

"Darling—you're not going to believe one word of this. . . ."

Peter Graham Scott was the original producer of the British television series *The Onedin Line* and *The Troubleshooters*, as well as three other major BBC drama series. He has also won four awards as a director of television plays. In the sixties he directed several episodes of *The Avengers, Danger Man* and *The Prisoner*, as well as six feature films. He recently adapted and produced Robert Louis Stevenson's *Kidnapped*, seen on television all over the world. He has written two plays for the theatre and several teleplays, but DRAGONFIRE is his first novel.

Peter Graham Scott lives quietly with his wife and four children in the English countryside.

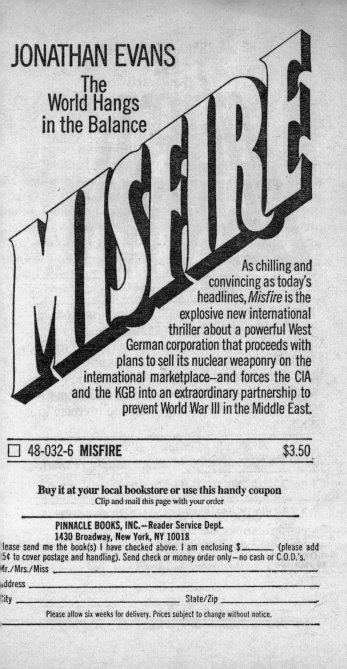